Pride Publishing books by Brian Lancaster

Single Books
Companion Required
Any Day
Salvaging Christmas
Famous Last
Don't Point at the Moon

I0598124

DON'T POINT AT THE MOON

BRIAN LANCASTER

Don't Point at the Moon
ISBN # 978-1-80250-745-4
©Copyright Brian Lancaster 2024
Cover Art by Kelly Martin ©Copyright August 2024
Interior text design by Claire Siemaszkiewicz
Pride Publishing

Published in 2024 by Pride Publishing, United Kingdom.

DON'T POINT
AT THE MOON

Dedication

Life forces us all to make painful decisions.

One of the hardest I have faced was leaving Hong Kong in 2022. Protests, handling of the coronavirus, and changes to the constitution aside, I have a deep respect for the people of Hong Kong, especially the ordinary folk I met socially or worked alongside. In my twenty-four years living there, I learnt so much from them, their sense of decency, their laughter and humility, their politeness and compassion and sense of orderliness — their humanity.

This book is my love letter to Hong Kong. If you are ever given the chance to visit, grab it with both hands and don't let go.

None of the characters in this story are based on the real people I know or have known, but a lot of opinions and ideas are borrowed from conversations throughout the years when Hong Kong was my home. They represent differing viewpoints of a diverse range of people and do not in any way reflect my own.

And at the heart of this story, please remember this is a multiracial love story between two consenting and wildly different men, something I understand with all my heart.

Prologue

He discovered the hidden path one Sunday morning during a solo hike to Hong Kong's Victoria Peak. Shaded by lush acacia trees and cooled by sea breezes, the well-trodden peak trail provided a welcome respite from the intense heat and humidity of subtropical summer days. The main route encircled the island's summit, with a cast-iron railing on one side offering occasional breathtaking views of the island. Discovered only by those bold or foolish enough to clamber over the barrier, a secret path led to a precarious ledge housing a massive boulder. Over the years, daring hikers had etched their thoughts and words onto its surface. Among them, a small, framed inscription made with a penknife read —

JASMIN
HONG KONG
I PROMISE.

For some, the inscription might have conjured tales of mystery and romance, a pledge left by one lover to another, a riddle of unrequited love worthy of a Shakespearian tragedy.

Only Mitchell Baxter knew the truth.

Six months into his Hong Kong placement, he had hit rock bottom. Mitchell did not make friends easily and had quickly come to realise that, for him at least, the life of a single expat entailed one of solitude. Long hours at work became his only solace. And during a probation period where he fought every day to prove himself, not only was the majority of his local-hire income flushed away on extortionate monthly rent but he spent most weekends alone, surviving on tea, toast, cheap takeout and Pearl TV.

On a stroll alone early that misty Sunday morning, he discovered the secret trail and the boulder before the sun had risen along with most of the population. Making a deal with himself that only he would understand, and entirely out of character for somebody who typically considered graffiti and hacking words into stone offensive, if not a crime, he carved his own pledge to the universe.

Just Another Six Months In
Hong Kong
I Promise

At the end of six more months, his working visa would expire and he would use the opportunity to return home to the poorly disguised smirks from family and friends. And once he was back in England, he would never ask for anything ever again.

But something happened that morning on Victoria Peak, something he couldn't explain that told him he was exactly where he was meant to be. After all, wasn't that how he ended up in Hong Kong in the first place? Something happening to change his life? All he needed to do was pay attention and make a bold choice when the time came. One thing he knew intimately was that low points didn't last forever, and as a local cab driver once told him, typhoons eventually blow themselves out.

Which is how Mitchell's six months in Hong Kong drifted into two years. Two years grew to five, five to seven with the approval of his permanent residency status, and the promise he had made himself faded. And slowly, over time, he rebuilt his world, forgot all about that life-changing moment at the top of the island and settled into a comfortable, if unremarkable, existence.

Until thirteen years later Tommy Chow came along.

Chapter One

In the nick of time, Mitchell caught hold of the taxi's backseat grab handle. The cabbie had floored the accelerator after nudging his car from the long queues of cross-harbour congestion into the empty lane heading towards the Aberdeen Tunnel. In the wing mirror, Mitchell watched the towering office blocks of Victoria Harbour shrink into the distance. For Hong Kong, as for many cities worldwide, the last day of April preceded the Labour Day public holiday, which inevitably led to after-work snarl-ups and long delays with commuters hurrying to be with family and friends.

On the approach to the tunnel entrance, his phone rang. As he pulled the device from his inside jacket pocket, he had a pretty good idea who the caller would be. Mitchell seldom left work before eight on weekdays, even though his contractual hours were nine to six. Such was the way of the working world in The City That Never Slept. That Tuesday night he had been invited to a kind of coming-out party and had managed to clear most of his work before slipping out of the door. He had not been able to find his boss and fully expected her to be on the line. But his phone had another name on the screen.

"Ellie? Everything okay?"

"Is this a good time, Mitch?" she asked. They called each other every Sunday. Or rather, she phoned, and he listened. He had come to view the conversations as her weekly therapy session. Mitchell usually browsed online newspapers while she grumbled about family or work.

"Well, I'm about fifteen minutes away from my drop-off," said Mitchell. "Being thrown around the backseat of a taxi by a wannabe Lewis Hamilton. So I'd say now is as good a time as any."

"Tell him to slow down then. Don't they have speed limits over there?" came his sister's stern but anxious voice. Mitchell bit his tongue. He hadn't been thinking. The last thing he wanted was to worry his sister by dredging up memories of Joel.

"I'm kidding, Ellie. He's perfectly competent," said Mitchell calmly. "He was just negotiating a curve in the expressway. The road system here is far less complicated than over there, barely any speed bumps or mini roundabouts, or those ridiculous ever-changing speed zones designed to catch drivers on cameras. Why are you calling?"

He could hear her taking a moment to breathe.

"Zane's been accepted into Leeds. For the mechanical engineering degree programme he wanted."

"That's great news."

And expensive, he mused, which was probably why she was calling. Their grandparents had set up education trust funds for her three children years ago, but fees had soared since then.

"I know, but he's now got time on his hands. He'll be living in the halls for the first year, but we don't move him in until August."

"What about a part-time job?"

"I wanted him to get out and socialise more. He's always been a bit of a loner. And the coronavirus years haven't helped. He's far more insular than Peter and Jules. I want him to take this time out and see the world. How would you feel about him coming to visit you?"

Mitchell had been hypnotised by the lights on the tunnel walls as they flashed past, and her question caught him off guard. How would he feel about sharing his space with someone?

"Here?" he asked, rather inanely.

"For part of the summer."

"How long?"

"A week. Maybe two. He can be with you at the beginning of June."

"A month's time?"

"If it's convenient."

Mitchell's mind went blank.

"I—I don't really know him, sis."

Referred to as the gay uncle who lived abroad, Mitchell had spent precious little time with his niece and nephews. On Ellie's advice he sent them cards and deposited money into their savings accounts for birthdays and Christmases. On his last trip back five years ago, twenty-year-old Peter had talked his ear off about rugby, while eleven-year-old Julie had asked a stream of questions about living in China.

Zane had all but ignored him.

"Isn't that the point? For the two of you to get to know each other? I'm worried that if he stays home he'll spend the summer in his bedroom glued to the internet or playing those mindless bloody computer games."

"Have you spoken to him about this?"

"Of course I have."

"And?"

"And he said he's okay as long as you are."

Mitchell had no idea what they'd talk about or how he would entertain Zane. As though answering his prayer, he glanced out of the window just as the taxi passed a giant billboard for the Ocean Park theme park.

"Just him? No friend?"

"Just him. I'm not sure he has any close friends. I thought he could stay until the twenty-third."

Three weeks, then.

"I'll have to work, Ellie."

"He's almost twenty, Mitch. He doesn't need babysitting. Just somewhere to set up camp. Give him a house key and he can find his own way around. And maybe the two of you can hang out at the weekend. If you can find the time."

He chose not to rise to the bait of the innuendo in her final words. He wouldn't have hesitated if she had suggested Peter, a nephew who could at least hold down a conversation. What did he know about Zane? Not much. Although he was sure he'd once overheard Jules talking to him about his work backstage on a school play.

"Okay, look," she said, clearly sensing his hesitation. "Cards on the table. Rob and I need to drive up to Newcastle to help move his mum into a care home and sort out her house, which is likely to take at least two to three weeks. Peter's holidaying with his girlfriend for a fortnight at the end of the month while Rob's sister's taking Jules to Spain with them over half term. Zane says he's happy to stay home and look after himself, but I want him to use this time, Mitch. And what better opportunity than bonding with his fabulous Guncle. Please say yes."

Mitchell took a moment to consider her plea.

"And I've managed to reserve cheap flights. All I need is a yes from you before I press go."

And there it was, the crunch. Mitchell sighed dramatically. Ellie loved a bargain.

"Yes, then."

"Fantastic. I'll send you the details—"

"No," said Mitchell firmly. "No, get Zane to email them to me. And tell him to let me know if he has any food allergies, dislikes or other quirks. Broadband is fibre and second to none here, so you can put his mind at rest there. And I want a list of the top five things he wants to do while he's over—"

"I don't think he knows enough about Hong Kong—"

"Then tell him to start researching. He's going to need those skills for uni. If he has a checklist, he can tick things off while he's here."

Right then, another caller's name popped up on his screen, one he had been expecting earlier.

"Thank you, Mitch," said Ellie. "Rob will be relieved—"

"Sorry, Ellie. Can we pick this up on Sunday? I've got my boss on the other line."

"Bugger off, then. I'll book his flights. Speak Sunday."

Brian Lancaster

Mitchell thumbed the incoming call.

"Mitchell. Where are you?" came the irritated voice of his boss, Pauline Ng.

"In a taxi. Heading to a friend's place for a family gathering. I tried to find you on my way out, but your secretary said you were busy."

"I was. I am," said Pauline, as dismissively as ever. "I wanted to speak to you privately."

"Do you want me to head back in?"

"No, no. There's no need. Do you have time to talk now?"

"Fire away."

* * * *

Half an hour later, holding a glass of red wine, Mitchell glowered through the floor-to-ceiling windows of Beth and Kate's lavish eighteenth-floor Repulse Bay apartment. The whole southwestern end housed a wall of enormous windowpanes. That evening they framed a spectacular fiery sunset across the South China Sea. At any other time, the sight might have lifted his spirits.

He should have ignored Pauline's call. Then again, she was like a terrier and would have kept ringing until he'd answered. Why did she always choose to confide unwelcome news late in the day? And just before a weekend or a public holiday? Why could she not let him enjoy his day off? Plans to close down their office in Hong Kong and relocate all departmental functions to Singapore or London told on Tuesday evening would still be the same gut-wrenching news come Thursday morning.

He knew why. Pauline wanted him to start getting his head around logistics and planning what would happen without being distracted by day-to-day work. Was it her fault if the strictly confidential news ruined his day off?

Her special initiative was going to be horrendous. There would be multiple redundancies. Statutory severance payouts bordered on pitiful, and unless the organisation matched the more generous British redundancy calculations — which was unlikely — many good local people would have a paltry handout and no livelihood. In the weeks and months following the end of the pandemic, they had reduced headcount by around five per cent. But in all his years in Hong Kong, working for the same bank, something felt different about this, brutal and final — and personal.

"What do you think, Mitchell, darling? About Colton Underwood? Mark says he should have stayed in the closet," said Harold, wrenching him away from his thoughts. Of all the group, sixty-eight-year-old Harold could read Mitchell's mood better than anyone, and honestly, he was grateful for the distraction.

"I don't know who that is," said Mitchell, half-heartedly but truthfully. "Is he Carrie Underwood's brother?"

He had not meant the remark to be funny but chuckled along with the men standing around him, whose earnestness had dissolved into mirth.

"Darling," said Harold, shaking his head. "You are very close to losing your membership —"

"Be nice, Harold," said Mark. "At least he knows who Carrie Underwood is. Surely that has to count for something."

"I suppose we should allow some slack. He is a banker, after all," said Harold.

Harold Choi had been Mitchell's best friend for over eight years. Now confined to a motorised wheelchair due to a rare spinal tumour, he stayed as active as his condition allowed. Always escorted by his long-term partner, William, he provided a voice of reason and sound advice in Mitchell's life. Long before the illness, Harold had worked tirelessly and sold his Hong Kong property business for a premium. With too much time on his hands and reduced mobility, he knew everything about the global entertainment industry but rarely paid any attention to the finer points of his friends' lives.

"I'm a human resources manager for Charteris Bank."

"Hiring and firing?" asked a grinning Mark—a simplistic view of his work but one that felt entirely accurate that particular evening. "Or are you a jack of all trades?"

Canadian Mark Doolen was the youngest and newest group member. He sported the kind of clean-cut and wholesome handsomeness characterised by young disciples of the Church of Latter-Day Saints. Mark had been in Hong Kong less time than any of them, and his introduction to the region had been a stint at a lacklustre quarantine hotel at the tail end of the pandemic pantomime. They had met only once before. Mitchell liked him and felt a mutual connection, more of respect than attraction. He sensed Mark was attracted to a particular type, a specific group into which none of their crowd fell.

"Jack of all trades," muttered William, stationed behind Harold's chair. "Master of none."

"Oft times better than a master of one," said Harold. And then there was William.

Mitchell had no idea how their relationship had stood the test of time. William exuded negativity and conversed in clipped, precise milliseconds, while the more optimistic Harold often rambled on in long, drawn-out, convoluted minutes.

"I do a little of everything," said Mitchell, focusing on Mark.

"A little, as in...?" asked Mark. Maybe he was making polite conversation, but he appeared genuinely interested.

"Strategic recruitment for specialist positions, providing advice when considering moving into new areas of operation. But I also get involved in everyday people work issues. Managing performance, employee engagement and training. I've been running awareness sessions at all levels on diversity, equity and inclusion."

"Pandering to the woke generation," said William.

"More like adapting old attitudes to a new world with a more enlightened workforce. There's a shrinking pool of talent out there. The new generation entering the workplace have choices and, naturally, want to work somewhere fair and culturally accepting. Even investors want to know they're putting their money into an organisation that has strong ethical values, including how they treat their employees. Unfortunately, some old-school directors running companies these days are just paying lip service to the concepts and, deep down, only care about the bottom line."

William pursed his lips and shrugged. "Profit is not a dirty word. Companies need to make one to survive."

"Of course they do, but—" began Mitchell.

"What kind of things do you include in diversity?" asked Mark, clearly interested and pointedly ignoring William. "The usual suspects? Tolerance? Discrimination? Equal opportunities?"

"They're all components. But there are other, more subtle areas like unconscious bias. Learnt assumptions or beliefs that we're not aware of, ones that might adversely affect our decisions and reinforce negative stereotypes. You know, like when someone voices their surprise that a Hong Kong native's spoken Mandarin is good. The statement might sound like a compliment, but the inherent bias is that, unconsciously, they believe locals only know how to converse in Cantonese. Many of the people I work with have parents who speak fluent Mandarin and Cantonese, and often other dialects. I've also had to cover something new for me, something called bystander intervention."

"Bystander intervention? Heavens, should we even ask?" said William, rolling his eyes.

"It's how we handle harassment, not so much as a perpetrator or a victim — something already embedded in our policies — but as an observer. Imagine you're at work and you witness someone being treated badly by another person, not necessarily physically or even overtly, but just something you sense intuitively. Like someone who singles out an individual and demonstrates bullying behaviour towards them. You have a choice whether to stand up and do something and actively intervene, or report what you see to someone in authority. Or you could walk away and say nothing."

"Speaking up is common sense, though, isn't it?" asked Mark, nodding thoughtfully. "That's what any decent folk would do."

"I like to think so. Although there's always the fear of misinterpreting a situation. But having something formally written into our policies rather than relying on common sense means that people have guidelines, which in turn means that anyone tempted to harass someone knows there will be consequences. In the past it's been all too easy to turn a blind eye."

"Yeah, I guess you're right," said Mark. "Sounds like you enjoy what you do?"

"Sometimes. Like any job, there are the good and bad parts. Too often these days you just keep your mouth shut, put on a brave face and do what you have to do."

Harold clearly noticed the change in Mitchell's tone. He turned the chair to face Mitchell using the joystick on his armrest. William took the opportunity to perch down on a wooden bench.

"Am I sensing a disturbance in the Force, darling?" he asked, reaching out to touch Mitchell's arm. "You don't seem your usual self tonight."

Mitchell couldn't disclose information about the upheaval coming down the line—not that Harold would care anyway—but he had other news that would most certainly grab Harold's attention.

"Enough with the Charles Xavier routine, Harold. My sister dropped a bombshell on the way here. My young nephew is taking time out before going to uni in September. She wants him to stay with me in Hong Kong for most of June."

"Oh," said Harold, skeletal fingers held over his lips. "What has she told him about you?"

"He knows I'm gay, if that's what you mean," said Mitchell with a shrug. "You know their generation. Whatever your preference, they couldn't care less."

"Unless you're fucking up their pronouns," said William.

"I have to admit to feeling a little disappointed by this self-proclaimed enlightened generation," said Harold. "I'd hoped they would finally retire labels, insist that people are people and love is love in whatever form that takes, and negate the need for the categorisation. But there appear to be more now than ever, each one vying for our attention and understanding. Sorry, getting off topic. Is this nephew of yours bringing a friend?"

"Just him."

"Isn't having him staying with you going to be a cock-block?" asked Mark.

"By cock-block, you're assuming I have a sex life," said Mitchell quickly before anyone else could.

"Definitely in danger of losing your membership," muttered Harold.

"What's he like?" asked Mark. "Your nephew?"

"That's the thing, I don't really know him. He was born and raised in New Zealand until the age of ten. They moved back to England around the time of the London Olympics, and I'd already been working here for a couple of years by then."

"You must have met him, though? On your trips back home?"

"A few times, but only enough to say hello. We've never spent time together." As he spoke, the realisation hit him hard. While he had pursued his career across the other side of the world, he'd missed out on the lives of his niece and nephews. "On most trips back, I'm rushing to meetings in London, or between family and friends. I'm exhausted by the time I board the plane back here. I mean, he's a good kid by all accounts, but he doesn't seem to have any close friends. My sister said he's intelligent but shy and not particularly sociable, if you know what I mean?"

"On the spectrum," said William.

"Not necessarily. And, for the record, I dislike that expression. If anybody's different these days, they get written off as being on the spectrum, as though they're borderline clinically dysfunctional or have a personality disorder. Not only is it a lazy way to explain away somebody's nonconformist behaviour, but it's often wrong and can be hurtful to the person in question. More importantly, it undermines those dealing with real issues of that nature."

"Excuse me, Mary," said William, holding his palms up. "What is with you tonight?"

"What kind of things does he like?" asked Mark.

"Again—and this is only what my sister tells me—he spends a lot of time playing online games like Minecraft or following his favourite internet celebrities on social media. You know, YouTube, TikTok, Snapchat. She's mentioned a few names in the past but they meant nothing to me."

"Well, there you are. You have the spare bedroom, don't you?" said Harold. "With a single bed, air-conditioning and a small desk. Set him up in there, plug him into your Wi-Fi, shut the door and forget about him."

Mitchell chuckled. Zane would probably be delighted with that arrangement.

"The plan is for me to help bring him out of his shell. I suppose I could drag him around the usual sights, but I wanted to do something that got him more, you know, involved locally with people his own age. Sports, or hiking or arts and crafts. I'm sure my niece told me he helped backstage with theatre productions at school."

"William," said Harold, turning to his partner, "you've always been an advocate of community theatre, haven't you? Always trying to cajole me into accompanying you to one amateur production or another."

"Before the crony-virus."

"Aren't the arts worldwide rising from the ashes like the proverbial phoenix? Surely there must be something on the horizon?"

"They're doing *Cabaret the Musical*. Early June. Started rehearsals in March."

"There you go, Mitchell, darling. Perfect timing. Find somebody who's on the production team or in the cast and ask if they need help working behind the scenes, if such is his wont."

"Actually," said Mitchell, "that's not a bad idea. Don't suppose you know anyone involved?"

"Kate's friend Shelly," said William. "She helps run rehearsals. Think she even directed a show once."

"Problem solved," said Harold. "Have a word with your friend Kate. Although Beth seems to have recruited her to remind people not to lean against walls or touch artwork, and to use coasters and napkins on pain of death. Surprised she isn't handing out latex gloves. On second thoughts, tonight might not be the best time to get Kate's attention."

"I'll send her a message," said Mitchell.

"Honestly," said Harold, peering around the room, "can you believe they're bringing a child to live in this mausoleum? I am so looking forward to being invited back one day in the near future and finding scribbles in coloured crayon and tiny strawberry jam handprints on their pristine white walls."

Despite his sullen mood, Mitchell had to suppress his laughter. Harold had a way of articulating what others were thinking. Even with the addition of clusters of pastel pink and pearl balloons framing the windows, Beth and Kate's apartment exuded all the homely cosiness of a Hollywood Road fine arts gallery. With no music playing, guests spoke in hushed tones. Only the jangle of Beth's polished glass earrings cut through the low hum of conversations like wind chimes as she ushered two servers across the bamboo flooring to offer around silver platters of colourful, tasteless vegan nibbles.

"Can we leave yet? My arse is going numb," said William, rising slowly from the bench.

"I'd suggest giving it half an hour after they've introduced Angel," said Mitchell, checking his watch.

"And how long is that going to take?" said Harold. "She told me seven-thirty. If I'd known it was going to be this uncomfortable I'd have brought picnic chairs. I blame you, Mitchell. You could have given us the heads-up."

"I told you what I knew, that they lived in one of the Repulse Bay luxury apartments, the block with the square hole in the middle. That should have been clue enough."

"Yeah, what is that about?" asked Mark. "The hole in the building."

"Feng shui," said Harold, rubbing one hand over the other. "A local superstition that dragons live in the mountains behind the apartment block. The opening allows them to pass freely through the building to get to the sea. Blocking their way would bring bad luck.

Leaving the space open means they can come and go any time they please."

"Unlike us," said William. "Hal, I demand hot food after this."

When he followed up with words in Cantonese, Mitchell could only guess their meaning from the tone and the face William pulled. Both men habitually ridiculed the Western tradition of serving cold finger food at drink parties.

"Could they not at least switch off the air-conditioning for a few minutes?" asked William, blowing heat into the fingers of one hand. "Or do they think the vegan pâté rice cakes might get warm."

"Is anyone actually enjoying this?" asked Harold.

"Tommy Chow," muttered William with disdain.

"Tommy's here?" asked Harold.

"By the bay windows," said William. "Wearing the expensive, tight-fitting Alexander McQueen shirt, if I'm not mistaken. In virginal white. Oh my, the irony."

"Mr Smoking Hot? I assumed he was one of the waiting staff," said Mark, his attention drawn to the figure William had pointed out.

Mitchell recognised him immediately. Tommy Chow, all smiles, networking the room like a vote-hungry politician. Mark was right, Tommy turned heads. Perfectly coiffed dark hair brushed up and with tapered sides showcasing his flawless, handsome Asian features. He looked like a Canto-pop celebrity in his fitted jeans and blue felt shoes without socks to show off his muscled legs and slim ankles. Mitchell had never been attracted to ostentatious men, but Tommy's many ensembles always seemed effortless, natural rather than cultured.

"Good heavens, Mark," said Harold, a hand pressed to his chest. "Are you telling me you've been in Hong Kong all this time and he hasn't tried to jump your bones? Tommy must be off his game."

Mitchell had never been able to figure out Tommy. On the rare occasions they'd met, Tommy had been civil enough, but his attention had quickly wandered elsewhere, probably on the lookout for something better. Mitchell had shrugged off the slight and didn't even find the behaviour insulting. He knew he wasn't Tommy's type. Too old and uncool. End of story. And that suited Mitchell perfectly because he'd already had the best. And nobody, not even Tommy the socialite, could compete or even come close. But that didn't stop Mitchell's faint admiration. Tommy might have flaws—who didn't?—and be considered vapid and superficial by their highly critical group, but on a night like tonight he put their antisocial elitism to shame.

"Don't be offended, Mark," said Mitchell, sipping his wine. "I've lost count of the number of times I've been snubbed by him. I'm not even sure he remembers my name."

"That, my dear Mitchell, is because you have singular tastes and impossibly high standards where potential mates are concerned," said Harold. "What is it Kate says about you? Mitchell is not one of those happy to dip his toe into many pools until he finds one he likes. He's someone whose idea of foreplay is intelligent conversation. And I'm afraid, my dear, that's enough to scare the shit out of most of our local gay community. Especially men like Tommy, who prefer to splash aimlessly from one puddle to the next like toddlers happy to be in the rain."

Mitchell chuckled at the image. Harold had tried to match-make Mitchell with a couple of his friends. Never successfully. And, yes, he was not a fan of online hook-ups, but neither was he a prude. During his first few months in Hong Kong he had swiped his way through a handful of no-strings encounters. But the selection had grown smaller every time, and the appeal had soon waned.

"At least Tommy's bothering to mingle," said Mark, his eyes still trained across the room.

"Tommy's a sexual butterfly," said William, plucking a slice of offending cucumber from the top of his finger food. "He's not mingling. He's flitting from group to group, trying to sniff out tonight's hook-up."

"I thought you said we were the only gay men at this party," said Mark.

"Tommy's an equal opportunity slut," said William. "Heterosexuality has never been a barrier."

"I know the guy he's chatting to," said Mitchell. "That tall, good-looking one with the light brown hair is Adam. He's an investment analyst. Plays rugby for a local team. And he's definitely straight. I work with his wife."

"Whereas the shady-looking gentleman standing next to him is single and will take whatever he can get," said Harold. "Not a particularly decent sort, by all accounts. Heaven knows how he got himself invited."

"Gentlemen," came Kate's clipped English voice from behind them. Mitchell noticed everyone stiffen slightly as though a teacher had caught them vaping in the cloakroom. "Thanks awfully for coming tonight. This was supposed to be an early gathering for everyone to meet Angel before her bedtime. An hour ago. Just hang on a few more minutes. She's finally decided which new dress she'll wear. Already turned her nose up and stamped her heel at four of our choices, the little madam."

"Taking after Beth, then?" said Mitchell with a smirk.

Although she giggled along with them all, Kate tilted her head at Mitchell to let him know that his comment wasn't far from the truth. Two demanding Beths in the same household would make for an interesting future.

Kate appeared to have been tasked with preparing and quieting the room, readying everyone for the entrance of the new starlet. Right on cue, the only child at the party appeared in the corridor leading from the bedrooms. Dressed in an ice-blue dress, like a miniature Elsa from *Frozen*, she was being urged forward by an uncharacteristically stressed Beth.

"Hi, everyone. This is Angel," said Beth in her crisp New York accent. "As you know, Angel's been living at a local orphanage for the past two years. You'll also know that Beth and I have been to see her on numerous occasions, and we've gotten to know each other really well. Anyway, she's agreed to come and live with us for six months on a trial fostering arrangement. And if she enjoys living here, well, maybe she'll agree to stay for good. But that's going to be her choice. Would you want to say a few words, Angel?"

Taking a step forward from Beth, Angel yanked her hand away, clasped both of her hands to her stomach as though about to sing.

"My aunties asked me to come and say hello to you all. After school we had a party with my school friends and we had special cupcakes. I'm afraid we ate all of those, but we left the balloons for you. Although you can't eat them, of course. Anyway, I hope you have a nice time, even if there's no cake. And thank you all for my presents that my aunties say I can open tomorrow morning. But for now, I need to go to bed, so good night."

To a chorus of good nights, the pretty little thing grinned a gap-toothed smile and waved a hand like royalty before turning away. But then, as an afterthought, she turned back.

"And Auntie Beth said nobody better spill a goddamn thing on her 'spensive rugs —"

"Yes, yes, Angel, hon. Time for bed now," said Beth, her eyes widening at Kate before she led their new arrival into the corridor to a murmur of titters. Yes, their little Angel was going to be a handful.

"Let's suffer through another fifteen minutes before making our escape," said Harold, peering over at the small group by the front door bidding their goodbyes to Kate and Beth. "Not sure if you noticed, Mitchell, but your colleague's drunken husband slipped out a moment ago. Led away by Tommy and the vampire. Heaven knows where they're off to, but I doubt it will end well."

Mitchell checked the open front door where Kate and Beth stood deep in conversation with an elderly couple. For all his wit and sarcasm, Mitchell trusted Harold's insights, and right then, something crystallised in him. He leant down to position his glass carefully on a coaster before straightening up.

"How long?" asked Mitchell.

"Sorry?" asked William, confused.

"Around five minutes," said Harold.

"Tell me you're not going to crash their party?" asked William.

"Quite the opposite. You asked earlier about bystander intervention," said Mitchell. "Well, this is a living example, me taking the initiative to stop Adam — and probably Tommy — finding themselves in a situation they might regret. Most of all, it's about me knowing all of this and bothering to offer my help. They might tell me to piss off, but at least I'll know I tried. Because if I woke tomorrow morning and found out something terrible had happened, knowing I could have intervened but did nothing, then I'd never forgive myself."

"You're an idealist. They're adults," said William, rolling his eyes. "They can take care of themselves."

"That may be the case. And maybe I am being oversensitive."

"Would they do the same for you?" asked William. Mitchell noticed that Harold had yet to pass comment. "I think not."

"Fine. Then let's just say I'm doing this for me," said Mitchell before holding a hand up in farewell. "I'll call you over the weekend."

"Good man," was all Harold contributed.

And with that, after a quick wave to the hosts, Mitchell slipped through the door.

Chapter Two

Tommy Chow perched on the corner of the faux-antique writing desk in his sister Sammi's Wellington Street aromatherapy shop, Candles in the Mist, flicking through a society magazine. Sammi trusted nobody else to unpack and check the deliveries of her stock, especially the artisanal ceramic oil burners. Half-past nine, she still had another half an hour before the doors opened for trade. There was something magical about the store with its musk-laden air and softly lit interior. Clusters of candles of various shapes, sizes, colours and scents sat on tabletops surrounded by regimented rows of aromatherapy oils, devices and other beautiful but wholly superfluous lifestyle curios. Everything had been arranged on Chinese antique rosewood tables or dressers amid hanging red lanterns.

"What do you think of this?" asked Sammi, holding an egg-shaped device in her palm. Tommy squinted a few times before shrugging.

"Looks like a sex toy."

"Barbarian. This is a mini humidifier — for travelling — combined with a diffuser, to slowly release essential oils. Comes with LED mood light settings."

"Wow, who doesn't need one of those? You should rename this shop Unessential Objects."

"And you should keep your opinions to yourself."

"Then you should stop asking for them."

He'd offered to help unpack, knowing she would decline because, being a control freak, she insisted on personally inspecting every item in her inventory. Instead, he had popped along to her favourite juice shop two doors down and bought her what he called her lawn juice — a mix of green apples, green vegetables and wheat grass. Until she had the ring on her finger, she reminded him repeatedly, there would be no more cream-topped iced caramel macchiatos.

"What did you get up to last night?" she asked, filling the silence. "Back to trawling the bars again? Or have you turned over a new leaf and decided progressing to cocktail parties or other grown-up activities is now your thing?"

He should never have told her. Almost three weeks ago Tommy had found himself attending a cocktail party in Repulse Bay, invited by a friend of a friend. Unsurprisingly, his sister knew one of the hosts, Kate Kirkby, who attended the same Pilates class. She and her wife had used the party to introduce the little girl they hoped to adopt."

"I did my one and only cocktail party, remember? Three weeks ago. An experience I would blank from memory."

"So you did. What happened again?"

"I told you. Pretty dull to begin with. But just as things started to look promising, this gweilo dickhead stuck his fat nose in."

"You know using the term gweilo for a Westerner is considered offensive these days, don't you?"

Tommy rolled his eyes. His sister preached political correctness when the situation suited her. He said nothing because she also invariably had his corner.

"Whatever."

"Anyway, go on," she said, her head buried in a box. "Which gweilo? There are so many."

Quite unnecessarily, Tommy turned away to smirk.

"I told you. You're getting worse than Grandma. Mitchell Baxter. One of Harold Choi's like-and-subscribe followers."

Sammi's head popped out of the box.

"Ah yes, Mitchell Baxter. Hang on, I remember this. You'd been chatting with two older guys, one a cute drunk and the other a little wild and uncultured, but they both seemed game for some post-cocktail fun. Did I get that right?"

"Exactly. Anyway, the roughneck invited us back to his place. We'd barely made it to the front of the taxi queue when this asshole friend of Harold's shuffles up. He starts chatting to Mr Handsome-But-Drunk, asking how his wife was and how many days left before their baby's due—"

"Wait! You never told me that," said Sammi. She froze with a newspaper-wrapped container in her hands, staring at him open-mouthed and horrified. "This guy's out partying while his wife's at home pregnant with their baby, about to give birth—"

"Chill, will you? He was attending on her behalf. And I'd hardly call it partying—"

"Honestly, brother. You are a total dick sometimes."

"Anyway, this friend of Harold's gets Daddy-To-Be all guilt-ridden until he cries off, saying he really ought to cab it back to Wifey. Meanwhile, this other not-so-hottie, Dash something, still seemed pretty keen—"

"Hold on. Dash? Not Dash Hernandez?"

"I didn't get his last name—"

"Honey, how many Dashes are there in this town? You never mentioned his name before. Otherwise I would have remembered. Did he look like an olive-skinned Captain Spock but with earrings and long, greasy, black hair?"

"Uh, yes, that sounds about right."

When he looked over, his sister had walked to the counter to search through a pile of old newspapers before pulling one out. After checking a few sections, she folded a page and held up a news article containing a small photograph.

"Now what?" he asked as she brought the paper over.

"Tommy, you have got to be more careful. Dash Hernandez is trouble. Look at this news article. There's an ongoing court case at the moment. One of his guests overdosed on the bathroom floor at a party he was throwing last September. Dear old Dash denies all knowledge, alleges the girl turned up with a friend and brought her own shit. But everyone close to him says Dash has even been rumoured to deal. If you want my opinion—and I know you rarely do—I think you dodged a bullet that night."

Tommy stared at the photo of Dash, who admittedly looked a bit like Jack Sparrow's less attractive older brother. When he had suggested they go back to his place for more drinks and a bit of fun, Tommy's mind had instantly latched onto the idea of sex. Drugs had never even crossed his mind. Perhaps his sister had a point.

At the taxi rank, Dash had simply shrugged off Daddy-To-Be bailing on them until Mitchell suggested Dash might want to make sure the man got home safely, offering to phone the hottie's wife and tell him they were on their way. And just like that, the after-party promise was flushed down the pan, with Tommy left feeling righteously pissed.

He had waited for Mitchell to finish the call before going for the jugular.

"What the fuck was that all about?"

Having just popped the phone back into his jacket pocket, Mitchell had looked reassuringly startled at Tommy's anger.

"I know his wife. We work together. He should be at home —"

"That's not your call to make, is it? He's a grown man. Who do you think you are? His mother-in-law?"

"Of course not, but —"

"And both of them don't have pregnant wives, do they? Why did you chase the other guy off?"

Even beneath the stark streetlight, Tommy had noticed Mitchell's face drain of colour. Maybe he'd had a sudden epiphany about being a prize asshole, but his argument for the defence had seemed to have evaporated.

"Just when I thought I'd salvaged something out of this car wreck of an evening, you come along and steal the tow truck. What gives you the right?"

"I — I'm sorry. I didn't think —"

"No, you didn't think, did you? I am sick of Harold and his judgemental queens thinking they're so much better than

everyone else and having an opinion about everything. You should all try looking in the mirror at some point. And keep your nose out of other people's business."

Tommy had twirled around and attitude-strutted down the pathway pretty damn confidently — a move he'd picked up from *Drag Race* — just in time to witness a red taxi pull up. Maybe he had overreacted a little, but his point had been made.

"Look — Tommy, isn't it?" Mitchell had called out. *"You probably don't remember me —"*

"I know who you are, Mitchell Baxter."

"Oh, I see. Then perhaps we can share the taxi? I'm happy to drop you off in town or somewhere. Just tell me where."

"Too late. Thanks to you I've lost my mojo." Tommy had stopped to look over his shoulder in disgust. *"And do you honestly think I'd get in a cab with you after you pulled a stunt like that? You'd probably dump me outside the Methodist church in Wanchai for an AA meeting. Or at the local police station citing parole violation. No, fuck you very much. Have a nice life."*

Okay, with hindsight, maybe he had been a touch overdramatic. Shit. Whatever. He was unlikely to see the guy again. Right now, he needed something to divert his sister's schoolmarm glare.

"On a brighter note, any updates on the wedding?" he asked, and noticed her stern features brighten.

"I haven't had a chance to tell you. You know what a pain the wedding banquet was becoming, because of the numbers and the date. Well, for the ceremony, we secured the front lawn of the Repulse Bay. But they're not able to cater the banquet. Eventually Daley's father stepped in and pulled some strings. He knows one of the owners of the Grand Hyatt and managed to book us the Grand Ballroom on the date we wanted. Four hundred and fifty guests. And we have preferential rates for a hundred rooms already blocked. At least that's one major headache out of the way."

Her fiancé, Singaporean Daley Tan, came from a wealthy family. His father owned commercial properties in Singapore and Malaysia, although Daley had found his niche in men's jewellery, mainly trading in high-end watches, his primary passion. The family was not in the top league of Crazy Rich Asians, but they were very comfortably off, and, more importantly, the money hadn't spoilt them. In fact, Tommy had always considered Daley a little nerdy with his designer but thick-lensed glasses and chubby face. And the few times they'd met in Singapore, Daley had taken them for lunch at his favourite spot, a dai pai dong open-air food stall, where they'd sat on plastic stools on the street slurping prawn noodles from chipped bowls.

"We'll put up close relatives from overseas in our parent's flat. Gran and Aunt Mabel have offered, too. And be prepared to be invited to join a message group for the bridesmaids, groomsmen and other organisers. And no, Daley and I are not included. One last thing. Mum asked if you could take your cello home. It's taking up space in their spare room."

"I'll pop over Saturday."

"And the string quartet I wanted for the ceremony is a bust. They accepted a better offer in Los Angeles the same weekend. I don't suppose you'd rethink getting up on stage and playing—"

"Absolutely not, sis. I am not looking like a dickhead in front of our friends and relatives."

Or any potential hook-ups, he thought, but said nothing.

"You used to be good, Tommy."

For a second, Tommy thought his sister meant his ability to hook up.

"Used to be. Past tense. I haven't practised in years. Move on. What other news?"

"Well, the hotel's organising the catering for the banquet — so that's one headache out of the way — and Mother's friend is sorting out the flowers. Bridesmaid's dresses will be a challenge, but I am working on a strategy. And can you believe that, despite his insane schedule, Alec has agreed to be Daley's best man. Oh, and you'll never guess who..."

Tommy heard no more. Dusty blond-haired, stunningly good-looking Australian Alec Janussen, complete with surfer bod and easy confidence, had been at Daley's thirtieth birthday celebration in Singapore. Alec and Daley had gone to university together in Sydney and remained lifelong buddies. Not often did Tommy get tongue-tied, but once left alone with the demigod, he had been unable to find anything remotely interesting to say in response to Alec's questions. Even though Tommy had sensed a definite vibe, staring at the light blond chest hair, the freckled skin beneath his open-neck silk shirt, and the well-defined pecs stretching the fabric, he'd been so embarrassed at freezing that he'd excused himself to use the restroom before heading upstairs and locking himself in his hotel room. Since then, he had told nobody and hoped Alec had written him off as a basket case. Were the gods giving him a second chance?

" — and I didn't know what to tell them, because you haven't told me yet."

"I'm sorry. Told you what?"

"Who you're bringing? Is poor Ming going to be hanging off your arm again, pretending to be your doting girlfriend? Or are you going to grow a pair and actually bring a man-date?"

Throughout the years—even though most of his immediate family knew he was gay—he had never brought a guy to a family event. Not that he had met anyone worth bringing along. But even if he had, would he have had the courage to introduce them to his critical extended family? Having a girl on his arm meant he could still scout the room for hook-ups without anyone suspecting. At his grandmother's seventieth banquet, Ming had sat chatting at the family table during dessert while he was in the men's room getting a blow job from a waiter.

"I hadn't thought that far ahead."

"Well start. I'm sending out save-the-date cards next Tuesday, and I'm putting you down as a plus-one."

Tommy waited a few seconds before voicing what he was aching to ask.

"Is Alec bringing anyone?"

He felt grateful when Sammi carried on unpacking items without looking up.

"No idea. But I don't think so. Just as well, really. He'll have his work cut out just keeping Daley to schedule. You know how unpunctual my fiancé can be, which is ironic considering he sells timepieces for a living? And did I mention the latest on the bridesmaid situation? Nightmare. Oh, but hang on, let me start by giving you an update on the current guest list dramas. So, Auntie Myleen has outright refused to attend if her ex-husband is invited…"

Tommy tuned Sammi out, his attention drawn to a two-page spread in the magazine, maybe because of her mention of timepieces. In the forefront there stood a beautiful man and woman, both actors he vaguely knew, and both clearly used to being in the spotlight. Chatting to a nondescript bald man in a white tuxedo, Tommy noticed they wore the same sparkling brand of sports watch. Were it not for the informal scattering of people, this could have been an advert for the watch company. A quick glance at the accompanying text told him the actors were attending the launch of a new range of elegant sports watches by a well-known manufacturer. Someone had gone to great lengths to pick the perfect Bali setting, with elegantly dressed people standing on a pristine lawn decorated with white pavilions and an ancient, moss-covered Hindu temple as the backdrop.

As Sammi droned on, Tommy refocused his attention on the people in the background, his gaze drawn instantly to the tall Caucasian man in the tan suit with the Arctic-blue eyes, chin dimple and long blond hair. Talk about coincidence. There stood the man himself, Alec Janussen, with Daley standing alongside. He was about to interrupt Sammi and show her, but something about the composition didn't feel right, and he leant forward to study the photograph in more detail.

A pretty but unknown Asian woman stood to Daley's right. The photographer — probably more concerned about the foreground matter — had captured the poor thing with her eyes closed. But that wasn't what had caught Tommy's attention. Whoever she was, the woman seemed overly familiar with Daley, leaning in close while holding his hand.

Had Sammi seen the picture? Did he dare ask or show her? Perhaps there was a perfectly innocent explanation. Having said that, she had enough on her plate right now without worrying about her husband-to-be's fidelity. But he had to know the truth. She was his sister, after all.

"Sammi," he began, holding up the magazine cover. "Did you buy this?"

"Please. Give me some credit. When have you known me to buy that sort of trash? Somebody left it in the shop. Why are you asking?"

"Do you mind if I take this copy? Not my kind of thing, but there's an article that might interest Devon."

"Be my guest. I was going to drop the thing into the trash where it belongs. Now will you please answer my question? Mum and Dad have been nagging me constantly about who you're bringing. They hate to be blindsided when people ask questions about you. And Grandma said she'll hit the roof if you bring another one of those pretty but dumb shop mannequins."

As Tommy tucked the magazine into his jacket, he looked up when the ping of a bell and a new voice — one he knew only too well — carried across the space.

"She will, too," came his grandmother's voice. "You are thirty years old this year. At your age, I had two children to raise and still did the accounts for all three of your grandfather's companies. And what do you have? Not even a casual boyfriend."

Tommy laughed again. His grandmother on his mother's side was the coolest person on the planet. While his mother and father had reacted with disappointment learning about their little prince's sexual orientation, his grandmother had embraced the difference and scolded his parents for being shocked at being blessed with such a loving child. Moreover, she never once commented on his private life.

"I have a job teaching kids to look after their physical well-being, Grandma. And what did Grandfather always say? Get a steady job first and the rest will follow later."

"And? You have the steady job. Now start worrying before you run out of time," she said, stopping to pick up and sniff at a French vanilla-scented candle. "It's gone nine. Why is the closed sign still on the door? Do you not want business? It's the weekend, in case you had forgotten. Everybody will be out shopping very soon."

"Morning, Po-po," said Sammi. "Shop opens at ten."

"Ten? I have finished most of my shopping by ten."

"That's only because I taught you to shop online. If you're talking about online shopping and shipping then my business is never closed."

"Smart girl has an answer for everything."

"Just like you taught me, Po-po."

Tommy made the mistake of chuckling. When his grandmother's attention swung his way, he noticed his sister grinning as she checked stock.

"Are you helping your sister in the shop today, Tommy?"

"Can't, Grandma. Having coffee with Devon in a minute. He has a special favour to ask. Then I've got a lunch meeting with a teacher colleague. We're discussing plans for the new play she's co-directing and I'm stage managing."

"Always helping other people. And will they return the favour and suggest a nice boy for you to bring to your sister's wedding? Would be good to enjoy the celebration without having to spend the day making excuses to our relatives about why my good-looking and eligible grandson is still single."

His sister snorted loudly while bending down to pull out a wrapped object. Tommy sighed and rolled his eyes. Okay, he thought, *most* of the time his grandmother didn't pester him about his love life.

"Don't worry, Po-po. I promise I'll bring someone to make you proud."

Two months until the big day. Battles had been fought and won in less time. And if he couldn't find a suitable hottie by then, there was always his best friend, Devon.

Chapter Three

With his small rucksack slung over one shoulder, Mitchell descended the concrete stairwell from his fifth-floor Kennedy Town walk-up after finishing his weekly household chores. Clothes and bedlinen hung in the tiny bathroom with the dehumidifier running on overdrive—otherwise, they would never dry in the cloying humidity. Everything would be ready for either ironing or folding away in the morning. With the quilt, pillowcases and bedsheet replaced and the bamboo flooring vacuumed and mopped, everything else had been dusted, polished, tidied away and made ready for the week ahead. Hardly a superhuman effort, with only three hundred and twenty square feet of living space. He'd even given the spare room a quick spring clean, tossing out old boxes and ensuring the space wouldn't need much work for Zane's arrival.

The thought evoked a sense of uneasiness. Mitchell had never had to bear responsibility for anyone other than himself—outside of work—in all his time in Hong

Kong. Having Zane around would obviously change that.

"Mr Mitchell. How are you today?" came the cheerful voice of Mrs Lau from the open doorway of her flat on the first floor. Harold had confided that many residents in his block considered her a nosy neighbour, referring to her as something that sounded like "butt-paw" in Cantonese. Mitchell found her cheerful and neighbourly, always smiling and checking in to make sure he didn't want for anything. She had even helped by translating for him the few times local workmen came in to complete renovations. His minor recompense had been in occasionally buying her Macau egg tarts from a little cake shop on Lyndhurst Terrace.

All communication with his landlady, Mrs Zhang, went through Mrs Lau. He assumed they must be friends or have been neighbours at some point. He had never seen the actual landlady in his six years living there, the original rental agreement having been signed in a local solicitors' office, where the man had stated his landlady's preference to have Mrs Lau act as their go-between. Mitchell, rightly or wrongly, assumed that Mrs Zhang preferred not to communicate in English. On the plus side, his rent had never once been raised. Many of his colleagues' landlords pushed for rent increases every time their contracts were renewed. Then again, on his part, he had paid out of his pocket to renovate the apartment's older features—obviously with Mrs Zhang's permission. He had upgraded the things he'd considered essential, like modernising the kitchen and bathroom, and installing double-glazed windows throughout the apartment.

"Morning, Mrs Lau. All good, thank you. I'm heading out to lunch."

Right then, the phone in Mitchell's pocket pinged with a message. Rather than read the text, he ignored the phone.

"You don't need to get that?"

"Probably my friend confirming."

Even though nothing had been announced officially, Mitchell suspected that Kate, as the head of finance, already knew about the upcoming redundancies and wanted to use him as a sounding board. They always worked better outside the office, being able to talk freely without fear of being overheard or interrupted.

"And how is the bathroom now?" asked Mrs Lau. "I haven't heard any more workmen upstairs with their banging and foul language. Are they finished?"

"Yes, thank goodness. And I'm sorry for any disturbance."

"Oh heavens, that sound is the background music of Hong Kong. Always buildings work going on, no matter where you live. Are they all finished now?"

"They are. And it means I don't have to use the gym shower before work. Can you please thank the landlady again for allowing me to complete the changes. They make all the difference."

In his most recent project, Mitchell had paid to get the bathroom updated – a slimline boiler installed and the tiny old bathroom suite replaced by a walk-in shower, a modern toilet and a washbasin. Even with the limited space, the functionality and efficiency of the room had improved dramatically. Of course, when he eventually moved out, his landlady could charge more due to modernisation.

"And can you let her know that my nephew from England is coming to stay with me in a few weeks? For a whole month?"

"Ayah, she won't care," said Mrs Lau, then sighed. "But I will tell her if you insist. Should be nice for you to have company for a change."

"We'll see."

"You don't sound sure."

He always found Mrs Lau easy to talk to, and explained that they hardly knew each other. She listened patiently and nodded her understanding as he told his tale, but then, as he finished, she held a finger up, indicating for him to wait.

"I have post for you. Wait here one moment."

Mrs Lau had agreed to take in his mail, citing her mistrust of the security of the block's ancient, wall-mounted mailbox.

"Here you are. Arrived this morning," she said, handing over a small pile of envelopes and leaflets. He tossed the menus and other flyers into the hall trash can before ripping open the envelopes. Two contained utility bills, and one was his official receipt for the month's rent. He made a mental note to apply for electronic bills for his utilities, but the landlady always preferred to send him a paper receipt. Inside, she had included a single card in bright red with the gold lettering of four Chinese characters. He lifted the cardboard out and handed the item to Mrs Lau.

"Would you mind translating?" he asked. "Maybe it's a late Lunar New Year greeting card?"

"*Yat gui leung duk.* No, this is an old proverb which means something like two benefits coming from one action. Mrs Zhang sent you this?"

"I guess so. Tucked in with the rental receipt," said Mitchell. "Does it mean something good?"

"Certainly auspicious. Maybe this relates to your nephew flying to see you and being able to travel and enjoy Hong Kong while you finally get to know each other. Two benefits from one action."

Mitchell smiled at the suggestion. His landlady didn't know about his nephew visiting yet. Like most proverbs, the saying could be applied to almost any situation. Mrs Lau must have seen his hesitation.

"Or could be just a happy wish card," she said.

"Well, thank her for me, will you? I'll stick it on my fridge door with the others," he said, placing the card with the bills into his jacket pocket. "To remind me to be thankful while he's here. Have a lovely day, Mrs Lau."

Situated at the northwest of the island, Kennedy Town housed the terminus for the trams that ran along the north of Hong Kong island, so he hopped on an almost-full one—Saturday trams, being a cheaper means of transport, tended to fill up quickly at the weekends—and found a vacant single seat upstairs.

As anticipated, when he checked his phone, Kate's message told him she was running late and asked him to grab a table in Coffee Maestro on Peel Street. Running much earlier than planned, he texted back before settling in for the ride.

After so many years, he still loved sitting on the top deck, listening to the rumble of the old tramcar on the tracks and watching the world float unhurriedly past. Kennedy Town had plenty of decent coffee shops, but Mitchell liked to head into bustling Central, to the area around Soho, which in Hong Kong stood for the small lanes up the hill and South of Hollywood Road. He had come to love the café society scene on a weekend lunchtime, bistros spilling out onto the narrow streets that made up Soho. Following severe restrictions imposed on businesses during the containment of the virus, many of his old haunts had closed down. But in true Hong Kong resilience, new ones were already opening up.

Coffee Maestro had an area with casual seating, soft leather sofas around low coffee tables, and a more regimented dining section. Along the back wall stood a row of tables and, with the café beginning to fill, he sat in the space reserved by Kate with his back to the wall and an eye on the shop door.

Five minutes later, he nursed a large americano while frowning into his laptop. He had pulled up the latest confidential regional headcount spreadsheet and was trying to figure out what the reduction would look like. With many of the workforce employed by the bank for their working lives, his department would have their work cut out, calculating redundancy packages.

When he saw Kate enter the shop, he snapped his laptop shut and slipped the device away. Instead of the usual smart business suits he had become familiar with at work, she wore a delicate white summer dress with china-blue peacock and floral designs. Only her face showed signs of a stressful morning. Mitchell watched her chat briefly with the barista, who pointed to his table.

"Mitchell. Do not ever consider adopting." She leant down and kissed him on each cheek. "Not. Ever."

"Bad morning?"

"Beth got up in the early hours, as she does, to use the apartment block gym before anyone else had risen," said Kate, placing her bag next to Mitchell and dropping into her seat. "And I don't know about you, but I relish Saturday and Sunday mornings, the only time I can treat myself to a snooze. Well, it looks as though that little luxury is out of the window. Our little Angel, it transpires, is an early riser too, and demanded to be entertained. So while Maria — our live-in nanny —

was preparing breakfast, the little madam decided to jump up and down on my bed until she fell against one of Beth's matching bedside lamps of vintage porcelain, which promptly fell to the floor and smashed into a thousand pieces. Beth tried to laugh the matter off when she returned but I can tell when she's pissed. After I managed to get Angel to eat breakfast, every time I tried to put a foot outside the door to come here she threw a tantrum. I almost called and cancelled."

"Where was Beth while all this was happening?"

One of the waiters dropped off a double espresso and an oversized cup of what looked like a café latte. Kate downed the shot in one go before answering.

"On a call with a client."

"She does know adoption is supposed to be a shared responsibility, doesn't she? Everything's not going to rest on your shoulders, is it?"

"Of course she does. But her job isn't like ours, Mitch. There are times when she has to be full-on, day and night, front and centre. I respect that. It's why they pay her good money. She's taking Angel to the clinic this morning so we can have our catch-up."

"Fair enough," said Mitchell. "Let's talk business and get that out of the way first, but you should know I've been sworn to secrecy by Pauline."

"We've all been sworn to secrecy. The handful that know. But we're going to have to talk at some point. May as well be sooner than later."

Kate knew the same as Mitchell but had a better grip on the redundancy packages on offer. Just as Mitchell had suspected, Charteris was offering nothing more than statutory amounts.

"They'll leave a skeleton staff behind," said Kate. "And find much smaller premises, but over eighty-five per cent of jobs will go. With your knowledge of the local market, they would be insane to let you go. But I've had a headhunter lining up interviews for me — "

"Already?"

"No point hanging around, is there? No doubt we'll be expected to handle the redundancy interviews."

"Not alone. You'll have someone from HR sitting in with you."

"No disrespect, Mitch, but that doesn't give me much comfort. Honestly, I would rather not be around to handle any of it. Hey, one of the banks I'm interviewing with is a relatively new outfit with their Asian operation headquartered here. They're also advertising for a Head of HR position. Do you want me to send you details?"

Even after three weeks, Mitchell hadn't fully processed the changes, not in his head. Ellie constantly teased him about his misplaced loyalty to the bank. And he had automatically assumed the restructuring would entail him staying put. Did he really have the enthusiasm or the energy to begin all over again learning the ways of a new company?

"No harm looking is there?" said Kate, digging out her phone. "I'll send you the details anyway. Delete them if you're not interested. Once I'm home, I'm bound to get swept up in one domestic dilemma or another."

While Kate fiddled with her phone, Mitchell's gaze scanned the room, and he shrank on spotting Tommy entering the café. Fortunately, the place had filled up, and Mitchell's table was hidden at the back. Tommy had a pretty, petite young woman with him, curly copper hair parted down the middle and reaching the shoulders of her white flannel shirt. For some reason, he liked her instantly. She had an openness and a sense of fun that shone from her smiling eyes. Tommy followed behind her, a good foot taller, his eyes scouring the spaces around them, probably looking for somewhere to sit. Mitchell noticed several women and some men turn to look at him. Fair enough, too. He was, without a doubt, a good-looking man, even if he was an asshole. Probably curious at what had grabbed Mitchell's attention, Kate twisted around in her seat, then sprang up with a squeal and waved them over.

Mitchell closed his eyes briefly with dismay before opening them and trying to centre himself. The last thing he wanted was another mouthful of abuse from Tommy.

"Shelly. Tommy. Yoo-hoo. Over here."

In true Kate style, she hugged and cheek-kissed hellos with both of them while Mitchell remained seated, flatlining a grin and holding a palm in salute. For once, Mitchell felt grateful that Kate had only managed to get seats on the row of smaller tables, with people already installed on either side. Otherwise, he felt sure, she would have invited them to join.

"Shelly and Tommy are teacher friends of mine. They're both at the SIA School on the way to the Peak. Shelly teaches science and Tommy teaches —"

"Physical education," said Tommy, avoiding Mitchell's gaze.

"Do you two know each other?" asked Shelly eventually, in all innocence, pointing a finger between Mitchell and Tommy.

"A little," said Tommy, who looked as embarrassed as Mitchell felt.

"Not really," said Mitchell at the same time.

"They have a mutual acquaintance. Harold Choi," said Kate, who looked quizzically at Mitchell and must have tuned in to his mood. "He's one of those people who tends to know everyone but keeps them in different silos. Although I'm surprised these two didn't bump into each other at our party. They both came along when we introduced Angel to the world."

"Oh, Kate. I am so sorry we couldn't make it," Shelly said earnestly. Mitchell sighed inwardly at the perfect diversion. "My hubby had this work thing—"

As the girls chatted, Mitchell caught Tommy's eye. Tommy tried for a lopsided grin, which seemed odd after the unpleasant things he'd said the night they'd last met. The gesture confused Mitchell, who did not return the smile. Instead—even though the action made him feel petty—he picked up his phone from the table and began checking messages. Eventually, he heard Tommy's voice interrupt the girls' chatter.

"Shall I grab us a table before they're all taken?"

"Can't we squeeze you in here?" asked Kate, looking down at the table.

"Kate, we've got work to do," said Mitchell, glaring at her.

"No problem. Tommy, can you get us a table?" said Shelly. "And order me a large, extra-hot, triple-shot soy cappuccino with extra soy foam on the side and two Sweet'N Lows. But make sure they put the sweeteners in first."

Mitchell peered up and almost snorted at Tommy's baffled expression.

"When you get served," added Kate, smiling sympathetically at Tommy, "point her out in the crowd and tell the barista that Shelly wants her usual."

"I'm on it."

Mitchell relaxed after Tommy moved away, and the girls chatted together. To pass the time, he opened his laptop and continued scanning the rows of numbers on his screen. Perhaps the café had not been such a good plan after all, the loud buzz of conversations distracting his concentration. Eventually, he lowered the lid and sipped his coffee.

"Okay, Mr Baxter," said Kate, sitting down again. "What was that all about?"

"What was—"

"Don't even. I know you too well. Your face dropped off a cliff when you saw Tommy. What happened? You left the party not long after him the other week. Did he finally try for a jump and hump?"

"No!" said Mitchell. After a quick glance across the café, he retold his attempt to help, which had prompted Tommy's after-party tirade. When he'd finished, Kate sat unspeaking, an infuriating habit of hers when she had something controversial to say.

"Come on," he said, picking up his coffee mug. "You clearly have an opinion. Do you think I was in the wrong?"

"No," she said hesitantly. "Not necessarily. I mean, if it were happening to me, I'm sure I would have appreciated the intervention."

"But?"

"Why do you have to be such a bloody Boy Scout all the time?" she said, putting down her mug and gently shaking her head. "Tommy is more than capable of looking after himself. Look, I know you well enough by now to know you meant well, but you have got to stop trying to nanny the world."

"Nanny? I thought you of all people would understand—"

"And I do. But you must know how you come across to other adults, especially men?"

Kate's response irritated him. He didn't mind being challenged on work matters, but had never considered needing to ask for permission when it came to doing the right thing. Maybe he would think twice in future.

"What are you doing tomorrow?" she continued.

"Oh no, you don't," said Mitchell, thumping his mug down and leaning back in his chair. "I've fallen for that before. Tell me what this is about first. Then I'll tell you what I'm doing with my Sunday."

Kate chuckled and matched his pose.

"I need your help. As you know, we've taken on a four-year-old typhoon with mild ADHD, so that alone is going to be a challenge with both of us working full-time." Mitchell knew the story behind Angel's mother, a single parent born locally with no living relatives or knowledge of the father, but a woman determined to give Angel a rich and happy life. She had died tragically in a road accident a week after Angel's second birthday.

"Part of the fostering arrangement is that we take her back to the centre every other Sunday for at least the first three months, for the sake of continuity, which would usually be fine. But this Sunday Beth has to head into work all day because of an urgent deal she's working on, and I agreed to help organise and participate in a charity event down in Shek O. On any other day we'd have asked her nanny, Maria, to take Angel, but Sunday is her day off and I'm loathe to ask her to change her plans. I just wondered if you would mind stepping in for me? For the charity event, I mean? It's nothing taxing, more of an early morning meet-and-greet. Getting participants to sign in and explaining what they need to do."

"For a moment I thought you were going to ask me to babysit. And I'm not sure I'm ready for that kind of responsibility just yet. But yeah, I'll help with the charity event, which sounds like my kind of thing. How early are we talking?"

"Eight-thirty until around midday. But you'd need to be there half an hour earlier to help get things set up. I'll message you the details. Are you sure you don't mind?"

Kate had no idea what lifeline she had just thrown him. With no other plans that weekend, he would probably have gone into the office to continue scoping out the bare bones of the retrenchment plan.

"Absolutely fine."

Chapter Four

Eight o'clock on any given Sunday morning was a foreign concept to Tommy.

Petticoat Lane nightlife in Central had resumed pre-pandemic closing times. After lockdown restrictions that lasted longer than most countries, Tommy savoured every breath of freedom. He had stayed until almost four before climbing into the back of a red taxi and heading home to bed. Alone. But at least he'd had the foresight to set two alarms across the bedroom to go off at seven-fifteen and seven-thirty.

An old school friend, Devon Lee, had roped him into helping to clean up Rocky Bay Beach. And if he was going to be perfectly honest, having something meaningful to do on Sunday morning meant not sleeping the day away. But he'd be damned if he was going to act bright and breezy.

Bleached blond Devon stood in the road outside his apartment block, grinning broadly, wearing tight white shorts and an equally fitted vest with the words Power Bottom Dweller in rainbow colours across his chiselled chest. In the bright light of morning, he looked sickeningly healthy. In his favour, he held out two huge cardboard coffee cups.

"Late one last night?"

Assuming the question to be rhetorical, Tommy focused on the cardboard cup Devon held out to him.

"You look like you might need this."

"That bad?" asked Tommy before taking a sip and letting out an obscene moan.

"There is a cosmetic surgery post-op vibe about you this morning. You look like death served cold."

Devon loved English idioms but often got them wrong. Tommy had given up correcting him.

"Nice."

"Public transport or taxi?" asked Devon.

"Taxi. Definitely taxi. Full air-con taxi. And can we not get a driver in a rush to be reincarnated? Or one of those old bastards who like to tap out stop-start-stop-stop-start Morse Code on the brake pedals? Unless you want to watch me puke milky latte," said Tommy before looking up at a couple of passing clouds. "Is it going to rain?"

"Doubtful," said Devon, stepping onto the road and flagging down a red taxi. "But I've got you covered. Packed a couple of North Face lightweight waterproofs in the backpack, just in case. Do you have a hat?"

"Shit."

"Thought not. I also brought a spare baseball cap."

"Do I want to know what obscene slogan I'll be sporting?"

"What do you care?" said Devon, opening the rear taxi door. "Are you ready?"

"As I'll ever be. Come on, before I change my mind. And on the way you can remind me why I am doing this at such an ungodly hour of the morning."

Tommy belted up in the back and slipped on his Ray-Bans, filtering out the offensive sunlight and letting Devon's voice lull him.

"Darling, it's a beach clean-up, to clear the trash away from the public area and the shoreline so people like us can at least catch rays and ogle tight Speedos on an unspoilt beach. Or swim in a relatively unpolluted sea without the fear of watching used condoms or dirty diapers float past."

"Ugh."

"I know, right?"

"Shouldn't the government employ people to do that? Isn't that why we pay taxes?"

"The government always has more pressing priorities. Like persuading the over-eighties that vaccinations are safe and a good thing."

"More to the point, darling, since when did you become all radical eco-warrior?"

Devon seemed to have been waiting for Tommy to ask. After twisting his upper body around, he removed Tommy's sunglasses, waiting until they faced each other.

"So..." he said, drawing the word out and giving Tommy his full, excited attention. "Tuesday night. Fruits in Suits. Talked to this gorgeous polar bear. Woke and hot. *Nat-Geo* gorgeous. Wrote his number down on this flyer."

Devon went on to explain how his new hottie spent weekends either doing punishing hikes around the New Territories, dragon boating or volunteering for one charity or another. Hanging on to the man's every word, Devon had enthused about how he had been considering joining a beach clean-up—a total lie, of course—and the guy had provided all the details, telling Devon how much he looked forward to meeting him there.

"Here you go," said Devon, handing him back his sunglasses and reading from the glossy sheet. Even without a hangover, Tommy could never read in a moving car. Trains and planes were fine, but never in a car. "Make sure to dress appropriately for the weather. If it's sunny, bring a hat and sunscreen—"

"I didn't—" began Tommy.

"Once again, darling, I've got you covered. Sunblock factor fifty," continued Devon. Tommy closed his eyes and let Devon's voice wash over him. "Next. Wear appropriate footwear such as trainers and definitely not flip-flops because there may be hazardous objects on the beach such as tin cans or broken glass. The events team will provide you with a goodie bag including gloves, trash sacks, an energy bar and a water bottle—a reusable one, naturally. They'll also furnish gay volunteers with a pack of ribbed condoms and sachets of lube—"

"They—what?" said Tommy, suddenly alert and straightening.

"Just checking you're still listening, darling," said Devon, throwing the flyer at Tommy.

* * * *

By the time they paid the cabbie and got out at the Shek O bus terminus for the short walk down to the beach, Tommy felt infinitely better. Why did nobody ever make a bigger deal about the healing powers of morning coffee? Clouds had moved off, and the hot sun sat centre stage in the clear blue skies. Humidity had crept up since the beginning of the year but had not reached Hong Kong's usual brutal peaks. All in all, they could not have picked a more perfect day. Signs had been posted on poles and fences, giving directions to the starting point. As they stood in line at the beach, shuffling forward to sign in and pick up their basic clean-up materials, Tommy spotted him.

Mitchell bloody Baxter.

Again.

People told him that Hong Kong was like a small village, but come on. A village with a population of over seven million? Was this some kind of cosmic joke? The man in question stood behind the officials' white plastic tables with four other officials, providing a smiling and enthusiastic greeting to volunteers. Devon stopped prattling on nonsense as they neared the bench, a sure sign he had spied his new beau. Tommy did his best to hide behind Devon and was fortunate to get another official to greet him. He scrawled his name on a clipboard before collecting his tag and hessian bag of goodies. But he couldn't help glancing at Baxter, who happened to turn his way at precisely the same moment. Except this time, Baxter glanced away.

The thing was, Mitchell was one of those men Tommy's attention would normally glide past. For goodness' sake, he wore black jeans and Dr. Martens on a day when everyone else wore summer shorts and brightly coloured trainers. And the Rugby Sevens polo shirt did him no favours, looking decades old. But when he bothered to look at Mitchell closely, he saw a naturally attractive man, handsome in a down-to-earth way, not gym-toned or obsessed about his hair or appearance, just an ordinary guy. Which was inconvenient in so many ways when all Tommy wanted to do was ignore him.

Once Devon had finished signing in and flirting — he'd made a beeline for an older guy — he joined Tommy, and they lost themselves in the small crowd of volunteers standing before a makeshift stage. Both had been given red wristbands to represent their clean-up group. Ten minutes later, Devon stopped speaking and a grin lit his face. When Tommy turned, the older guy had taken the stage. Smiling broadly at everyone, the man gazed briefly at Devon, and he winked. Devon emitted a soft whimpering sound and wilted against Tommy before straightening up as the man began his speech.

"Every year, millions of tons of rubbish end up in our oceans, threatening our marine wildlife." The man had a deep, rich voice, and Tommy finally understood the attraction. Even more impressive, he stopped after each sentence to repeat the words in very passable Cantonese. "I am sure many of you have seen pictures of turtles trapped by plastic can holders or seals tied up in nylon netting. Marine litter is not only a problem for us here in Hong Kong, but is a challenge the world over and something everyone needs to urgently address. And every little bit helps. So thank you all for coming along today. Small acts like this clean-up, when multiplied by millions of people, can transform the planet. And while we thank you for assisting us in cleaning Rocky Bay Beach, we urge you to commit to a more sustainable lifestyle by reducing consumption of plastic and reusing and recycling what you have. If enough of us push to change the way we live, to reject convenience in favour of sustainability, then corporations will have no choice but to sit up and take notice."

A murmur of approval rumbled through the crowd.

"A note on logistics. If you find any oversized objects, things like wooden pallets or concrete blocks, don't touch them but call over one of the marshals. The last thing we want is any of you hurting yourselves trying to lug heavy objects around. We have a team who will deal with those. At the finishing point, there are restrooms with washing facilities. Once you've cleaned up, come to the sign-out bench for hot and cold beverages and something light to eat, which is our way of saying thank you. Can I also ask you to be respectful of anyone enjoying the beach today? By all means, explain what we're doing if asked and offer to take away any litter. And something I urge you all to do is to take a good look at the beach before we begin, then do the same at the other end once we're finished. Any mothers here with a teenage son or daughter will know the feeling when they've cleaned up their kid's bedroom—"

"And how long does that last?" called a female voice from the crowd, raising laughter among the group.

"Good point. And I'd imagine not long," said the smiling man after the crowd had quietened. "And neither will this. Because more rubbish will begin to be washed up onto the shore as soon as we leave. Even more so if a typhoon hits the region. But does that mean we shouldn't bother? Somebody has to care. Somebody has to take a stand. And today that person is you. Which is why I ask you to see beyond today, to take a careful look at your lives and rethink your waste habits."

This time the guy got a round of applause.

"And when you do look back to survey the cleaned-up beach today, I hope you enjoy the same sense of achievement I always do. And, in particular, understand the difference people working together for a good cause can make in a single morning, that we can be the solution to the problem. A simple life lesson for us all."

After a few more words about logistics, the man invited the volunteers to meet with the marshal assigned to their coloured wristbands. Once in groups, the marshals arranged everyone, volunteers forming lines across the depth of the beach, from the water's edge to the rockier dunes, moving methodically and systematically forward over smooth sands and boulders like police officers doing a ground search for a missing person. Working unhurriedly and chatting amiably, some participants positioned along the sea's edge ventured out into the shallows and plucked out all manner of junk.

Devon and Tommy filled six large black plastic sacks between them. Items included the usual culprits of cigarette butts, plastic shopping bags, soda cans, various sizes of plastic water bottles and some more unusual finds such as a rusted pushchair, a cracked toilet seat and the headless upper torso of a female shop mannequin. Devon hugged the plastic model to his chest and briefly entertained those around him with a song and dance performance from one of his favourite diva artists before a laughing marshal salvaged the item from him.

As they approached the clearing at the end of the beach, having finished for the day, Devon excused himself to trot ahead and find his prize. Tommy was walking alone, sipping from his water bottle, enjoying the sun and feeling more awake than ever, when a familiar voice caught his attention.

Walking directly ahead, Mitchell chatted and laughed with another volunteer. They were talking about cars, because he'd heard Mitchell mention something about a BMW. At first Tommy thought about hanging back and letting them finish, but then he decided he needed to be the bigger man.

"Mitchell," he called out, once within range.

When Mitchell turned and clocked Tommy, the humour drained from his face. Tommy took a deep breath.

"Could I have a word, please? In private?"

After assessing him for a moment, Mitchell turned and spoke a few words Tommy couldn't hear to the other man, who briefly turned to eye Tommy before walking on. Mitchell stood his ground, clearly waiting for Tommy to catch up.

"Look," began Tommy as soon as he was close enough to speak without others hearing. "I wanted to apologise for the last time we spoke. After the cocktail party, I mean. What I said was harsh. And my sister rightfully scolded me. One of those guys turns out to be a not particularly nice sort. You probably did me a favour. And even though, in all likelihood, you think I'm a total asshole—"

"I don't think you're an asshole. And I really hope you don't think I'm a self-righteous prick. But Adam doesn't hold his drink well. And his wife really *is* almost ready to give birth."

"Anyway, what I wanted to say is, I apologise. And thank you for saving me from the crackhead."

"Harold might have mentioned him being a little shady, but I assumed you were friends."

"Absolutely not. His kind of thing is definitely not mine."

Mitchell nodded his understanding, and, finally, his smile returned. Beckoning Tommy to join him with a tilt of his head, he began walking again towards the finishing bench.

"What brings you out here?" asked Mitchell. "Beach cleaning? Is it something you do often?"

"Are you kidding? This is a first for me. But my friend roped me in after he was invited by his soon-to-be boyfriend, the one who arranged the event and gave that rousing introductory speech—"

"Oscar."

"If that's the name of the guy stood to your left at the welcome table. Is he your friend?"

"Not really a friend. More someone I bump into at these kinds of events." Mitchell rubbed his chin, clearly finding the information amusing. "But your friend is the one with the blond hair? Up ahead brushing shoulders with Oscar? I was walking behind and heard them discussing various Handover Day marches. I think I overheard your blond friend arguing that protestation is the thief of time. Or maybe I misheard."

Tommy looked ahead while laughing. Just the kind of saying Devon would misstate. In front, he saw Devon grinning at Oscar, clearly in awe at something he'd said. His friend did not waste any time.

"No, that definitely sounds like Devon."

"How about you?" asked Mitchell. "Enjoying yourself?"

"You know what? I am. Surprisingly. Can't believe how much crap gets washed up on the beach. And I must say I like the kind of 'pay-it-forward' mentality of the organisers. As in us not just helping out this one time but consciously making an effort to reduce our consumption of plastic and other waste, and spreading the word."

Tommy noticed people stopping and turning around to stare at them. He wondered what had happened until Mitchell directed him to turn and do the same.

"Look."

At first glance Tommy didn't understand what he was supposed to see apart from a pristine-looking beach. Only then did the penny drop. People weren't looking at something specific but at the absence of the discarded litter, mottled blue plastic and random ugly lumps that had almost become a part of the beachscape. Many people enjoying the beach that day had thanked him and asked for details of the subsequent clean-up. For a change, he felt as though he had done something worthwhile with his Sunday.

"We helped do that," said Mitchell, and even though the remark was spoken plainly enough, Tommy felt a sense of pride inflate his chest.

As they made their way towards the finishing post and the parking lot beyond, Mitchell stopped when his phone pinged with a message.

"That's my sister," he said. "We speak every Sunday, but she's tied up this afternoon."

Mitchell continued walking, but he appeared distracted.

"I don't suppose you know anybody who's involved in the English-speaking theatre scene?"

"Me. Our Head of English and Dramatic Arts directs shows for the local community theatre and I help to stage-manage the productions. Building sets, acquiring props and coordinating lighting and scene changes —

that kind of thing. Why? Are you going to tell me you're an aspiring thespian?"

"Heavens, no. My sister's son, my nephew, is coming to stay with me for a month in a couple of weeks and I haven't a clue what to do with him. But my niece texted me to say he'd worked backstage on a number of school plays. I don't suppose you could use an extra set of hands?"

"Are you kidding? We're rehearsing the musical *Cabaret* with performances in June and we need all the help we can get. Actually, the way the rehearsals are going, Shelly thinks we could use some divine intervention right about now. Recruiting stagehands is the last thing on anyone's mind. Always is. Then it's a frantic rush to get everyone up to speed."

"Really?"

"Absolutely. This nephew will understand it's not paid work, won't he?"

"Of course. I'd even offer to pay you, if it means keeping him busy."

"Hang on. How old is he?"

"Nineteen."

"Okay, that's fine. We may need to ask him to sign a few forms for insurance, if that's okay."

"Brilliant. Thank you. Can I give you my number?"

Tommy blinked for a second but then caught himself. Mitchell simply wanted a favour, nothing more. They stopped walking while Tommy unlocked his phone and asked Mitchell to type in his number. Once finished, Tommy fired off a quick message and heard Mitchell's pocket ping.

"We're probably heading to Soho for Sunday afternoon cocktails," said Tommy. "Or a coffee, if you'd prefer. You're more than welcome to join."

Mitchell turned to frown at the horizon. Maybe Tommy wasn't entirely forgiven yet. They continued strolling towards Devon and Oscar, who stood together by a motorcycle bay in the car park. Devon appeared amused about something, probably assuming Tommy was trying to pull Mitchell.

"Honestly, Tommy, I'd love nothing more than a glass of red right now," said Mitchell eventually, stopping by one of the motorcycles. "But I have this work dilemma that I need to sink my teeth into before tomorrow morning. And I'm driving, too. Some other time, perhaps?"

"Sure, no problem. Hey, I wasn't snooping but I thought I heard you telling that guy, Oscar, that you own a BMW," said Tommy.

"I do," said Mitchell, putting his hand on the black leather seat. "This here's mine. Two-fifty-four cc engine, top speed of two hundred kilometres — "

Tommy's mouth dropped open as he did a double take between the shiny scarlet, black and chrome bike and mild-mannered Mitchell.

"And here's me thinking you were gay," said Tommy, watching as Mitchell unlocked a bag and placed a black crash helmet onto the seat. Mitchell laughed good-naturedly before adopting an admonishing expression.

"You should know better than to reinforce wildly inaccurate stereotypes that gay men can't possibly be into fast cars and motorbikes. I've had this baby for three years, and let me tell you, it has turned out to be a godsend navigating Hong Kong's traffic jams."

"Are you giving Tommy a lift back on that?" asked Devon, who had sidled up to them.

Tommy let out an involuntary gasp and turned to see Mitchell equally stricken.

"I could. I mean, I do have a spare helmet—" began Mitchell, stopping while throwing a black leather jacket around his shoulders.

"There is no way on God's green earth you're getting me on the back of that thing," said Tommy simultaneously. "No offence, Mitchell."

"Wuss," said Devon. "Faint heart never favoured the bold."

Tommy turned to see Mitchell trying to suppress a smirk while pulling on black gloves.

"See you guys around."

Mitchell pulled his jacket zipper up and secured his helmet on before swinging his black-jeaned leg over the bike. After flipping down his dark visor, he leant forward and started the machine. With a twist of the throttle and a roar of the engine, he rode the powerful beast out of the parking lot.

Tommy stared after him, after mild-mannered Mitchell, his throat going dry and his imagination ramping up with the distant up-change of Mitchell's bike's gears.

Chapter Five

Mitchell glanced down at his phone. Usually he wouldn't care about the time. After all, he worked late most nights. And Hong Kong locals didn't seem as obsessed with punctuality as their Western counterparts. But for his boss to keep everyone sitting around in a conference room until almost seven, like the accused awaiting the jury's verdict, felt nothing short of cruel. None of the nine managers in the room spoke or made eye contact, each playing with their mobile phones, everyone probably suspecting something serious without realising how bad things had become. The smell of fear and foreboding would have been tangible even to someone not employed by the bank. Such was the suspense that when the conference door finally opened, at least one person dropped their phone.

Pauline Ng once confided in Mitchell that any interview candidate who said their desire to work in human resources stemmed from their love of humanity or because they considered themselves a 'people person' would instantly raise a red flag. In their business-critical department, she argued, staff witnessed the very worst of human nature. Even what should be considered the positives of a business, things like promotions, wage increases or bonuses, were all too readily met with jealousy, or grumbles of dissatisfaction or inequality, which often resulted in escalations. Pauline's thirty years in the business may have jaded her to the positives, but some of her team swore she relished the opportunity to dish out bad news.

"I've come directly from a call with the global head of operations. What I am about to tell you is in the strictest confidence. You are here because this involves you in your role within this department. Nothing I tell you can be discussed with or communicated in any form to anyone outside of this room without my explicit consent. You all know a privacy clause is included in our terms and conditions of employment, but due to the sensitive and confidential nature of what I am about to divulge, I need you all to sign a separate non-disclosure agreement before I continue. Mitchell, if you will, please."

Mitchell handed out the soft folders containing the NDAs produced by their legal department. He already knew the agreement prohibited the person from disclosing details to anyone, including family members, friends, colleagues and, in particular, to members of the press. If anyone in the room had not grasped the seriousness of the meeting before, they did now.

Pauline waited patiently until everyone had signed the agreements and handed them back to Mitchell, and he had checked them and nodded his confirmation. All the while, the room remained deathly silent.

"The board has come to a decision about the future of operations here in Hong Kong. Our job is to make changes happen as smoothly and efficiently as possible with the minimum disruption to business. In a nutshell, the bank will move regional operations, such as support departments and the China desk, to Singapore. All other core roles will be absorbed back into London. Hong Kong will become a satellite office — like Seoul and Tokyo — with minimal staffing. The board want everything completed by the end of the second quarter."

Even as hardened HR professionals, nobody could have anticipated the extent of the change and the inevitable consequences. He'd had the same reaction in the back of the taxi when Pauline had first divulged the news.

"That makes no sense." Helen Cheong, Pauline's assistant regional manager and an Australian expat, had been brought up and educated in Sydney and tended to be vocal in meetings. Mitchell wondered why Pauline had not confided in her before the meeting, but his boss always had her reasons. "Even in the wake of the recent turmoil, Hong Kong is still — commercially — the main gateway into the China market. Our Singapore office doesn't have the talent to run a China desk."

"Not yet. But they will. We'll be enticing key staff members to relocate with the right incentives. And there are plenty of other banks operating there with skilled staff who might welcome the opportunity to work for a more global organisation. Moreover, the business language of Singapore is English, and plenty of people in the workforce speak two or three other languages, including Mandarin, Cantonese and other Chinese dialects. And many speak Hindi and other Indian languages, as well as Bahasa Indonesia and Malaysia. It's a no-brainer."

Helen did not seem satisfied but, surprisingly, let the matter go. Mitchell wondered why she did not mention the strict entry criteria for foreigners to work in Singapore. Nobody knew more about regional labour laws than Helen. How they would meet the deadline to get everything done was anybody's guess.

"Look," said Pauline, softening her tone. "We all know the board has been nervous about the mainland's influence over the region for years. In this way, we're future-proofing the organisation against any developments or changes to Hong Kong's regulatory framework, changes that might adversely affect the way we do business. The point is the decision is final. It's our job to make things happen as smoothly as possible. Members of the board understand the critical nature of your involvement and have promised financial incentives. I'll be flying to London to meet with my counterparts and discuss the realignment of key positions. While I'm away, Helen and Mitchell will hold down the fort. Going forward, they will manage all retrenchment activities and, once we have the green light, help run them alongside senior staff. The rest of you will help to coordinate them for all other staff. When I return from London, I expect to have a full list of exactly who will go and who will remain."

"Who else in the office knows about this?" asked Helen.

"Upper management, naturally. And heads of department heard the announcement Tuesday. They, too, have signed NDAs and will be pivotal in ensuring this is executed smoothly."

"And what about us?" asked Helen, a question everyone was probably thinking. "What's going to happen to us once we've done the dirty work and this is all over?"

His boss appeared to have been expecting the question because she began nodding even before Helen had finished asking her question.

"Clearly, we're no longer going to need such a large team. Along with other professionals, you will be given a choice wherever possible. For those willing to relocate, we will try to find you similar positions in Singapore or other offices around the network. If you prefer to take a redundancy package, then that will also be made available."

Pauline had not said those exact words to him, but suddenly, the depressing reality hit home. Undoubtedly, he would be invited to apply for a job back in the bank's head office in London—which would unquestionably entail a demotion—or he would be offered a payout.

"After everything we've done to make this bank an employer of choice?" said Helen. "What kind of message is this sending? Not only to investors, but to those considering a career with us?"

"I understand how you feel, Helen," said Pauline. "And believe me when I tell you that I've done my level best to argue our corner. But the decision has been made."

Mitchell could almost touch the negative energy in the room. Although he understood Helen's pain, he felt more for the local staff who had silently absorbed the news. And because of the NDA, they wouldn't even be able to confide in their close family members.

"What's important during these times," said Mitchell, dragging up memories from past experience, "is for us to keep things professional. Some people will welcome the payout, those who may have already been thinking about moving on. For others, our more institutional employees, those who have only ever worked for us, this will be a bombshell. And with that shock often comes inertia and the inability to see a way forward. If we're going to do our jobs properly, then we'll need to provide all we can in terms of counselling, talking to recruitment agencies on their behalf and assisting them with their interviewing skills. A part of our responsibility is to help them discover a way forward and visualise a new future."

Even Helen nodded her agreement.

"In the meantime," said Pauline, "'it's business as usual. I called this meeting to ensure you're all aware of what's coming down the line. When I return from London, I will have all the headcount and financial information we need to begin planning our approach. In the meantime, Mitchell and Helen will set up brainstorming meetings for us to decide how we will run retrenchment meetings. Remember, this development is strictly confidential. You are legally bound by the agreement you signed not to disclose anything with anybody. Do I make myself clear?"

Pauline waited until everyone in the room had nodded their understanding.

"What do we do about ongoing recruitments?" asked one of the managers.

"There shouldn't be any. We have a hiring freeze at the moment. But for any business-critical roles, let them continue for now. We must do everything we can to avoid rumour and speculation."

At the end of the meeting, Pauline asked Mitchell to remain behind for a brief chat, but before they could speak, Helen cornered her. Mitchell stood by the window at the far end of the conference room, giving them relative privacy while looking out over the calming Victoria Harbour nightscape. Even though they lowered their voices, Mitchell could discern the barely restrained anger in Helen's tone. When she finally left, Pauline beckoned him over before letting out an exaggerated sigh.

"Anybody would think I enjoy being the bearer of bad tidings," she said, using her back to push the conference room door closed. "This decision affects me, too."

Mitchell said nothing. Pauline would land on her feet. She always did.

"Look, a quick heads-up. When the announcement is made publicly, Helen will be one of the first to be laid off. You and I will manage that particular meeting. And I'm sure I don't need to tell you how important it is that this particular piece of information remains strictly between the two of us."

Another bombshell. Not only did he consider Helen a friend, but they worked well together. Sharing the burden of the retrenchment interviews with her would have helped keep him sane.

"You're letting her go when we need her most?"

"I don't trust her to remain impartial. And if I'm going to be perfectly honest, I don't trust her not to leak this information to employees or the press. Whereas I am confident you will remain professional throughout. We're going to need people like you to see us through this rocky time and to provide continuity once we've moved to the next phase of operations here."

* * * *

Mitchell eventually left the office at eight-thirty but didn't feel like returning to his empty home. Pauline's pointed comment about providing continuity kept nagging at him. Did she mean he was being considered to head up the downsized operation in Hong Kong? Or had the comment simply been an observation? After any late-in-the-day meetings, Helen would usually drag him for coffee or a drink to decompress. Tonight he didn't want to sit and try to make nice with her, knowing what Pauline had just told him. Instead, Mitchell phoned Kate, but the call went straight to voicemail. He was about to scroll down to Harold's number when a message appeared on his screen.

Tommy: *Play run-through this Thu. Want me to snap photos for ur nephew?*

He considered ignoring the message. After all, he had seen Tommy the day before and still didn't feel entirely comfortable around him. Tommy taking the initiative to apologise had felt both gracious and genuine, but would they ever be friends? Doubtful. They were, after all, total opposites. But Tommy was following through on his offer to help get Zane into the theatre scene. Maybe Mitchell needed to be the better man this time. Before he could talk himself out of the idea, he texted back.

Mitchell: *Sounds excellent. Don't suppose you're up for a coffee or a glass of wine right now?*

Almost instantly, a message popped up on his screen.

Tommy: *Brief Encounter. Half an hour.*

Mitchell checked the time. Maybe an innocent chat with someone unconnected with his work was just what he needed. One of the many things he loved about working on the island was that a person could get to most places quickly at night, either on foot or in one of the plentiful, air-conditioned public taxis. Brief Encounter was a bar off the network of escalators that rose from the Central business district up to the dizzy heights of Conduit Road. Moreover, the bar was on his walk home.

Mitchell: *Perfect. See you there.*

* * * *

The nighttime air had turned pleasantly balmy as Mitchell neared the familiar watering hole. Hidden in a small courtyard down a narrow lane, Brief Encounter — once an exclusively gay bar — had become a popular haunt with locals and expats of all persuasions and somewhere only tourists in the know would find.

When Mitchell drew close, he saw Tommy sitting outside on one of the high tables, checking his phone. Only a handful of people had ventured out Monday night, but Mitchell noticed three men at a nearby table blatantly appraising Tommy. As Mitchell approached, one of the group stood up, goaded on by the others, and picked up his beer bottle, ready to walk over.

"Tommy," he called out, noticing that when Tommy looked in his direction and waved, the man aborted his approach.

"I appreciate this," said Mitchell at the table. Tommy had a champagne flute of something sparkling. "Let me get you another. What is that? Prosecco?"

"Let me buy. Still haven't thanked you properly for saving me. And this is ginger ale because it's a school night."

"After the day I've had, I could use something stronger, but I'll have the same."

While Tommy headed inside, Mitchell took a deep breath of humid evening air and peered around. He loved the sensory bustle of Hong Kong. Accompanying the sound of distant traffic, a vaguely familiar Cantonese pop song sounded from deep inside the bar. Somewhere along the lane, light shone from the back door of a café, the odour of frying noodles from the kitchen mingling with the night's musk and making his mouth water. Thick branches of an ancient banyan tree overhung that section of the lane, and when he looked up through the trellised limbs, he could see a full moon. Tonight, a beautiful halo accompanied the celestial phenomenon.

"What are you looking at?" asked Tommy, placing a glass of red wine in front of Mitchell.

"There's a full moon tonight," said Mitchell, prodding his forefinger into the night sky.

"You shouldn't do that. Point at the moon," said Tommy as he sat down.

Ever conscious of being culturally insensitive, Mitchell pulled his hand down and peered around to see if anyone else had noticed. His mood of wonderment had dissolved into one of mild embarrassment.

"Why?" he whispered.

"Nothing to worry about," said Tommy, grinning impishly. "A superstition my Taiwanese grandmother taught us as kids. Those who point at the moon risk having bits of their ears fall off."

"What?" Mitchell choked, which made Tommy's smile broaden. "I've heard superstitions about not looking at the full moon through glass, but never that one."

"Honestly, I think it's a way to teach kids not to point at strangers. But according to my grandma, legend has it that Chang'e, the Chinese goddess banished to the moon for stealing her consort's potion of immortality, didn't like people pointing at her. If she caught anyone doing so, her vengeance was to cut off bits of their ears."

"Brutal."

"That's Chinese mythology for you. Filled with cautionary tales."

"Whereas in Europe the Brothers Grimm only wrote happy and cuddly stories with loveable characters to give children sweet dreams. You know, like Red Riding Hood's wolf and Hansel and Gretel's witch."

"Fair point." Tommy had a nice laugh, unaffected and infectious. Mitchell took a sip of his drink and peered quizzically across the table.

"You bought me red wine," said Mitchell. "I asked for ginger ale."

"Didn't you say you wanted something stronger? We can switch, if you want."

"No. This is a good call. Only the one, though."

Such was his limit. Time had taught him that any more than two alcoholic drinks and his usual tightly belted self-control might come undone a notch or two.

"Bad day?"

Mitchell let out a sigh. "The worst. And thank you. For the drink and the company."

"You want to talk about it?"

"I wish I could," said Mitchell. "But it's all highly confidential. Tell me about your day."

"Usual Monday chaos. At lunchtime our head teacher called me in for a chat and mentioned that she'd overheard other teachers commenting that when I start projects, I get easily distracted. One of them suggested ADHD and another said I might be somewhere on the spectrum."

Mitchell groaned. "Everyone's a professional psychiatrist these days."

"I told her not to worry, that I'm not on the spectrum, not even close. Tommy Chow is over the fucking rainbow."

Mitchell laughed aloud for the first time that day, and it felt like a weight had been lifted from him.

"You didn't really?"

"Not in so many words, but she got the message. Hey, let me tell you about the staging of this play. Then you can let your nephew know what he's in for."

Mitchell knew the synopsis of *Cabaret*, but Tommy filled in small details about the set design and the staging for the play. He ended by explaining how Mitchell's nephew, Zane—Tommy had remembered his name—would be needed for quick set-changes and to help ensure the props were always in the right place at the right time.

"Is Zane gay?" asked Tommy out of the blue.

Mitchell stared at him over the top of his wine glass.

"I'm just curious," said Tommy. "I'm not prying. We have a very inclusive theatre community. Everyone's friendly and welcoming, but if you're concerned, I can keep an eye on him and fend off any unwanted attention."

"Like I said, I know hardly anything about him. But what I do know is that he's my sister's kid, and as such can take care of himself. He'll also behave himself because he knows what it's like to face her wrath."

"Fair enough. And if you want, I can show him around when you're busy."

"You don't have to do that."

"I'd be happy to. Or if it makes you feel better, how about we agree to a trade-off?"

"Trade-off? What kind of a trade-off?"

Across the table, Tommy began drawing a circle in the condensation on his tall glass.

"My sister's getting married this year…" he began, but appeared unable to make eye contact with Mitchell. Eventually, he sighed deeply before continuing.

"Okay, look. Total transparency. My sister's getting married in July and the groom's best man is his best friend, this gorgeous Australian hunk. We've only met once, but I got a vibe from him. And the dude totally slays the surfer beach bum look. Think of a blond, blue-eyed, pumped-up version of Henry Cavill. Yikes. The thing is, I don't really know how to engage him and I don't want to come across as completely superficial—"

"You're doing a pretty fine job right now—"

"Will you listen? They're having the bachelor party in Singapore, but the wedding will be here. The thing is, I fell to pieces last time I was in his presence."

"I find it hard to imagine you being lost for words in anyone's presence. You've certainly never been with me."

"That's because I don't find you—uh—intimidating."

Mitchell knew precisely what Tommy meant. He didn't find Mitchell attractive.

"Anyway, I wondered—" began Tommy.

"You want my help."

"Yes."

"At the wedding?" asked Mitchell.

At least Tommy had the decency to look and sound tentative, as though he knew he was probably asking too much.

"As what? Your date?"

"If you're free."

"While you romance some other guy—"

"Alec."

"Let me see if I've got this right. You're suggesting introducing me as your plus-one while trying to hook up with the best man. I'm sure I won't be the only person in the room who might find that behaviour a tad unchivalrous."

"Details. We can work out motives and mechanics later."

"And you're going to just introduce me there and then? Some random guy you just met on the streets? Are your family going to buy that?"

"Maybe. Okay, we might need to tidy you up a bit."

"Should I be offended right now?"

"No, I just mean the guys I tend to go for are more fussy about their appearance. We might need to work on your hair, clothes, grooming—"

"Stop right there. You are not *Queer Eye*-ing me. If you want me there, you take me as I am or not at all."

Tommy paused to assess Mitchell for a few seconds.

"I suppose that might make the breaking up part a little more convincing."

"Remember, I'm doing you a favour here. How old are you, Tommy?"

"Twenty-nine."

"I'm thirty-eight. Which makes me nine years your senior. Have you considered the reputational damage that might cause?"

Mitchell watched as Tommy stared down at his drink, a deep furrow between his brows.

"I'll survive."

"I meant me, not you."

When Tommy's gaze swung back, Mitchell began to laugh, which had Tommy joining in.

"You're a dick."

"Seriously though, Tommy. Shouldn't we at least be seen together before the event?"

"We're here right now, aren't we?"

"For nobody to see."

"Come to the play run-through this Thursday."

"The way work's going right now, that might be difficult. What are you doing Sunday?"

Tommy grinned, probably thinking Mitchell meant brunch in town or a drink with friends. But something in Mitchell's expression must have given him cause for caution.

"Why?" he asked, his eyes narrowing. "What did you have in mind?"

"Oscar's taking a group of us on a hike Sunday. The first two stages of the MacLehose. Early start, though.

The trek takes around six hours, and the second section is supposed to have some steep climbs."

"I usually catch up on sleep Sunday mornings."

"Shame. Would have given us a chance to swap stories about each other. And your friend, Devon, will be disappointed."

"Devon's going? Are you serious?"

"Gospel. According to Saint Oscar."

Mitchell watched the cute little knot form between Tommy's brows again as he looked away to consider Mitchell's words. Eventually he returned his gaze and heaved out a sigh.

"If it helps promote the illusion, then I'll come."

"Excellent. I'll let Oscar know. He's arranging a minibus to take us there and bring us back after we've finished. They're picking us up is from outside pier three in Central at six. Do you need an early morning call?"

"I can wake up on Sunday mornings," said Tommy indignantly. "I just usually choose not to. About my proposal. Do we have a deal?"

"We do. Where's the wedding?" asked Mitchell.

"On the front lawn of the Repulse Bay hotel for the midday ceremony and cocktails. But my sister's fiancé has managed to snag the large ballroom at the Grand Hyatt for the banquet. Middle of July."

"The Repulse Bay front lawn in July? What if it rains?"

"They have this wonderful invention called a marquee. And before you say it, we still have the Hyatt ballroom if there's a typhoon. But it had better be a super-typhoon. Otherwise, some weather god or another will have to answer to my sister and grandmother."

Mitchell hadn't considered the family angle. Would he need to be friendly to Tommy's family members only to be dumped on the day of the sister's wedding? Maybe he would have to be the one breaking them up to make sure Tommy ended the day smelling of roses. Except Mitchell was hopeless at lying. Always had been. And on top of that, Hong Kong had a way of making sure you ran into people again, even those you might not want to see.

"Listen, my sister's looking for recommendations for wine to serve at the hen night dinner. You're a wine buff, aren't you? I noticed you savouring a glass of red at Beth and Kate's place."

Mitchell smiled down at the tabletop, not because of the veiled compliment but at the thought that Tommy had noticed him.

"I wouldn't exactly call myself a connoisseur, but I know what I like."

"What about the wine you're drinking right now."

"This? Italian red. Montepulciano D'Abruzzo. Dry and quite young, a recent vintage."

"Wow. Spot on. I'm impressed."

"You shouldn't be. I often come to this bar and Montepulciano D'Abruzzo is the only house red they serve by the glass. And always a recent vintage. You don't have to be a connoisseur to know that, just familiar with the bar's drinks menu. Or as your friend, Devon, might say, there's more than one way to skin a banana."

Tommy laughed again, a sound Mitchell was beginning to enjoy.

"You know, Devon might have a habit of mixing up sayings—"

"Malaphors, I believe they're called. A blend of aphorisms and malapropisms."

"If you say so. But first of all, you should know that he is the nicest, kindest guy I know, with not a bad bone in his body, and, secondly, I am fairly sure that sometimes when you think he's mixing them up, he actually knows exactly what he's saying."

"I look forward to hearing more on Sunday morning at six during our first official date."

Tommy merely groaned. "Hell, what have I let myself in for?"

Chapter Six

Robbed of Sunday sleep again and running late, Tommy rounded the corner to the Central ferry concourse skirting Victoria Harbour and stumbled to a halt. He slid his limited-edition Ray-Bans down his nose to witness a group of jolly-looking people togged out in a mishmash of unflattering fluorescent hiking gear. Instead of doing the sensible thing of spinning on his limited-edition Nike heels and heading back home, he huffed out an irritated sigh, fixed the sunglasses back in place and forged onwards. Bright colours and cheerfulness ought to be banned on Sunday mornings. Or at least minimised until the serving of brunch cocktails. But a deal was a deal. After several scans of the crowd, he finally spotted Mitchell in a dark brown top and tan shorts, standing out like a millionaire's shortbread in a sea of Smarties.

"I didn't think you'd show," said Mitchell, daring to grin at his approach.

"Don't speak to me."

"Not a morning person?"

"Not a Sunday morning person. There's a difference."

"Here." Mitchell reached to the ground, where a cardboard coffee cup sat. "Devon said you might need one of these to improve your mood."

"Latte?"

"With a double shot."

"You are marginally forgiven," said Tommy, taking the cup and attempting a smile. "Where is Devon?"

"He went on ahead in Oscar's car. Some of the hikers are getting to the starting point under their own steam. Oscar wanted to be there to meet and greet."

"Of course he did."

"People are boarding the bus. We should go."

"Sit next to me. And let me take the window seat. I don't want some jovial rando talking my arse off on the way. I will have my earbuds screwed in tight, my playlist on max and my sunglasses fixed in place, doing my best to catch up on sleep."

"This is going to be fun."

Once they settled on the coach and had rumbled some way along the expressway, Tommy pushed his sunglasses onto his head and removed one of the earbuds. Next to him, Mitchell had his hands folded in his lap, eyes shut as though in meditation. When Tommy nudged him gently on his shoulder, Mitchell's eyes popped open and he turned his head to Tommy.

"I apologise for being a grinch," said Tommy. "I promise I'm not always like this. But this is the second successive Sunday morning sleep-in I've been denied. My mood will have improved considerably by lunchtime. And thank you again for the coffee."

"No need to apologise. This is all excellent fodder for my Tommy Chow character file. You know? For your sister's wedding."

Tommy groaned and lowered his sunglasses. "We really are doing this, aren't we?"

"As instructed."

By the time the bus dropped them off at Pak Tam Chung, the start of the trail, Tommy felt infinitely better. Oscar met them at the bus door, recording people's names as they stepped off. His smile broadened when he saw Tommy standing behind Mitchell. Devon must have said something.

"Where's Devon?" asked Mitchell. Tommy had been about to ask the same question.

"He said he was going to join us for the walk," added Tommy.

"Did he?" said Oscar, shrugging while he looked down at his clipboard. "Sorry, he volunteered to accompany the other novice hikers. They wanted to get a head start and not be responsible for holding up the rest of us at the end of the hike."

Tommy's heart sank. Although he had agreed to accompany Mitchell, he'd counted on having Devon as a buffer to chat with in case the conversation with Mitchell became stilted. Strangely enough, Mitchell appeared equally crestfallen. Maybe he'd hoped for the same thing. Just as Tommy was about to break the awkwardness by asking Mitchell about the route, Oscar called the crowd together.

"It's going to be another hot one. Don't push yourselves—this is not a race—and please make sure you stay hydrated. I find it's best to sip fluids continuously. On the route, there are a few places with potable water outlets to top up your bottles. Can I also ask you to take a few small plastic sacks with you, to place your litter in and pick up any items you find along the way. You can tie them up and dump them into the public bins lining the trail."

Tommy almost rolled his eyes at Mitchell. Oscar never seemed to be off duty. But he noticed Mitchell nodding in agreement.

The first part of the trek entailed walking up a gently sloping road. In silence, they trailed the chatter of other hikers who had set a pleasant pace. Once again, they had lucked out on a cloudless day, which at that early hour was comfortably cool. Surrounded by the soft chirping of woodland birds, a gentle breeze and the absence of traffic sounds, everything conspired to improve Tommy's mood.

At one point, when they drew level with a group of stragglers, he chatted to them in Cantonese for a while. Unsurprisingly for his fellow Hongkongers, their main topic of conversation was about the food they planned to eat when they reached the famous seafood restaurant a short bus ride from the finishing line. He laughed along with them before realising Mitchell strolled beside him, not understanding a word. After a quick introduction, everyone transitioned to English, and they continued chatting, this time including Mitchell.

As they made their way towards the High Island Reservoir, the largest in the territory according to Mitchell, trying his best to contribute, and with the sparkling blue ocean of the South China Sea on their right, they gradually peeled away again, both relaxing and opening up. Tommy found he enjoyed listening to Mitchell even though they were polar opposites.

In the spirit of getting to know each other and helping pass the time, Tommy suggested they play a question game, five quick-fire personal questions posed by each of them that both had to answer. And as he had come up with the idea, he insisted on being the first to pose questions. Mitchell nodded, correctly judging that doing otherwise would be pointless.

"Let's start easy. Favourite colour?"

Mitchell took time to answer, as though afraid of answering incorrectly. Even when there was no right or wrong answer. Tommy noticed him staring at the cloudless sky then at the other hikers.

"Blue."

"What shade of blue? Azure, cyan, cobalt, teal?"

"What shade of blue is the jacket the woman in front is wearing, the one with the orange baseball cap? I'm no good with hues."

"Royal blue. Conservative but predictable, I suppose."

"Why? What's your favourite?"

"Hot pink, of course."

"Of course." Tommy noticed Mitchell shaking his head but smirking.

"Best female singer of the noughties?"

"Adele," said Mitchell.

"Adele?" said Tommy, stumbling on the path. "Seriously? Out of all the fabulous new millennial divas, you pick Adele?"

"Yours?"

"Beyoncé."

"You do know she's older than Adele, don't you?"

"Mitchell, she is a goddess. That girl not only sings and dances, but has acted. Did you not see *Dream Girls*? She's the whole package. More than. Untouchable. Preferred cocktail?"

"I don't drink much, and then only wine. But if I had to choose I'd go with gin and tonic."

Tommy mimed a yawn.

"Mine's Moscow Mule," said Tommy. "The local convenience store used to stock small bottles and cans of ready cocktails, most of them sugary sweet and disgusting, all except Moscow Mule in a blue and silver can, which was sublime. But they seem to have phased them out. Sorry. Off topic. Favourite animated movie of all time?"

"*Toy Story.*"

"Mine too. Which one?"

"All of them."

"You have to pick one, Mitchell."

"Why?"

"Because the question is which movie, not which movie franchise."

"All right then. Three."

"Wrong. Four transcends them all." Mitchell huffed aloud, but Tommy noticed him smiling fully this time, clearly enjoying the repartee. "Okay. Last question. What's your preference. Top, bottom, verse or side?"

Mitchell quietened then, and Tommy thought he might have overstepped. Before he could ask a different question, Mitchell answered.

"No preference, really. Versatile, I suppose."

"I see."

"What about you?"

"Whatever gets me laid."

"Heavens. Such high principles."

"We did agree to honesty. But that's my last question. So today's your lucky day. You get to ask five burning questions of yours truly. No holds barred."

Scents of salt and seaweed mixed with a faint undercurrent of diesel wafted off the sea. Neither pleasant nor unpleasant. Mitchell cleared his throat before beginning his own mini-interrogation.

"Favourite Asian movie with a gay theme?"

"Easy. *The Iron Ladies*. Thai movie. Matchless." Devon had put him onto the classic, which had become a firm favourite.

"Oh. I haven't seen that one."

"Really? About a Thai men's volleyball team that includes gay and transgender athletes? Based on a true story? Fabulous."

"Never seen it, but it's now on my watchlist. Mine's *Happy Together*."

"Hmm. So dark and gritty and disjointed."

"That's what makes it a classic. Most attractive Hong Kong male actor?"

"Chen Hing Wah."

"I don't know who that is."

"Edison Chen?"

"Ah, him. Personally, I prefer Tony Leung."

"Of course you do. He's a bit old, though, isn't he?"

"But still hot. Preferred men's scent?"

"Anything by Tom Ford," said Tommy. "And in case you're ever thinking of buying me a present, the most expensive will do. Yours?"

"Armani."

Tommy nodded. He had noticed the classic scent on Mitchell when they'd met for drinks, a more traditional cologne but one that suited him perfectly.

"How about best cuisine in the world?"

"Italian."

"Italian?" This time, Mitchell stopped walking and stared open-mouthed at Tommy. "You live in China. How can you possibly choose spaghetti over noodles?"

"Is this about me, or not?"

"Of course."

"Well then," said Tommy, pouting. "Besides, spaghetti is just noodles stolen from the Chinese by the Italians, put in different packaging and given a new name. What about you?"

"Sichuan. Or is it Szechuan? I'm never sure which is the correct pronunciation. But I especially love Dan Dan Noodles. My go-to comfort food. As long as they're not too heavy-handed on the chilli oil."

"Noted. Last question."

Tommy noticed Mitchell tapping a forefinger on his lower lip.

"Okay. This might be a little tougher. Favourite author of classic English literature?"

"I need time to think. You go first," said Tommy.

"Well, for me, it would have to be a toss-up between Charles Dickens and Thomas Hardy. I love the realism of the era that both depict in their works, almost like an historical account of the time, but each using very different styles. Let's go with Dickens. What about you? Thought of anyone yet?"

"JK Rowling."

"J—?" began Mitchell, turning to stare incredulously to Tommy.

"What?" said Tommy, meeting his gaze. "What?"

"Nothing," said Mitchell, grinning smugly.

Tommy had begun to enjoy this fun side of Mitchell almost as much as he liked walking behind him, watching as he climbed steps in his tight tan shorts, the muscles of his backside and hairy thighs straining the stretch cotton fabric. Not that Mitchell was at all his type.

With the fun questioning over, Tommy suggested they share more mundane facts about each other.

Mitchell talked about his family, comprising one sister and an estranged mother. Mitchell's father had died of a sudden stroke two days after Mitchell's eighth birthday. When his mother had crumpled under the pressure of loss and responsibility, his father's parents — his grandparents — had stepped up and raised him and his sister. Today his mother lived with her boyfriend in Croydon, a racist and homophobic coach driver who only ever left the flat to go to work. At her insistence, he never visited her at home when he returned to the UK. Instead, she would meet him for the occasional coffee in town. As for Mitchell's love life, he'd only ever had one serious boyfriend in college, but refused to go into any detail. Tommy half suspected the ex had dumped him, which explained why Mitchell had ended up halfway across the world in Hong Kong.

When Tommy's turn came, he silently thanked his loving and tolerant family. He felt almost guilty telling Mitchell how normal they were — his mother a housewife, his father an accountant, his sister a shop owner. Mitchell seemed more concerned about who he needed to impress at the rehearsal dinner if he was going to convince them that the confirmed bachelor, Tommy Chow, finally had a boyfriend. His sister Sammi sat at the top of that list — Tommy had already decided against telling her about their arrangement — but then, of course, there were his grandparents. Mitchell listened attentively when Tommy told the story of how his grandmother on his father's side had been born in Taiwan back when the island was still under fifty years of Japanese rule and how his grandfather had escaped from Northern Guangdong to Hong Kong as a young man during the famine that ravaged China in the late nineteen fifties. By the end of the retelling, Tommy felt a new pride in his ancestors' struggles, something he often took for granted, and looked forward to Mitchell meeting them.

"Tell me about this best man, Alec," asked Mitchell, who appeared to have been emboldened by their exchange.

"He's a demigod."

"Yes, but what kind of things does he like? I think we've established you have the hots for him and his mere presence does a number on your libido. My question is about Alec the person. What other things do you know about him? Or are you planning to stand in his presence again, gawking like a goldfish and drooling onto his lapel? How did that work out for you last time?"

Tommy stopped walking and glared at Mitchell.

"Rude!"

"I'm trying to help. How much do you actually know about him?"

Mitchell had a point. Tommy recalled a conversation with Daley about how Alec had planned to set up an extreme sports travel company straight from college.

"He has a sister. Or maybe two? His family are definitely Australian, but I'm sure he told me they come from Newcastle. That's in England, isn't it?"

"There are lots of Newcastles around the world. Canada, the US, Jamaica, Barbados and Australia. I imagine he meant the Australian Newcastle in New South Wales. Supposed to be beautiful. Around a hundred miles north of Sydney, I believe."

"Oh, yes. That would make sense. He does have a great tan."

Mitchell turned to Tommy with an expression of disbelief.

"You don't seem to know much about him. Is he actually gay? Or are you hoping he finds you so irresistible that he decides to jump—"

"Stop already. He's gay. Or possibly homoflexible. Daley told us he'd been popular with girls in college but secretly dated a guy, a jock on the soccer team. So yes, I am fairly sure he bats for our team. But I'm not sure how out he is, if you know what I mean? And at college he talked about starting his own specialist travel company."

"And did he?"

"No idea."

"Then it seems you have some homework to do."

"Are you suggesting I cyberstalk him?"

"No, I'm suggesting you phone Daley. Far more efficient and less creepy. And they're best friends, aren't they?"

"Good point. And Daley owes me."

"What for? Marrying your sister?"

"Finding a plus-one to bring to his wedding," said Tommy with a smirk.

"Finding a plus-one to *dump* at his wedding, I think you mean."

Tommy chuckled again. They settled into a peaceful stroll and this time the silence felt companionable rather than awkward. Tommy noticed signs popping up announcing the imminent end of the first section of the walk.

"How about you?" asked Mitchell, after a considerable pause. "Any long-term relationships I should know about?"

"Define long-term?"

"A year. Maybe two or more."

"I think the longest I've been with anybody is two months."

"Not something I would publicise, if I were you. Anyone the family got to meet?"

Something in Mitchell's words niggled at Tommy.

"No. Look, I've been told I'm picky. Overly picky, if you know what I mean?" Tommy realised his tone had begun to sound defensive. "But nobody has held my attention longer than a couple of dates. We've normally run out of things to say to each other by then. That doesn't make me a flake."

"I never thought for one second you —"

"But the thought of being with the same person for the rest of my life makes me break out in hives. Waking up next to the same face. Having sex with the same person. It's an unnatural state of being."

"People do, though. What about your parents and grandparents? What about Sammi and Daley?"

"That's different."

"Because they're straight?"

"No, that's not it. I've met gay couples who fit together the same way. Your friends, Harold and William. As though something happened to them. You'll understand when you get to meet my family. I know this sounds like a cliché, but they were always meant to be together. They make sense. I couldn't imagine them with anyone else."

"They're two halves of a whole?"

"Another cliché, but exactly."

"And you don't see the same thing for yourself?"

"Nope."

"And, just to be clear, none of your family have never met any of your past two-month dates?"

"Absolutely not." Tommy turned to see Mitchell smiling at him again. "What?"

"I'm going to be the first man you've ever introduced to them? Wow, I'm honoured."

"Yeah, well," said Tommy, staring ahead. "Don't let it go to your head. It's a temp job, remember?"

Mitchell chuckled, and they continued on again in comfortable silence. Ahead of them, the route reached an apex, and the hikers in front disappeared over the top. They would be descending soon.

"Hey, Tommy," said Mitchell, sounding pensive again. "I appreciate you sharing this personal stuff with me but you might not want to be as candid with Alec. Not to begin with. Find out more about him and what he wants first. Plenty of gay men are looking for that one person to share their lives with."

Tommy hadn't thought that far ahead. Mitchell had a point.

"Are you?" he asked Mitchell.

"I used to. But for some of us those things are not in the cards. Besides, I'm happy with who I am."

Tommy could see the truth in Mitchell's words. Somewhere during his life, he had made peace with himself.

"My sister thinks there's something wrong with me," said Tommy.

"There's nothing wrong with you. We're all put together differently, which is what makes people so amazing. And I'm sensing commitment doesn't appeal. If things work out with Alec, and his life is in Australia, you could consider keeping things long distance. People say it's a way to keep a relationship fresh."

* * * *

At the end of the hike, Tommy collapsed onto one of the benches the authorities – or maybe the Red Cross – had kindly provided. For goodness' sake, he taught physical education for a living and was no stranger to exercise. But after strolling along the beautiful beach at Long Ke Wan, the second leg of the hike had become progressively crueller, steep and relentless. They'd continued to chat until forced to make the not-so-difficult choice between talking or breathing. With his shoes and socks removed, the heels of both feet hanging off the end of the bench sported bloody blisters.

Despite Mitchell being the more experienced hiker, he had stayed by Tommy's side the whole way, matching him pace for pace. Only on the steep climbs, often over rocky terrain, did Mitchell excel, his shorter, sturdier form navigating the ascent effortlessly. Even so, he, too, was laid out on a bench seat and breathing heavily.

Devon appeared to have fared better than either of them, togged out in unflattering but clearly functional walking boots and something equally unfashionable that Mitchell labelled a caped hat, the kind with a flap at the neck worn by nerdy hikers to protect them from the sun. No doubt Oscar had schooled him on what to wear.

"What do you expect," said Devon, standing over Tommy, holding out a tube of a thick and pungent antiseptic cream called Rambler's Relief, "designer Nike trainers? Do you not know the old saying about hiking? Sun shines on the right shoes."

To emphasise his point, Devon lifted a leg and thumped a heavy boot on the seat next to Tommy's head. Mitchell's barely suppressed laughter turned into a choking groan as he clamped his arms around his ribcage.

"Yeah," said Tommy, unamused. "I'm fairly sure that's not a saying, but a head's-up might have been nice, friend."

"Didn't invite you, darling. Therefore you are not my responsibility."

"In my defence," said Mitchell, "I have never attempted that second stage before. Otherwise I might have suggested something more practical like — uh — "

"A taxi?" offered Tommy, the comment making Mitchell laugh again before groaning in pain.

"Honestly," said Devon, hands on hips. "You two should get a room."

Chapter Seven

Mitchell stood at the metal barrier in the familiar arrival hall of Hong Kong's international airport, staring into the spacious heavens at the wooden replica Farman bi-plane suspended from the ceiling, wondering what the next month would bring. The British Airways flight from London Heathrow carrying his nephew had just landed.

He took a deep, calming breath.

When Zane had emailed his flight details and five ideas for his visit — something he had clearly copied and pasted from an old travel blog — Mitchell had replied with what he hoped were clear instructions to help him navigate the airport. Even in that short communication, with his nephew's use of lazy abbreviations, he'd sensed the gaping generational chasm between them.

And he only had himself to blame. Every human relationship he had cultivated since arriving in Hong Kong thirteen years ago had been with adults. Ellie had once told him, half-joking, that he might as well be living on the moon. While building his career in Asia he had missed out on the young lives of his niece and nephews and knew little of their triumphs and challenges. Here he stood, welcoming his youngest nephew as a grown adult. Moments like this reminded him of his ineptitude in connecting with people unless explaining policies or procedures, which hardly constituted small talk.

If only he had an ounce of Tommy's ability to connect with others. Tommy had an uncanny knack for striking up conversations and making people feel at ease, whether he was attending a formal gathering or during a casual hike. Just remembering that fun day made Mitchell smile.

They had ended the hike hobbling back to the minibus, which had dropped them at their starting point in Central. After sharing his packed lunch with Tommy — ciabatta bread filled with Brie and Branston pickle — he had fallen into a delicious sleep. Tommy had nudged him awake as the bus crawled through the Cross Harbour tunnel, informing him that he, Mitchell, would be buying the first round of drinks at a hole-in-the-wall bar opposite one of the piers. Oscar and Devon would be joining them. Mitchell knew better than to argue, although as he'd struggled to stand amid the grunts and groans of others trying to depart the bus, he'd wondered if alcohol might be such a good idea.

Once again, Tommy had been right. Not only had the first plastic cup of chilled red wine relaxed him as they'd sat chatting on stone steps looking out over the harbour, but Oscar had guided them through a series of stretching exercises to ensure they would not wake too sore the following day.

After two drinks, Tommy had helped him to a taxi and had even leant in to buckle his seatbelt. Mitchell had dared to inhale Tommy's scent, the subtle mandarin and spice smell of shampoo in his hair, then held his breath when the back of Tommy's hand had brushed against his upper thigh, leaving a tingling sensation. On the way home, he had beaten down his rising attraction, which would only be doomed to failure. A little giveaway remark kept echoing back to Mitchell.

Tommy didn't find him attractive.

Mitchell scanned the arrivals board again before checking his watch. Passengers from the flight would be collecting their luggage soon and exiting onto the concourse. He would keep an eye out for the distinctive British Airways luggage tags. Hopefully Zane had not been delayed.

He checked his phone and saw the message Ellie had sent overnight, a simple line telling him to take good care of her son, following up with two pieces of advice—Zane was known to wander off sometimes, and was hopeless at remembering to charge his phone.

Not for the first time, Mitchell wondered what he had agreed to.

That morning he had also received another card in the post from his landlady, this one with gold-embossed letters on a red background. With two lines, each bearing four Chinese characters. His neighbour Mrs Lau had read the words aloud for him in Chinese before smiling, humming her approval and translating the slogan as 'Don't Miss Opportunities: Time Doesn't Come Round Again'. His landlady knew about his nephew coming to stay. Was this her subtle way of telling him to make the most of the visit? Or something else?

He spotted Zane immediately. Since their last meeting, he had grown taller. His father, Robert's, ancestors were natives of Antigua. Zane had inherited his father's solid frame and masculine good looks, although his skin bore a lighter tone, a warm chestnut hue. Dragging a well-used luggage of pale blue, he looked as though he had just woken. Perhaps he had. His thick hoodie with faux-fur lining and baggie jeans might have been a good choice when boarding at Heathrow, but not in the ninety per cent humidity of Hong Kong. Mitchell decided not to say anything, but to let Zane find out for himself.

When Zane locked eyes with him, Mitchell could see Ellie's brooding gaze, how she used to single him out when she had something bugging her that needed venting.

Mitchell stepped forward to greet him, then faltered. He had no idea of the familial protocol. Should they hug, or might that be too intimate? But would a handshake be too formal? Fortunately, Zane answered by shuffling to a stop and thrusting out a hand.

"Uncle Mitchell."

Mitchell shook hands and tried to lighten the mood.

"Do you think we could drop the uncle moniker while you're here?"

At least the remark raised a slight smirk and got a nod.

"Come on," said Mitchell. "I'm splashing out on a taxi."

"Thought you had a motorbike."

"I do, but you have luggage. We'd normally take the Airport Express train into Central but I'm sure you're tired, so we'll cab it home. Is that okay?"

Zane shrugged. Mitchell did his best to engage him but, after a while, began to question whether the passage from the concourse to the Hong Kong island taxi rank had always taken so long.

"You might want to lose the jacket. It'll be hot outside."

"S'fine."

"How was the flight?"

"Cool."

"Any turbulence?"

"Some."

"Did you manage to get any sleep?"

"Not much."

"How did you find the instructions I gave you for the airport?"

"I'm here, aren't I?"

Mitchell decided the curt responses were a result of tiredness and deferred to silence after attempting a few more questions and getting abrupt responses. When the doors to the climate-controlled airport slid closed behind them and they strolled out into the sunlight and stifling heat, he noticed Zane unzipping his jacket. Zane waited until they had settled in the back of the air-conditioned taxi and Mitchell had rattled off his home address in Cantonese using words and tones Mrs Lau had taught him.

"Look, I know why I'm here. Mum and Dad need to sort out Gran and the last thing they want is me tagging along, getting in the way. And they don't trust me to stay home and look after the house. So here I am. I don't want to be here, and I'm pretty sure you don't want me here either—"

"Hold on a minute. That's not true—"

"Uncle—Mitchell. I'm young but I'm not stupid. Mum never stops talking about your high-powered bank job that keeps you busy all year round. I wouldn't want me here either. Aunt Pat—Dad's sister—is taking Jules to Spain. Nobody asked me if I wanted to go. Probably because they thought I'd be in the way. And they're probably right. They've got young kids and don't want to have to fret about me, too."

"Hang on. Would you have gone to Spain?"

"I dunno. Maybe. Maybe not. Would have been nice to have been asked."

"Did you say anything to your mother?"

"She's got enough on her plate, hasn't she?"

Mitchell had only ever heard his sister's perspective of her family. Maybe their time together would prove insightful. At nineteen, Zane seemed to be on the verge of resigning himself to people not wanting to engage him.

"Mum probably told you I don't have friends. I do. Plenty. Other gamers. We chat regularly, almost every night."

Mitchell did not consider online friends real friends, but kept that judgement to himself. Instead, he chose to give Zane some local facts.

"Fair enough. But if you want to continue gaming here, or whatever you call it, remember we're eight hours ahead of the UK."

When Mitchell turned to him Zane was frowning, appearing to process what had been said. Eventually he emitted an exaggerated sigh, as though Mitchell had delivered yet another death blow.

"You mean it's one o'clock in the morning right now?"

"It's nine in the morning here in Hong Kong. Get your head around that first. You may experience jet lag, which is quite natural. But I find it's best not to keep converting back."

"My friends are online from eight or nine at night. At home."

"Which will be four or five in the morning here. You get to have a good night's sleep before you join them."

The lighthearted comment fell on deaf ears.

"Look, Zane, try to relax. You'll figure things out and adjust like I had to when I got here. As for Spain… When you've finished your studies, you'll have plenty of chances to visit Europe. You're out here now, on the other side of the world. Not many youngsters get to experience this, so I suggest you make the most of it. Let's get you settled back at my place. Then, if you're up to it, we'll go meet some of my friends for lunch. Okay?"

Next to him, Zane said nothing.

"Zane?"

"I suppose."

"Fine, then."

One thing in Zane's favour — he didn't seem fazed at all about lugging his case up multiple flights of stairs to Mitchell's apartment despite the heat and humidity flooding the stairwells. He seemed more put out by Mitchell's rule that shoes were not to be worn in the flat. Showing Zane around the tiny apartment took no time, with Mitchell saving Zane's room for last.

"This will be yours for the duration. Not much, I know, but you should have everything you need. There's a bath towel at the foot of the bed. There's also an Octopus card with two hundred dollars loaded. Keep that in your wallet. You can use it on buses and trains —"

"I know the deal. We have Oyster cards back home."

"Similar concept, except you can use this one in convenience stores to buy drinks or snacks. For the record, all forms of public transport, including taxis, are fairly inexpensive. And most taxi drivers speak a degree of English. But just in case, I've got a laminated card — business-card size — for you to keep in your wallet, which has our address in English and Chinese.

If the driver doesn't understand you, just show them the card."

Mitchell had adopted a work colleague's tip a few weeks after arriving in Hong Kong. Flashing the card had gotten him home on numerous occasions. There were also phone apps that did the same thing, but Mitchell preferred the card version.

"Now, I'm not sure what your mum does for you back home, but I won't disturb you in your room unless you're screaming for help. You can keep it as clean or as messy as you like. I won't be making your bed or doing any tidying for you. I machine wash clothes on Saturday so leave anything out you need cleaning. A lovely Filipino lady called Grace — a domestic helper employed by my landlady — comes in once a week, every Wednesday. She vacuums, mops and cleans the flat from top to bottom, as well as ironing any clothes and changing the bedlinen. She'll go through this place like a mini typhoon, so don't get in her way. But I suggest you let her tidy your room. She has her own set of keys, and if you're in at the time, best to make yourself comfy on the living room sofa while she does your room. You'll probably be treated to her wonderful laugh and, if you're really lucky, to her mezzo-soprano rendition of Mariah Carey's greatest hits with her own interpretation of the lyrics."

"I'll go out."

"If you want. But she's really nice. Speaks English, if that's what you're worried about."

"No, it's cool."

"The controls for the air-conditioning unit are on your bedside cabinet. It's a super quiet unit, barely makes a hum. At the moment you'll probably need to keep it going at night. Do you want to grab a shower and change?"

"I'm good."

Mitchell pushed out an exhausted sigh.

"Zane, you've just travelled halfway around the world. Do your uncle this one favour, will you? Go shower and change into something more comfortable. I promise you will feel infinitely better."

Although Zane did not appear to be entirely happy, he nodded his agreement.

"Is this restaurant posh? Can I wear shorts?"

"I'd say shorts are a good choice. And as long as you're wearing a shirt with sleeves, long or short, most restaurants here are fine with shorts."

* * * *

They arrived at the venue just after midday. Mitchell's first experience of local dim sum restaurants had been a mix of shock and awe. Chipped bowls and saucers, chopsticks and china spoons tossed carelessly onto the table, and a server spilling tea onto the starched tablecloth were all part of the experience. More importantly, his usually polite and subdued work colleagues came to life. Once seated, conversation dialled up a couple of notches, everyone speaking excitedly and simultaneously. From early on, he had learnt to sit back and enjoy the Cantonese banter at his own table and across the restaurant floor. He didn't care that he couldn't understand a word. The sound was pure joy. Laughter punctuated conversations. Working in London he would have been hard-pressed to find a colleague who wanted to leave their desk at lunchtime. Not so in Hong Kong. He likened the experience to the excited buzz of after-work Friday night drinks with colleagues back home.

Harold preferred more upmarket establishments. Crisp white tablecloths, spotless cutlery and obsequious waiting staff were a bare minimum. Mitchell half suspected accessibility was also a concern. Not all smaller eateries had a serviceable lift big enough to house a wheelchair. When they approached the round table, Mitchell noticed Harold and William had invited along a couple he had not met before, who were already in a heated conversation with William.

"—naive stupidity," barked William. "Running through the streets waving the British flag. What were they thinking? Blatant provocation. No wonder the police came down hard."

"What do you think, Harold?" asked one of the guests as Mitchell ushered Zane to take the seat between himself and Harold.

"They were voicing their desire for self-governance," said Harold in his usual calm way. "Nobody was advocating that Hong Kong would be better back under British rule, God forbid. One would hope those days of tyranny and suppression are well and truly behind us."

"Then why not hold up something meaningful? A symbol that represents the birthplace of democracy?" asked William.

"Forgive me, dear, but I believe the subtlety of waving the flag of Greece might be lost on the authorities and most definitely on your average Hong Kong policeman."

Seeing they had a full table, a server came to take their order, and the subject was dropped. Mitchell took a moment to introduce himself and his nephew.

"Are you okay with chopsticks, young man?" asked Harold to Zane.

"Yes," answered Zane, a little brusquely.

"Excellent. Do you mind if I order?"

"Fine."

Having lunched with his friends many times, Mitchell was familiar with Harold's choices, a selection of popular steamed and fried dishes and including some Mitchell had sampled but did not particularly care for — steamed chickens' feet and tripe served in bamboo steamers. He loved other items like sticky rice wrapped in lotus leaf and steamed pork ribs. And he had instantly relished the local green vegetables, particularly seasonal dao miu stir-fried snow pea shoots served plain or with crabmeat. Growing up in England, his mother had boiled green vegetables into a soggy mulch.

Mitchell noticed Zane eyeing nearby dishes with suspicion. He glowered at Mitchell when Harold plucked a dumpling from a steamer and dropped the item into Zane's bowl, like a parent feeding a child. But such was the custom in Hong Kong. Mitchell realised too late that he should have warned Zane. While conversation continued around the table, Zane picked at his food, pushing a few of the things Harold had served him onto his side plate.

"Have you had dim sum before?" asked Harold during a lull.

"Course I have," said Zane. "Many times. Chinatown in London. Just not like this."

"I admit, some of these more local dishes are an acquired taste. Tell us then, what's your favourite dim sum dish back home?"

"Satay chicken."

William laughed aloud.

"What?" asked Zane, glaring daggers at him.

"Satay is Indonesian," said William, as blunt as ever. "Dim sum is Chinese. We don't mix and match here. No curry and chips in Hong Kong."

The two other friends at the table had the decency to laugh behind their napkins.

"William," said Mitchell, "lay off. He's just arrived—"

"Don't apologise for me, Uncle Mitchell. I know what fucking dim sum is."

"Ooh, feisty," said William.

"William, hush, dearest. How about I order us some stir-fried chicken with cashew nuts? And something sweet and sour?" asked Harold, trying to soften the mood.

Harold flashed Mitchell a sympathetic smile before diverting the conversation to something he had read in a media magazine about a closeted celebrity. While waiting for the extra dishes to arrive, Zane pushed half a fried spring roll around his plate but refused prawn dumplings, fried turnip cake or green vegetables. Even with Harold's extra choices getting Zane's grumbled approval, the meal ended on a frosty note, with Zane ignoring Harold and his guests as they left the restaurant.

"Is everybody in Hong Kong gay?" asked Zane, the only words he spoke in the taxi on the way back home.

Mitchell didn't dignify the question with an answer. As soon as they arrived home, Zane went straight to his room and closed the door. Seconds later, the air conditioner started running. Mitchell lay back on the settee and sent a text message to let Ellie know Zane had arrived safely, then stared up at the ceiling fan, taking a few breaths. Maybe introducing Harold and William immediately had been a mistake. However much he enjoyed their company, he realised they were a bit like the exotic dim sum — an acquired taste.

He had planned to take Zane to a restaurant famous for Peking duck that evening but wondered if Zane might be put off by too much Chinese cuisine. Ellie had informed him that her son had no food allergies, but he had not asked her about his preferences. If they were going to survive the month, Mitchell would need reinforcements. He pulled the phone display to his face and tapped out a text message. Around fifteen minutes later, instead of getting a return text, his phone rang.

"I take it your nephew's arrived?" came Tommy's voice.

"That's why I messaged you. Sorry, I didn't want to take up your time. But I could do with your advice. Any suggestions for where I can take him to dinner tonight?"

Tommy's laughter broke the tension inside Mitchell.

"Surely someone like you has a plan?"

"I do. Well, I did. Beijing Garden. But now I'm not so sure. Where would you suggest taking a nineteen-year-old English kid who just turned his nose up at authentic dim sum?"

The line went quiet for a few seconds.

"I'll answer that question," said Tommy. "If you answer one of mine first."

"Go on."

"What beats a gay ménage à trois?"

"I'm being serious, Tommy."

"So am I. Answer the question."

"I have no idea. What beats a gay ménage à trois?"

"Five Guys."

"Huh? Oh. Yes, of course."

"Johnston Road, Wanchai. See you outside at six-thirty. After which we can show him the dubious delights of the Wanchai bar scene."

"Are you sure? You don't have to. I don't want to hijack your evening."

"Please. You've done me a favour. My sister is taking her bridesmaids dress shopping and I do *not* want to be there to clean up the mess after they've finished."

Chapter Eight

The stainless-steel spoon Tommy had been holding clattered into the glass mug housing the remains of his bubble tea. A guy at another table turned at the sound and smiled at him. Only Tommy's sister, Sammi, remained oblivious, continuing to check messages on her phone while sipping occasionally on a matcha green tea. That morning Tommy had dropped into her shop and dragged her out for a break. She had been almost relieved to see him, rather than irked at the unscheduled interruption.

"Georgie?" he asked aghast.

"Yes," replied Sammi, not really paying attention.

"Supermodel, Georgie Yeung?"

"I'd hardly call her a supermodel. She's tall and slender, I suppose."

"You've finalised Georgie and Kiki as bridesmaids. Do you not see the problem?"

"They're my best friends. I'd have had the Kwong twins, too, but their older sister is getting married on the same day in Taipei. So it's Georgie and Kiki."

"And as stunning as they both are, sister dearest, Georgie is a chopstick and Kiki is a dumpling. You are never going to find bridesmaids dresses to keep them both happy. It cannot be done."

That remark finally got her attention. She looked up, her mouth dropping open.

"I cannot believe my own gay brother would body-shame my best friends. I should disown you. Besides, I am going to let them decide what they wear."

"There is no way in this lifetime they are going to say yes to the same dress."

"I'm bringing along a couple of bottles of bubbly. To help oil the wheels. We've booked the shop for the whole afternoon and early evening. It'll be fun."

"It'll be carnage," said Tommy, scooping out the last of his drink as a thought came to him. "Could you at least insist on full-length gowns, then persuade Georgie into sandals and Kiki into wearing high heels?"

"Why?"

"To ensure you're all around the same height. And that any wedding photo of the three of you standing together doesn't resemble a stepladder."

"What is with you today?"

"Sis, those photographs will be stuck to your wall or propped up on your sideboard for years to come. You need to make sure they're fabulous."

"Look, I am not making everyone uncomfortable for the sake of photos. Give me some credit. I want them to be lasting memories with everyone genuinely happy, and if that means having Georgie in a grass skirt and Kiki in a kaftan, then so be it."

Tommy thrust his hands over his eyes and grimaced at the mental picture.

"You might as well call Disney right now," he said through his fingers, "and offer them the movie rights. You'll have the perfect cast in place for a Pixar animated movie."

"Do you know how much effort goes into planning a wedding? Do you? And don't you think I should be able to do whatever I want on my special day?" she asked before muttering something.

"Is everything okay?" he ventured, not wanting to seem too concerned. "Between you and Daley?"

"Of course," she replied. She appeared confused by his question. "Why wouldn't it be?"

"You seem unusually stressed today."

"Seriously? Let me see. Apart from having had less than a sixty per cent response rate to our invitations and fussy bridesmaids to please, some of our relatives are already demanding where to be sat for the banquet. On top of that, the Hong Kong observatory has forecast amber rainstorms that weekend. And don't get me started on my brother."

"Do you mean your wonderful brother who has not only managed to book the Melody Triplet String Trio to play at your ceremony, but has agreed to accompany them on the cello for your grand entrance. Although you have to tell me what song you want because I'll need to find time to practice."

Sammi squealed and jumped up, craning across the table to hug his head.

"Thank you, thank you, thank you," she said, letting him go. "What would I do without you?"

"Well, for starters, you would inherit our parents' money."

"They can donate everything to charity. I'd rather have my brother."

"I'm serious, Sammi. Let me know what song you want. I don't want to look like a total amateur up there. And the guest list will sort itself out. Don't let anything spoil your big day preparations, or get in the way of the fight club this afternoon."

They smirked at each other across the table, an effort for him because in the back of his mind he could still see the photograph of Daley and the anonymous woman in the society magazine. He really needed to talk to Daley and get the whole thing resolved.

"Why are you not working this morning?" she asked, back to sucking on her paper straw. "I thought you said this Saturday was the schoolgirl's regional football league competition or something?"

"We had to drop out. Four of our players came down with bad colds during the week and, you know, we can't be too careful these days. Don't want to be accused of infecting kids on the other teams. More to the point, why are you not working this afternoon?"

"My new manager started this week. Asked if she could have the chance to run the show alone. She didn't say as much but I think she wants to see how she gets on without me constantly looking over her shoulder. Does that mean you're free this afternoon?"

"Whatever you're thinking, the answer is no." Tommy knew Sammi's smile only too well.

"Spoilsport. You're supposed to be helping."

"I am. I just agreed to play cello at the ceremony. I've even found a male plus-one to bring."

"No," said Sammi, the word sounding more like disappointment than surprise. "You can't have."

"Why not? You're not trying to fix me up with someone, are you?"

"Of course not. I don't hate anyone enough to do that to them," she replied. "Who are you bringing? Not Devon?"

"No, Devon's got a new man. I'm bringing someone you haven't met. It'll be a surprise."

"Never use that word on a bride-to-be. Who *is* it, Tommy?"

The phone in Tommy's hand pinged with a message. For a second, he wondered if Devon was cancelling lunch, but when he dragged the display to his face, he couldn't help smiling. "Talk of the devil. My date-to-be."

"Who?" asked Sammi sternly.

"Mitchell. He's my date to your wedding."

"Mitchell?" Sammi appeared genuinely shocked. "Not the same Mitchell you balled out after the cocktail party? I thought you despised him?"

"We called a kind of truce. He's not my usual type. A bit stiff and formal."

"Real, then?"

"And he still thinks I'm an asshole —"

"I'm liking him more and more."

"But, yes, he's agreed to be my plus-one on the day." Tommy read the message and smiled.

"Oh my God. You like him, don't you?"

"Not like that. He's a friend, Sammi. And we're helping each other out."

"Whatever. I don't want to know the details. You have my approval," she said, with a smile that aroused Tommy's suspicions.

"Hold on. You've never even met him. Do you not need a background check? Or a private investigator to assess his suitability?" When she smiled sweetly at him, he stood up from the table to collect their cups. "I'm off before I get roped into any more favours."

"Give me one minute. I need to pee. Don't leave without me."

Tommy huffed out a sigh and plopped back down. His sister hated being alone in public — arriving at anything first or being the last to leave. He thought about calling Mitchell but decided to wait until he was on his way. To bide his time, he pulled out the *StarAsia* society magazine with the picture of Daley and the unknown woman, something he had stored in his bag as a reminder of unfinished business, an additional responsibility he had taken on. When he saw Sammi appear, he stuffed the paper back inside, but not before she spotted him.

"I thought you said you didn't read that vanity trash," she said as she picked up her bag from the table. "They're little more than glossy comic books for grown-ups who prefer pictures over intelligently written editorials."

"I wouldn't buy them. But I find they help to pass the time."

"If a customer decides to litter my shop with any more, I'll save them for you."

As Tommy stood and kissed her on the cheek, a thought came to him. What if the customer who left the magazine in her shop knew about Sammi and Daley's wedding? Had someone done so out of spite?

"Let me know how you get on today," he said, pulling his bag onto his shoulder. "Now, I really need to go. Devon's buying me lunch because he's in a flap about something."

After escaping and phoning Mitchell to help solve his nephew's problem, Tommy hopped on the MTR train and headed to Central for his lunch meeting with Devon. On the short journey, he pulled out his phone and dialled Daley's Singapore number once again. When the call went straight to voicemail, he decided to call later. Again. Maybe he would discuss the matter with Devon—just to unburden himself. Devon might provide some interesting observations and advice, even though he was hopeless at keeping secrets.

A short stroll from the Mid-Levels escalator, Pink Propaganda Brasserie was nestled among the parade of bars and restaurants along Wyndham Street. A popular venue, Thursday to Sunday evenings saw revellers spilling out across the pavement until closing time. During the day the kitchen served a range of mid-priced bar foods, and the place had become Tommy's second home. He faltered to a stop when he spotted Devon seated at a table outside the café with someone.

Aaron, one of their occasional friends, sat with him, talking and gesticulating wildly with his hands. The three had gone to school together. Coming from an orthodox family, Aaron had suppressed his innate queerness growing up and had been unassuming and aloof during their schooldays. Tommy remembered standing next to Aaron in the playground during Halloween as they'd both watched Devon, kitted out in a witch's costume and green makeup, arms apart, on one of the lunch benches belting out a fabulous rendition of *Defying Gravity* from *Wicked*. Aaron had made his disapproval plain to those around him, but even then Tommy had been able to tell the distaste had been used to deflect attention from himself and mask his jealousy.

When Aaron's parents had migrated to Vancouver, he and his sister had chosen to stay behind to finish their studies and look for employment in Hong Kong. Aaron's newfound independence had allowed him to rise from the fires of suppression like a feather boa phoenix. He had quickly become a much-discussed member of the gay community. Relatively hot, financially independent and promiscuous, he had been Tommy's main rival for a time. They had only remained lukewarm friends because Devon insisted that members of the tribe needed to have one another's backs.

"Tommy Chow," said Aaron, rising from his seat and blowing air kisses. "Gorgeous as ever."

Aaron had made no bones about his desire to sleep with Tommy. Unfortunately for Aaron, Tommy found his indiscretion and pushiness—more than his flamboyance—a total turn off.

"Hello, Aaron. And how are you?"

He should have known better than to ask the question. Aaron—someone who never reciprocated by pausing to ask a person how they were—took the greeting as an opportunity to soliloquise. As they listened, Devon looked over at Tommy and shrugged an apology. Tommy caught a waiter's attention and ordered sparkling water and a green salad. A good twenty minutes later, as Tommy tucked into his food, Aaron finally stopped speaking when his phone rang. After an elaborate eye roll, he stood and moved away to take the call in private.

"Before you say anything," said Devon, "he was passing and saw me sitting alone. I think he decided to play the Good Sumerian and keep me company. Now quickly, let me tell you my news."

Devon talked at length about Oscar, about the sex between them being amazing and how, after one prolonged session, he had told Oscar that they ought to set up their own OnlyFans channel, except Oscar had had no idea what that meant. Finally Devon got to the point, which had him hot and bothered.

"You know the lease on my place comes up next month?"

"Yes. And your landlord's putting the rent up by thirty per cent, the crook.

"To make up for rent freezes over the past few years."

"Don't make excuses for him. It's still extortion. Have you found a new place yet?"

"No, but—"

"I can help you with the deposit, if you want."

"Thank you, but—"

"And help move your stuff in over a weekend, if you need me. As long as it's not the weekend of the wedding—"

"Oscar's asked me to move in with him."

Mitchell took a moment to process what Devon had said and noticed his terrified expression.

"But that's great, isn't it?"

Devon blinked. And blinked again.

"He's asked me to move in. With him."

"I heard you the first time. What's the problem, Dev?"

"The problem is we've only just met. It's a huge step, don't you think? And I like him so much. But we're both independent, both used to having our own space. I'm worried that if we're sharing the same flat and he gets to know the real me, he'll lose interest and end up throwing me out."

"Is that it? Is that what's got you all wound up?"

Mitchell wanted to say something more about the insecurities of gay men but sensed that now was not a good time. Besides, he knew his sister shared many of those. Perhaps everyone did.

"How have you left things? With Oscar?"

"I told him I'd think about it."

"And how did he take that?"

"Honestly, he seemed a little disappointed. I think he thought I'd jump at the chance."

Tommy thought back to a conversation with Mitchell about people who were meant to be together. Although he had only known them as a couple for a short while, Devon and Oscar fell comfortably into that category.

"Let me show you this through Oscar's eyes. He really cares about you — any fool can see that — and he's also a decent person. When he sees his lover in a predicament, of course he wants to help. But he also respects you, which is why he hasn't pushed you to make a decision. I'm pretty sure he was nervous enough about asking you in the first place. As for living together, well, you never know until you try. But I'd say the most crucial thing is that you talk to each other, tell him your concerns about living in close proximity and maybe about setting boundaries or ground rules on personal space. Tell him you'll want to move some of your furniture in and put your stamp of fabulousness on the apartment, with his help, approval and assistance naturally —"

"I'm not sure I could do that."

"Has he been to your place?"

"Once or twice. His apartment is much bigger."

"Listen to me. You resuscitated that squalid little flat in Tin Hau. I remember when you first moved into that hole with its stark white walls, chocolate brown woodwork and whitewashed windows. Two weeks later the place was unrecognisable. Walls in shades of terracotta, gold and apricot. Diffusers with amazing scents. Rows of musical theatre posters lining the walls, colourful chiffon draped over table lamps, and who would have thought self-assembly furniture could look so chic and fashionable? You have a knack for making things fabulous, Devon. That's your thing."

Devon sat thinking for a few moments before his sadness melted away.

"I know you don't do relationships, Tommy, but Oscar and I are at that point where neither of us can do anything wrong in each other's eyes. And you're right, we do need to have a chat. Thank you, darling. If only you and I were compatible, we would make an awesome couple."

Sammi had once said the same thing. But neither Tommy nor Devon had ever felt anything more than friendship for each other, as though they were siblings.

"Good. Then it's my turn. I'm considering hitting on Alec, the best man at my sister's wedding. What do you think?"

"Is he attractive?"

"Stunning as a Hemsworth. Mitchell's going to help. He's agreed to be my date to the wedding."

Tommy didn't miss the insinuation behind Devon's grin.

"Let me rephrase that. Mitchell Baxter has agreed to be my *pretend* date—"

"Mitchell Baxter?" came Aaron's voice high-pitched voice. He had returned unnoticed and stood now with his hands braced on the back of Devon's chair. "Tell me

128

you don't mean Emperor Harold's foot soldier, Mitchell Baxter?"

Tommy nodded, picking from his plate of green lettuce and avoiding eye contact.

"Oh, dear. Are you sure about that, Tommy?"

"We have an agreement."

"Do you seriously not see? To say the man is barely average is being generous. He stands out like bad shoes. We're catwalk, darling, and he's not even on the reserve guest list. Have you not noticed his complete lack of style? And don't, whatever you do, accidentally let him into your bed, because that is the kind of mercy fuck that will end up with the words stalker written all over it."

Aaron's words seemed unnecessarily harsh, even for him. Tommy wanted to brush them off, but his brain had stalled.

"Have you even thought about how that kind of association might affect your already waning reputation? You know what our tribe is like once they start talking. Look, if you really want, I could move a few things around and come with. A far more appropriate choice, don't you think? What date is this wedding thing?"

Tommy looked to Devon for help, at a loss for how to respond.

"Mitchell agreed to escort Tommy," said Devon, after a quick wink to Tommy, "because we want to make sure my Oscar has a friend to keep him company while Tommy and I are showcasing our *Strictly Come Dancing* moves out on the dance floor. Unless, of course, you're happy to chat to Oscar, in which case I hope you're up-to-date with the latest developments in environmentalism and conversation."

"And conservation," corrected Tommy.

"That, too," said Devon.

Tommy remained straight-faced while Aaron's expression—as he stared at the top of Devon's head—morphed from surprise into disgust. Every now and again Devon could pull something extraordinary out of the bag.

"Ugh. In which case I'll pass, thanks," said Aaron, taking his seat. "But mark my words, Tommy. I've heard people saying you're off your game. Maybe you and I should go out sometime."

"Maybe. I have your number."

"And before you ask," he said, smiling triumphantly and royal waving his phone, "that was a call from a cabin crew hottie I met a few months back. He's in town and wants a repeat hook-up tonight. The thing is, I already have one in the bag this evening. Kirk from High Five Fitness. Might have to juggle things around to fit them both in. Have I told you about Kirk?"

Without waiting for a response, Aaron launched into a tale about the personal trainer who had—apparently—all but stalked him. Eventually the hour nudged four and Tommy, realising he would never get the chance to talk privately to Devon, decided to escape. Aaron finally stopped wittering when he rose to leave.

"Where are you going?" asked Aaron. "Cocktail hour starts in half an hour."

"Not for me."

"Since when?"

"Since I have better things to do. Devon, are you coming?"

"I'll stay. Oscar's meeting me here. Call me tomorrow."

"Come on, Tommy, darling," whined Aaron, hands on hips now. "I haven't told you about flyboy yet. I'll even buy the first round."

"Sorry, Aaron, I need to go," said Tommy, lifting his bag onto his shoulder and giving Devon a quick wave. "I've got to get home, shower, and make myself look respectable before my Five Guys date tonight."

And with that little morsel hanging in the air, Tommy marched away without turning back, absolutely sure he could feel Aaron's glare burning into him.

Chapter Nine

Sunday morning, still in his pyjamas, Mitchell sat cross-legged on the sofa, blowing on the surface of a mug of freshly brewed coffee while checking work emails. At two-thirty, he had woken with a gasp to the sound of the toilet flushing and someone moving about his apartment—until he remembered having his nephew stay. He'd need time to adjust to another living soul in his space, just as Zane needed to adapt to the time difference.

They had returned from their night out around midnight. After dinner, Zane had come to life as a second wind kicked in and, with Tommy's encouragement, had agreed to continue enjoying the cooler evening air and the delights of Hong Kong's nightlife. Despite his tiredness, Mitchell had agreed. At least his sister might get a positive report from her son about his first night away from home.

Maybe he shouldn't have been surprised that Tommy would be such a big hit with Zane, but the two had clicked like long-lost brothers. Moreover, his suggestion for Five Guys had been frighteningly accurate. Zane's expression had lit up on seeing the wall menu, and he'd devoured his burger, fries and milkshake as though he had not eaten in days.

Instead of heading into Wanchai, Tommy had led them to the nearest MTR underground station, where they had travelled across the harbour to Tsim Sha Tsui. He would not reveal their destination until they approached the waterfront outside the Hong Kong Cultural Centre, where crowds had already gathered. At first Mitchell had assumed they did so for the vantage point, the unique panorama of Hong Kong island seen from the other side of the water. Until the penny dropped. At precisely eight o'clock, synchronised with orchestral music from speakers installed around the quayside, colourful lights had flickered and danced across skyscrapers and other structures around the harbour while laser beams lit up the sky, something Tommy announced as the symphony of lights. Mitchell had noticed the nightly display before, usually through a restaurant window while eating dinner, but had never enjoyed the whole experience in the open.

They had taken the Star Ferry back to Central, and Zane had checked another item off his bucket list. But Tommy had not finished and had led them to Lang Kwai Fong, where revellers—many around the same age as Zane—filled the pedestrianised road. Once again Tommy had demonstrated his popularity, stopping to chat with familiar people along the way and introducing Mitchell and his nephew as friends in fluent English or Cantonese. At one point during the evening, Mitchell remembered smiling his gratitude to

Tommy and getting a shrug and a smirk in response. At well after midnight, they'd bade goodnight on the street above the nightlife, where Tommy had made no bones about looking for his bed filler for the night. Sitting in the back of the taxi, Mitchell had envied the stranger who had yet to know he would be sharing Tommy's bed that night.

Just then, the bedroom door across the living room cracked open. A bleary-eyed Zane in ruffled grey sweats pants and a plain white T-shirt poked his head out. Despite his tiredness, he smiled. Mitchell guessed that at some point during the fun of the past evening, he had decided to relax into the holiday.

"How are you feeling?" asked Mitchell.

"Demolished. Mind if I use the bathroom?"

"Be my guest."

Zane padded across the wooden floor with a towel over one shoulder and his wash bag in hand. Mitchell turned away and continued checking his messages.

"Did you sleep?"

"At first, yeah. But then, not so much."

"Thought we'd try the little coffee shop around the block. My haunt on a Sunday morning. They serve the best range of international breakfasts and pastries."

"Cool."

Mitchell heard Zane open the bathroom door.

"Tommy's dope," came Zane's voice from the doorway. "He's the main character, you know? Said you don't hang out much."

"We're very different people."

"Shame. He's into you."

The remark blindsided Mitchell, and he looked up into Zane's mischievous grin.

"Is that what he told you?"

"No, but the way he takes the piss and you retaliate is better than standup. And he's more relaxed around you, more like his real self, I guess. Not like when he meets his other friends and becomes a kind of on-duty Tommy, if you know what I mean?"

Mitchell wasn't sure he did.

"You picked all that up in one evening?"

"What can I say? I pay attention. He said me and him can hang out when you're busy. Is that going to be okay?"

"I don't see why not."

"Cool."

When the bathroom door closed, Mitchell smiled to himself. Tommy had made Zane think their hanging out was his idea, which worked better. Zane wouldn't feel manipulated.

* * * *

Just before nine-thirty, they headed down the stairs to Mitchell's apartment, and as Zane walked on ahead, he plucked a red envelope from his letterbox. Mrs Lau's door was firmly closed, so he thrust the card into his pocket and caught up with Zane.

They strolled the already busy streets of Kennedy Town, fierce sun and humidity warming their skin. Unlike the previous Sunday, grey clouds filled the horizon in the distance, a sure sign of rain later in the day. Mitchell enjoyed watching Zane — perked up after his shower — absorb the local hustle and bustle during their short walk along the road bordering the harbour. Mitchell had been wrong about him. Once he opened up, he had a lot to say. He just needed time to thaw out.

Mitchell opened the café door to a mix of ice-cold air-conditioning and the scent of freshly ground coffee. A server squeezed them into a free table at the window, waiting patiently for them to settle before taking their order.

"Now, before we eat," said Mitchell. "I have something for you."

Zane looked apprehensive, but Mitchell smiled, brought his hand out of his pocket and let a set of keys clatter onto the table.

"Keys to the castle. Yours for the duration. Now you can come and go as you please."

"Oh," said Zane, picking them up. "Cool."

"Now that you're here, let's talk about some of the more unusual things I think you should consider doing or seeing. Things you can easily do on your own. You'll have plenty of time during the week while I'm working."

"Can I take notes on my phone?"

"Of course."

Zane pulled out his phone and tapped away as Mitchell went through his suggestions, which included a visit to the Man Mo Taoist temple on Hollywood Road and a stroll along the nearby Cat Street Market, getting the bus to various beaches along the south of the island and riding the electric tram from beginning to end, all the way along the north side of the island from Kennedy Town to Shau Kei Wan in the east.

"We hit the Mid-Levels escalator last night, but you're likely to go there again, and when you do, keep an eye out for a place called Rednaxela Terrace. Grab a shot of the street sign on your phone. There's an urban myth that the Chinese street sign painter at the time reversed the name Alexander, which is actually an easier mistake to make than we Westerners appreciate. Unlike English, written Chinese is pretty versatile and can be written vertically or horizontally, and can read from right to left."

"Cool. I'll add that one to my original list."

"Start a new one. The five things on your original list were to take a red taxi, ride a ferry across the harbour, take the Central Mid-Levels escalator and visit the Jumbo Floating Restaurant—which, as I told, has already floated away. The only thing left is to take in the views from the Peak Lookout, which is simple enough to do on your own. And I hope you, along with the rest of the tourist population of Hong Kong, enjoy yourself."

"Not worth the effort?"

"I didn't say that. On a clear day you can get spectacular views and shots of the territory. Just be warned that there are endless tourist shops up there, and that you have to pay to get access to the best views on the terrace."

He was interrupted by a member of the waiting staff who approached the table, balancing a tray stacked with food.

"Full American breakfast, apricot Danish and a large wild berry shake," came her amused voice. Zane held his hand in the air.

"Hope you've got an appetite?" she said, putting food down before him.

"Watch me."

Mitchell grinned. He remembered his college days when he could eat to his heart's content, day or night, without worrying about putting on a pound.

"I also have an order of a wholemeal bagel and a pot of English breakfast tea."

"And that, I'm afraid, will be me."

The woman smiled and gave Mitchell a sympathetic look while placing the items. Once she had gone, they ate in companionable silence for a while.

"I thought we might take a ferry to Lantau Island today. We can visit the Big Buddha and nearby monastery," said Mitchell. "After that, we'll take the glass-bottomed cable car down from there to Tung Chung and catch the tube train home. How does that sound?"

"Cool."

Mitchell had begun to recognise the sincerity of Zane's enthusiasm by the depth or lack of emotion he used to utter that single, monosyllabic word. The visit to Lantau was met with lukewarm to middling excitement.

"And if I let you choose dinner tonight, what type of food would you pick? What's your favourite?"

"Out of anything?"

"Anything. But please. Not Five Guys two nights running."

Zane snorted. "Ribeye steak —"

"Mitchell!" rose a voice from across the café.

"Hold that thought," said Mitchell.

He had recognised Kate's voice instantly. He looked around, bewildered, at the other tables until Zane pointed over his shoulder. Kate stood at the counter, balancing a cardboard cup of coffee and a bottle of something orange. Her cheeks glowed red either from the warm morning or her efforts to control Angel, who pulled at her hand. At least Kate seemed pleased to see him. When he stood up and waved them over, Angel turned in their direction and appeared to calm.

"What are you doing slumming it in this part of town?" asked Mitchell after giving Kate a peck on the cheek, waving a hand at Angel and taking his seat. "Do you want to join us?"

"Can't, I'm afraid. Tons to do this morning," said Kate, tilting her head to Angel. "Beth asked me to drop some papers off. One of her clients lives out this way."

"Is Beth working again?"

Kate smiled with resignation. "Isn't she always?"

"This is Kate," said Mitchell to Zane, who nodded a welcome. "We work together. And this is Angel, her—"

Mitchell looked to Kate for help. How was he supposed to introduce their new addition? Kate snorted at Mitchell before taking up.

"We're not using specifics for the time being," she explained before addressing Zane directly. "Angel's living with us right now while she decides whether she wants to stay permanently. She thinks of me as her auntie."

"Auntie Kate," said Angel, playing with the paper straw in her drink and not paying attention.

"And this is my nephew, Zane," said Mitchell. "He arrived yesterday from England."

"Which means Mitchell is Zane's uncle," said Kate.

"Are you 'dopted?" asked Angel, suddenly interested.

"No," answered Zane patiently, but Mitchell noticed a slight frown crease his brow.

"You don't much look like your uncle," said Angel, glaring at Zane. "You're a different colour."

"Zane looks like his daddy," said Mitchell without missing a beat, but Kate had already begun to lead

Angel to an open space away from the table before crouching to whisper to her.

"Yeah, I don't think so," said Zane to Mitchell.

"Don't you? I do. I think you've lucked out on the gene pool front with Rob's good looks and my sister's intelligence. A pretty lethal combination, in my honest opinion."

Zane shrugged but did not smile. Had he experienced problems at school being biracial? Was that a part of why he didn't socialise much? Mitchell remembered watching an interview with Barack Obama where he talked about the difficulties of being accepted by people. But both of Zane's siblings seemed to have thrived without any problems. Moreover, Ellie had mentioned nothing and very little managed to get past her. Maybe Mitchell would broach the conversation with Zane at some point.

Kate returned to the table and eyed Mitchell an apology. Mitchell didn't miss the frown Angel sent Zane's way and wondered what Kate had said to her.

"We won't disturb you any longer. Angel's going to a princes and princesses party this afternoon in Clearwater Bay. We still need to visit the fancy dress shops on Pottinger to pick out some finishing touches for her outfit. But you'll have to bring Zane over for dinner one night when you're both free. I'll pop by and speak to you in the office early Monday morning. Also, I have some news I need to share."

"Sounds ominous."

"Monday. Enjoy your weekend."

Kate gave him a cryptic smile and a wink before instructing Angel to bid them goodbye and heading out of the door. Zane continued eating his food while Mitchell poured himself another cup of tea.

"They're planning to adopt Angel," said Mitchell. "Poor little thing has had a difficult childhood."

"Whatever," came the icy response.

Mitchell had placed his phone on silent but noticed the device buzzing on the table's surface. Pauline's name appeared on the display. He had learnt to quash his annoyance at seeing her name, especially at the weekend.

"Give me a minute, Zane," he said, snatching up the device. "I need to take this."

Mitchell pushed out of the café door into a wall of humidity before thumbing to accept the call.

"Mitchell, I know it's Sunday, but I need you to come to work."

"I have my nephew with me."

"I'm sorry, but this can't wait. I fly to London late tonight for the board meeting tomorrow and I need you to help me collate figures and access personnel files before I leave. Forearmed, and all that."

"What time do you need me?"

"I'll be there around midday, but I've got a couple of things of my own to do. Can you be here for two?"

"Fine. Have you asked Helen?"

"Just you. And please don't call her. The fewer people that know, the better. I'll see you soon."

While Mitchell was talking, the clouds had moved closer to shore, and he felt a few raindrops on his skin. When he returned to the table Zane had finished his food and lounged back in his chair, checking his phone.

"I'm sorry," said Mitchell, taking his seat. "We'll have to take a raincheck on the Big Buddha. Although, by the looks of the weather, that's not such a bad plan. I need to go to work this afternoon."

"On a Sunday? Is that even legal?"

"It's not illegal and it doesn't happen often. This is kind of an emergency."

"Man, your job sucks."

"Sometimes. Are you going to be okay on your own?"

Disappointment flashed momentarily across Zane's face, something he quickly masked by nodding his understanding before peering out of the café window. Mitchell felt a mix of anger and remorse — anger at his boss for being cold and unsympathetic and guilt for leaving his nephew alone in a foreign country.

"Sure. I'll find something to do."

"Hang on. I have an idea."

Mitchell hesitated only a moment. Would he be out of line calling in a favour from Tommy at ten-thirty on a Sunday morning? Tommy's previous Sunday mornings had been hijacked, and he might take exception to having another one disturbed. And what if his hook-up was still there? But he had gotten along so well with Zane the night before. And they had, after all, agreed to help each other out, with Tommy promising to show Zane around.

Just as Mitchell unlocked his phone to find Tommy's contact number, the device vibrated with Tommy's name showing on the screen.

"Tommy Chow? Are you psychic?" asked Mitchell, and he noticed Zane's mood soften.

"Sorry?" replied Tommy with what sounded like a snort of humour.

"I was just about to dial your number. Purposely resisting until after midday under pain of death. Yes, I hadn't forgotten. And here you are calling me."

This time Tommy chuckled with amusement.

"Yes, well. Looks like I cannot resist your charms."

"Yeah, right. What's up?" asked Mitchell. "You sound good. Must have had your morning coffee."

"Don't push it, Mitchell. Coffee's only just brewing. But I'm calling on the off chance you could do me a favour. Are you and Zane free this afternoon?"

Chapter Ten

A thick slat in one of the horizontal wooden blinds in Tommy's bedroom had broken a while back. Sunshine shone through the gap, cutting across the teak headboard of his bed, onto his pillow and straight into his eyes. Most days he could guess the time by the invasion of light. No matter how much he turned away and squeezed his eyes closed, the blaze would nag him until he surrendered to waking.

He opened his eyes and instinctively turned his head on the pillow. Memories from last night floated back. Half of his double bed remained unused. He breathed out a sigh of relief. No awkward morning pleasantries or forced conversations. After he pulled himself onto his elbows, he noticed his jeans and shirt from the night before hanging neatly on the back of the bedroom chair.

Was Aaron right? Had he lost his touch?

There had been that good-looking daddy, a New Zealand investment banker with his friend, in town for a weekend conference. The friend, a handful of years younger, had clearly been smitten with the older man. Enjoying their banter, Tommy had let them ply him with drinks while they asked questions about the gay scene in Hong Kong. The older Kiwi had clearly wanted Tommy. All the signals had been there. But there had been something about the young friend, the sadness and desperation at being overlooked by somebody he worshipped in silence, that had tugged at Tommy's heart. In much the same way Tommy yearned for Alec.

And there it was. He was saving himself for the best man. Simple. Eventually, as the place had become crowded, he'd faked a toilet run and escaped.

Last night had not been a complete bust. Up until his itch to get laid had surfaced, he'd enjoyed being with Mitchell and Zane. There was something to be said for easy and uncomplicated company.

Fully awake now, he staggered out of bed to his open kitchen and popped a capsule into the coffee maker. While the machine whirred and glugged, he plucked his phone from the charger, rested his back against the countertop and checked messages. Almost midday, and nothing. Perfect. His eyes slid down to an earlier message from Mitchell, probably sent from the taxi after they'd parted ways, thanking him for the evening and including a link to the biography section of Alec's extreme sports website. After scratching a hand across his scalp, he fired off a quick thank you and ran through the things he needed to do. After he'd showered, he would try to phone Daley again about the magazine article. The sooner he found out the truth, the better. If all went well, maybe he'd ask about Alec, too.

Before he had a chance to dial the number, his phone rang. Shelly from school. He groaned. A call from her on a Sunday usually entailed one of the teachers being away sick or on unscheduled leave the next week, and he would have to cover their lessons. That also meant he would need to spend the afternoon going through lesson plans. He braced himself and took the call.

"Tommy. Sorry to disturb your Sunday. Can you help out with the play this afternoon? We were supposed to be doing a full run-through in the gym from two, but the bloody director has food poisoning. Inconsiderate bastard. She suggested spending the time running through the musical numbers and choreography, something they did to death last Thursday evening. As the assistant director, I eventually persuaded her that we could spend the time more wisely blocking movement with the actors while your team moves parts of the set around between scenes—"

"The set isn't finished yet, Shell."

"I know, I know. But couldn't we use tables and benches to represent moveable parts? We've been working in an open space so far. Using objects will help the actors become familiar with the space they have available to them, with entrance and exit points, what is going to be where, and also what happens when. We did the same sort of thing back in Auckland when I directed a school production. Turned out to be time well spent."

Shelly had a good point. They'd been known to leave that kind of detail until the technical rehearsal a few days before opening night.

"Excellent idea. And sure, I can be there. All the crew I've cobbled together so far will be there. But we don't have everyone in place yet."

"Yeah, I thought today might be a good chance for the cast to see what goes on behind the scenes. You mentioned that friend of yours, Mitchell, and his nephew wanting to help out. I know it's a bit of a cheek, but can you get them to come along? You could also use the opportunity to ask the cast if they've got any friends or family members who might be willing to help."

"Actually, that's not a bad plan. Okay, bugger off and let me phone around. I'll see you at one-thirty."

Before anything, Tommy called Daley. Once again, the call went to his voice messaging service. He considered leaving a detailed message but instead asked Daley to call back. Once he had rung off, he sighed and shook his head. This issue of the mysterious woman was messing with his usual good mood. He decided to shelve the problem and concentrate on Shelly's idea. He sent a quick note to the messaging group he'd created for the crew to tell them about the afternoon run.

Once he had finished, he thought back to what Shelly had said about Mitchell wanting his nephew involved. Apart from not remembering telling her, Zane had only just arrived. But they needed hands, and they did have a deal. Mitchell answered on the first ring, his greeting making Tommy smile.

"Wait a minute," said Mitchell. "Can I put you on speaker? I've got Zane here with me."

"As I was about to say," continued Tommy, "we're having a rehearsal of the play this afternoon. They want the backstage crew to get an idea of set-changes, stage furniture and props placement. Last night Zane said he'd be interested in helping out and I thought it might be a good chance for you and him to come meet the gang and get an idea of what's involved. Only if you don't have anything else planned. It'll be from one-thirty until around five-ish. After that we usually stick around for a drink and a chat. I know it's your day off, Mitchell—"

"He's been ordered into work," came Zane's voice. "On a Sunday afternoon. Can you believe?"

"Not ordered," said Mitchell, sounding a little defensive. "I told you. It's—"

"That's fine. Then how about just you, Zane?" said Tommy. "Are you up for the challenge? We'll have some fun. Or are you planning to head back to bed and sleep the day away?"

"He's not you, Tommy," quipped Mitchell.

"Sounds cool. Count me in," called Zane. "Where shall I meet you?"

* * * *

Tommy met them at the appointed location outside an MTR station a few minutes later than arranged. When Zane spotted Tommy, he brightened noticeably, standing up from the road bollard he'd been perched on. Next to him, Mitchell appeared flustered as he stared at the pavement while taking a phone call. Clouds hung low in the sky now, seeming to match Mitchell's mood.

"Ready to flex those muscles?" Tommy asked Zane as he approached.

"Ready to do something," said Zane, looking bored.

Mitchell peered apologetically at Zane before breaking off from his call to speak to Tommy.

"Thanks for this, Tommy. I'll call or text you later when I'm done. I owe you big-time."

"Yes, you do. And I'm keeping tabs," said Tommy, which made Mitchell smirk and Zane chuckle. "Come on, Zane. We've got some magic to work."

On the way in the taxi, Tommy read down the messages from all of his team who had agreed to show up that afternoon. They were a range of ages, some a little older than Zane. His principal lighting engineer was bringing a friend, and even though they would be stuck in the lighting control room for each performance, they had agreed to help with the staging during the afternoon.

Their taxi climbed the steep Peak Road until they rounded a bend and entered a lane leading to the school, their rehearsal location. Built in the late fifties, the Sino-Anglo International School where Tommy worked sat high up on the north of the island overlooking the Kowloon peninsula. Over the years, they had invested heavily in upgrading classrooms and facilities and providing top-quality school equipment even though the exterior of the building maintained a fifties municipal vibe with its weathered grey concrete broken only by intermittent blocks of light-blue tiling beneath windows or walkways.

Tommy felt particularly proud of their new school gymnasium, where he spent most of his time. Renovated and refitted at the tail end of the coronavirus break, they now had the addition of fully computerised overhead lighting and four mobile banks of auditorium seating that could be moved and positioned easily to suit various indoor activities. Today they had been set up with three banks around the staging area, like an arena theatre, even though the actual venue for the play would be a small theatre in town.

Clusters of cast members lounged in them now, chatting or rehearsing their lines. Shelly had acquired several wooden gym benches, foldable tables and plastic chairs to represent parts of the set and props. From a quick conversation Tommy learnt that some of the cast were still reading from scripts and that the blocking — directions for where actors would stand, sit, move and how they would enter and exit — had begun only three or four rehearsals ago. Shelly kicked the proceedings off with a quick explanation.

"As most of you know, the set will be a fairly simple and static design. The Kit Kat Klub in Berlin is the main setting, but we'll use stage right and left to represent other locations. The musical numbers are performed in the club downstage. I think you know most of this from your read-throughs, so I'll ask Tommy Chow, the stage manager, to come up and explain some important staging points."

At Shelly's prompting, Tommy gave a speech introducing his team of stagehands and emphasised his list of essentials, such as actors listening carefully for their cues and picking up and returning props to the correct tables. He explained the goal of the afternoon's rehearsal to perfect blocking. His crew had marked out the stage boundaries with masking tape to ensure the actors stayed within the confines of the stage. Always a great idea when you were not rehearsing in the actual venue. Once they had arranged the make-do furniture, some actors appeared unhappy, grumbling about the reduced space.

Without prompting, Zane stepped forward and checked the cast members' understanding of stage directions. He explained how he had been initially confused when working on his first play because he had always assumed the left of the stage meant from the audience's viewpoint. Even though Shelly or the director would have done the same during early rehearsals, Tommy was impressed. Today, those directions needed reemphasising. Zane came across as genuinely friendly and humorous, never talking down to anyone, physically pacing out each of the nine positions from upstage right to downstage left. Shelly looked over at Tommy and gave him a thumbs-up at one point. He could also see that some of the younger players really appreciated the reminder, especially when he went on to explain the importance of being in the right place at the right time for several reasons, including lighting prompts, other actor's' positioning and, most important of all, so that the audience could see and hear everything. Zane played a quick game to see who could name the spot where he was standing then asked them where he should move to if given a specific stage direction.

The afternoon flew by. Adding movement to the scenes always provided another element to rehearsals, often a little chaotic, but with practice everyone eventually understood their places. After that, they could begin to weave dialogue and action together and the production would elevate to a new dimension.

Three hours in, they called a break. Tommy and Shelly found Zane sitting with three stage-crew members around his age. Shelly's team always laid on hot and cold drinks and simple snacks for everyone, and Zane's group appeared to have been handing around a pork bun, a local speciality with sweetened dough and a char siu pork filling.

"I'm surprised," said Tommy as they stood over the group. "Mitchell told me you're not a fan of local food."

Zane turned his head away and muttered something under his breath before excusing himself from the group and coming over to talk privately to Tommy and Shelly.

"Do you know Uncle Mitchell's friends, Harold and William?"

Tommy and Shelly shared a look.

"We both do," said Shelly. "More by reputation."

Zane told them about his first day in Hong Kong and being whisked off to lunch at a fancy local restaurant with Mitchell's cronies. All Mitchell had told Tommy was that Zane disliked local food. Zane's version of events told a different story.

"And my uncle just sat there and let them throw shade at me. My own uncle."

"Throw shade?" asked Shelly.

"Embarrass. Made me feel like some dumb hick from the sticks."

"Harold and his entourage can come across as judgemental, maybe even a little elitist," said Tommy. "Devon calls them Hong Kong royalty, queens who think the rest of us should curtsey to them."

At least that managed to wrangle a chuckle out of Zane. "You crack me up."

"You know I have a friend called Kate who works with your uncle?" said Shelly.

"I didn't know you were friends, but I think I met her this morning."

"I'm not sure if it changes your opinion," continued Shelly, "but Kate told me Harold was there for Mitchell when he needed a friend. As much as people tend to view us expats as transients—here temporarily and passing through—the reality is that life can often be lonely, especially for those who are single, maybe something Harold recognised in Mitchell, and why he brought him into his group of friends. That might be something you want to bear in mind."

"Harold's not my friend."

"No, he's not," said Tommy. "Nor is he mine. But he is your uncle's. And he still will be after you've returned to England. And I think you should respect that. Look, your uncle's agreed to put you up, so maybe bite the bullet when you're invited out with them. Do it out of respect for him."

Although Zane's attention appeared to drift off, Tommy noticed his head bobbing slowly as he listened. Shelly winked at Tommy and used the opportunity to slip away and mingle with the troops.

"Actually," said Zane, "Harold did order some half-decent chow in the end. If only I hadn't had to listen to their bullshit."

"Mind if I give you a free piece of advice?" said Tommy, feeling himself slipping into teacher mode.

"Go on."

"You're going to meet people like Harold and his friends at university, older and younger, people with their own sense of self-worth and unshakeable opinions on any number of subjects. Some of those are likely to contradict yours. Listen to what they have to say, but don't let them get to you. Learn to stay calm, rise above any comments. Be the better person. I often find a simple smile, a nod and silence is better than a full-blown argument, one that, frankly, nobody ever wins. Smiling and nodding doesn't mean you're agreeing. It simply means that you've heard them."

"Not always easy to do," said Zane.

"No, it's not. And it seems to me these days that a lot of people ask for your opinion about something because they want to hear their own reflected back. I find it best, especially if they bluntly disagree with what I've said, to maintain my composure and ask for theirs. Hear them out. Some people may have facts we didn't know or make a point we hadn't considered. But like I said, it's fine to agree to disagree because, believe me, you are going to hear a whole heap of factually inaccurate bullshit from some corners. For me, once I've parted ways, and if the bothersome bee of annoyance is still buzzing around in my chest, I go to the local gym, find the nearest hanging punch bag and spend an hour knocking all kinds of shit out of the damn thing. It's my go-to stress reliever, as well as a great way to stay in shape."

"I prefer to jog," said Zane. "Five miles. Totally clears my head."

"Perfect. If that works for you."

"Listen," said Zane, peering over at Shelly and his group. "I wanted to say thanks 'cause I'm really enjoying this afternoon. Think I passed the vibe check with the crew. They tell me they're rehearsing Thursday and Sunday each week until the performances. They also told me about this cool virtual reality venue they're hitting later this week and the fancy dress junk boat trip in a week's time for the cast and crew to get to know each other better. I'm going to join them but can you do me a favour and mention the idea to Mitchell—"

"Mitchell already thinks you being involved in this is a good thing. He'll be fine—"

"He might get funny about the boat trip because he knows I can't swim. But he'll definitely agree if it comes from you. He's into you, man—"

"He's—what?"

"Don't worry," said Zane, grinning. "He's too chicken to say anything, but I can tell by how his mood improves when you show up."

"We're just friends —"

"Chill, Tommy. He knows he's not your type. Thinks he's not good enough for you, even if he was interested. Mum says he steers clear of relationships, anyway. Says he once had his heart broken beyond repair."

"What happened?"

"If he hasn't told you, then I'm not sure I should say anything."

"Whatever you think is right. But you do know I'm not going to repeat anything, Zane."

Zane looked away to think before nodding.

"Look, it was long ago, and I don't know all the deets. I was barely three when it happened. But he had this friend — more than a friend, if you know what I mean — called Joel. My mum and dad really liked him. Joel and Mitchell had all these plans and things. I think it was at the end of their college year. They'd done their finals and were out celebrating. Mitchell came home early, but Joel stayed out drinking with friends, said he'd get a cab home later. Then Mitchell was woken the next morning at their student digs by Joel's parents, calling to say the cab Joel had been in had collided with an articulated lorry. The lorry driver had been asleep at the wheel. They rushed Joel to hospital, but he didn't survive. Mum reckons Uncle Mitchell was never the same, and thinks that's why he took the job in Hong Kong."

Tommy stared at the young cast and crew, their lives barely beginning. They would eventually have stories to tell, but some would be harder than others. Had

Mitchell really made peace with himself? How did you ever get over something like that?

"Poor Mitchell."

"It was a long time ago."

"Some things stay with us for life."

"That's what Mum said. She thinks he never really gave himself time to deal with his grief. Thought he could run away to Hong Kong and that would be that. Says he's stuck feeling guilty that he didn't insist on Joel coming home with him that night. I used to think he just didn't like us. He rarely visited and when he did, he spent most of the time ignoring us and talking to our parents. "

"Remember he's also not used to having kids around. Not at work or at play. Whereas I have to put up with you little shits all day long."

Zane laughed. "He seems to put up with you okay."

"Careful, Zane. Or I won't speak to your uncle for you."

"Will you do it, then?"

"There's actually no need, but I will."

"Cool," said Zane before heading back to his group.

Tommy pulled out his phone, and was ready to send Mitchell a note when he saw a message from a newly set up group called Daley & Sammi Club. When he checked the group members, they included the two bridesmaids, Daley's brothers Liam and Cho, Best Man Alec—*gulp*—and Daley's Aunt Florence, who was an event coordinator in her day job and had been working as the wedding organiser. She was the one who had set up the group. As he looked on, a string of messages came through from her.

Florence: *Welcome to the group, everyone.*

Florence: *Big news.*

Florence: *Daley's father agreed with the editor-in-chief of StarAsia Monthly*

Florence: *They're doing a photoshoot of the wedding day for their August edition.*

Florence: *Apparently, they're good friends.*

Florence: *How amazing is that?*

Cho: *Fantastic. Defo wearing our velvet tuxes*

Tommy stared at the screen for a full minute. *StarAsia* was the magazine that had published the photograph of the mysterious woman holding Daley's hand.

Florence: *DO NOT say anything to the bride and groom. It's going to be a huge surprise.*

Of that, Tommy was absolutely certain.

He *really* needed to talk to Daley.

Chapter Eleven

Pauline loaded paper files into her wheelie document case—she preferred to view and amend physical documents when flying rather than try to work from her laptop—and, citing her need to get home and pack for her evening flight to London, hurried out of the door, leaving Mitchell to clear up the mess and switch everything off.

Once she had gone, he took a moment to breathe and centre himself before switching his phone from silent mode and firing off a quick message to Zane. Another half an hour, and he should be ready to leave. Maybe his nephew had been right. His job did suck far too often of late. Having gone through spreadsheet after depressing spreadsheet containing the personnel history and financial remuneration of almost every staff member—people he had worked alongside for years and knew personally—coldly ensuring their redundancy figures added up, he felt emotionally drained.

Worst of all, Pauline would return to the office on Thursday morning and her number two, Helen Cheong, would be the first casualty. Pauline had reminded Mitchell that he would be sitting in the meeting as an observer, something he dreaded. Naturally, Pauline alone collated redundancy packages for the senior managers, the information sensitive and confidential, entailing more considerable sums she would need to negotiate and get approved by the directors in London. Not that anybody would challenge her. She had a reputation for being unerringly parsimonious in financial matters.

Somewhat out of character, she had talked him through Helen's remuneration package and asked his opinion. Considering Helen's long service for the bank's operation back in Australia, he had suggested she push for the maximum. Pauline had agreed, and Helen's payout would be fairly generous. Maybe the lump sum would not compensate for losing her livelihood, but would hopefully be enough to give her options. Mitchell wondered if his boss had agreed to the sum to ensure Helen left without creating too many waves.

During the afternoon, Pauline had installed him at the small table in the corner of her office, collating reports as she printed them off her computer. Unneeded pages lay scattered around the room, confidential data that he would need to shred. Before anything, he stood and stretched, then walked around the space, collecting papers from surfaces or the carpet and turning off devices like the standalone computer she had been provided to print confidential data, her desktop scanner, her aroma air purifier and the snazzy black and chrome coffee machine.

When he reached her desk, he realised she had left her desktop computer signed on. He plonked down in her leather seat and tapped a key to stop the screen from timing out. Then he grabbed the mouse, ready to shut everything down, when one of the folders on the bank's customised desktop caught his eye.

HR Senior Mgt Decisions.

During the afternoon, she had asked him to update and print out details of staff members in all departments. Apart from Helen — and she had only read the proposed package to him — they had not looked at any of their own departmental staff. He'd assumed she'd already dealt with senior employees, maybe done the work from home. Then again, one of Pauline's admittedly few flaws was that she was hopeless with technology and would probably have struggled to access confidential documents on the bank's secure network from her home.

But then he remembered. Midway through the afternoon, Pauline had given him money and asked him to go out and get drinks and cookies from the artisan coffee shop a couple of streets away. Told him to treat himself to his favourite choice of coffee in the biggest cardboard cup they had, even though she had a swanky coffee machine in her office. Had she used that opportunity to print the senior management files while he was out of the building? That would undoubtedly be her style.

Maybe the file housed something innocuous, an updated departmental organisational chart. Although bearing in mind the current state of affairs, that seemed unlikely. One click would reveal the truth.

Would anyone know? Would Pauline? And did Mitchell give a damn if she did?

He clicked into the folder, which brought up a short list of spreadsheets, each with the names of senior staff. Both Kate and Helen were there, but listed in alphabetical order by family name, Baxter sat at the top. Without hesitating, he clicked to open the file.

Name: Baxter, Mitchell Angus.
Title: Senior Human Resources Manager, Asia
Other: DOB: 31-08-1985 | Status: Single | Base: Hong Kong
Largely operational experience. Joined Charteris straight from university. Fifteen years with the bank, thirteen worked in Hong Kong supporting the Asia region. Four minor promotions during those years. Loyal staff member, if unremarkable. Risk potential to bank: low.
Options:
1. Remain and rehire: Local head of HK ops position? Knowledgeable and well-respected by staff. Good connections with local recruiters. Extensive international labour law knowledge. Lack of broader management and finance skills. English only, no local or Asian languages. Unlikely to be suitable.
2. Relocation: London office, Canary Wharf. Upcoming junior HR management position. Twelve month maternity leave cover.
3. Redundancy: Statutory severance package. Standard local terms.
Proposal: Second option, due to knowledge and experience. But only once transition to reduced office completed in six months.

And there it was, in her own words. Not only was Mitchell not being considered for a role in the reduced

Hong Kong operation, but he was expendable. And unlike Helen, he would only have been offered a minimal payout, which would have amounted to no more than a few months' salary. No special treatment because he was considered low-risk and unlikely to cause problems. Even the position in London would be temporary. And he knew only too well from calls with repatriating colleagues that London might sing the praises of overseas experience, but treated returning colleagues at best like prodigal children, at worst like pariahs. His fate had been sealed. Another six months and he would be shipped back home. Jasmin Hong Kong, he had once carved in a stone on the peak, the word Jasmin code for just another six months. Ironic that the memory of that dark time should come back to haunt him today. Worst of all, seventeen years working for the bank and she had summed him up in that one word.

Unremarkable.

Anger, hurt and a sense of betrayal seethed in his chest. The years of dedicated service, working long hours, often being called during his vacation about work matters and sacrificing weekends had meant nothing. Tirelessly recruiting only the best for prime positions. Never a single day's sick leave, even working from home while he battled through a nasty dose of the coronavirus. Everything he could do to shine a positive light on the bank. And for what? He wanted to call someone and share the hurt bubbling inside him. Kate might have been the perfect listener, but she had problems of her own. If he called his sister, she might be sympathetic but would always try to find a positive spin, most likely that he would finally be returning home. And he did not want to hear that right now.

Then he remembered somebody who would not only give him sound advice but would probably have forgotten all about the call by morning.

Harold Choi.

The call picked up after two rings, but the voice was not Harold's.

"William?"

"Yes."

"Is Harold there?"

"We're at Queen Mary's Hospital. Harold's talking to a specialist surgeon about having spinal surgery."

"Oh, I'm sorry. I had no idea."

"Nobody did. It's all last minute. Is there anything I can help you with?"

"No, no. I just wanted to chat."

"Well, I'm afraid he's better at that than I."

"Of course. And you both have more important things. Give him my best when you see him."

"I'll let him know you called."

"Thank you. And take care."

After ending the call, he took a few breaths, squeezed his eyes shut and leant back into Helen's plush chair. People close to him had worse problems than his own. Even though he felt no better, he decided to finish and leave the office. Closing the spreadsheet file and folder, he shut down the computer and left Pauline's keyboard, mousemat and calendar squared off how she liked things.

As an observer in meetings with her, he had learnt that there was no point arguing a critical decision she had made. In some elemental way, he felt a sense of closure, and was no longer tethered by the inertia of living under the illusion or hope that he might be asked to remain. At least now he knew the truth and could finally plan his future.

His phone buzzed with a message.

Zane: *Super dope group. Two hours to go. Finish by six-ish. Taking us for drinks and snacks after. Wanna come join?*

Mitchell felt sure he would not be good company. And he did not want to spoil Zane's fun.

Mitchell: *Best decline. Feeling a little tired. But you go. Can you find your own way home?*
Zane: *Of course. Sure you won't come? Tommy's here.*
Mitchell: *Not today. Takeout food okay tonight? Pizza, maybe? My treat.*
Zane: *Cool.*

After running through permutations of the tone of Zane's last word in his head, he began feeding sheets of confidential papers into the industrial-sized shredder. The final thing Pauline had asked him to do was to unplug and hide away her coffee machine in a cupboard. She preached clear desks to her staff, and having the machine on display sent the wrong message. Most likely she didn't want anyone else being tempted to use the device while she was away. The unit wasn't hefty, but he first knelt on the floor and opened the cupboard doors beneath the device to check for space.

Apart from the perfect area to store the machine, all manner of colourful bottles of spirits, wines, beers and mixers filled the cupboard. Peppered in a light coating of dust, many looked like they had never seen the light of day. On the rare occasion when the department had done something exceptional or the bank had performed above expectation, she would invite staff to her office for an hour of after-work drinks and stilted conversations.

He could count those occasions on one hand, which was why he had forgotten about her stockpile. After fitting the coffee machine into place, he began to close the doors.

And stopped.

Sensible Mitchell would have left things alone, locked up and headed home. But reasonable Mitchell had gone to a quiet corner of his head for a well-earned sulk.

Didn't he deserve a consoling drink after sacrificing his afternoon and learning about his worth to the company? Nobody would be any the wiser, would they? And who would even know, especially if he took something from the back of the cupboard?

Crouching down, he reached in and brought out an opened bottle of something called Baxter Whisky — surely a sign. The label announced a twenty-five-year-old malt, whatever that meant. He was not a whisky drinker. But his brother-in-law drank the stuff and swore that anyone who added ice or any kind of mixer to a malt whisky should immediately have their drink confiscated — along with a list of other punishments too painful to mention.

After staring at the amber contents for a few seconds, he leant over, grabbed the empty shop-bought cardboard coffee cup from the waste bin, popped off the lid and poured in the remains of the whisky almost to the top.

What harm could one drink do?

Chapter Twelve

At the end of rehearsals, when the first live performance date was in sight, those participating rarely rushed to go home. Tommy had seen the effect countless times. Adrenaline, combined with excitement, had everyone buzzed. A little like when his school soccer team won a challenging game against another school.

But the gym needed clearing and to be made ready for the school day, so he and Shelly put their teacher's hats on and instructed everyone to stop chatting and help put things away. After that, they decided to head to Tommy's regular haunt on Wyndham Street, the café where he'd met Devon and Aaron the day before. Had the weather remained rough, they'd have phoned for taxis, but the rains had finally stopped, and even with the pavements steaming in the cloying humidity, they chose to walk.

"Your boy's a star," said Shelly as they strolled arm in arm down the hill towards the entertainment district.

"Not only likeable, but he knows his way around a stage."

"He's not my boy — he's the nephew of a friend — but I know what you mean," he said. Ahead of them, Zane chatted to a small group, two boys and one girl around his age, occasionally laughing together.

"Is he into one of them?"

"No idea. He's only just met them."

"Only takes a minute. Young love. Melts the heart, doesn't it?"

"You're asking the wrong person."

"Have you never been in love?"

"Does double chocolate cheesecake count?"

"Idiot."

"Actually, I'd better contact Zane's uncle. Let him know how things are going."

Tommy held back a pace or two while typing a message to Mitchell.

Tommy: *We're done. Want to join us? Heading to Wyndham for a drink. I'm sure you could use a glass of vino by now.*

He began to put his phone away, thinking Mitchell might be busy and unable to respond, but an incomprehensible message pinged onto his phone.

Mitchell: *Hd drink whisker. At world*
Mitchell: *Worm*
Mitchell: *Work*
Mitchell: *Shut*
Tommy: *Are you okay?*

Reply bubbles popped up a couple times and stopped. Eventually, after standing and waiting for a response for a full minute, Tommy dialled the number. The phone rang continuously before Mitchell finally answered.

"S'okay. Mm fine."

"Where are you, Mitchell?"

"Mm fine."

"Mitchell."

"Taxi stan' near Kowloon fle-fle-ferry. But m-fine."

"You don't sound fine. Stay where you are. I'm coming to get you."

"Is that Mitchell?" asked Zane, coming up as Tommy ended the call.

"Yes," said Tommy.

"I texted him already. He told us to go on without him."

"Sounds like he's — uh — unwell. I'll pick him up and take him home."

"I can do that," offered Zane, looking naturally concerned.

"No, Zane," said Shelly, nodding at Tommy and holding Zane's arm. "Let Tommy go. I'm sure your uncle would be mortified if you missed out on the fun because of him. Tommy's got this."

"Shelly's right. I'm sure it's nothing. Probably a stomach bug. He just needs medicine and rest. I'm sure it won't take long. He did insist you stay and get to know the crew. Do you have money?"

"Yes," said Zane, reaching a hand into his pocket. "I have Hong Kong dollars and my bank card."

"Good for you. I suggest you also buy yourself dinner. I'll take care of Mitchell. It'll give me and him a chance to have a chat about you, okay?"

"Oh. Yeah. Cool."

"You have my phone number, in case you need me. Can find your own way home?"

Zane rolled his eyes.

"Uncle Mitch — Mitchell — asked me the same thing. I'm nineteen, not nine. Are you sure you don't want me to come with you?"

Tommy looked down the hill and saw Shelly had already moved off, her phone clamped to her ear.

"No. Go and catch up with Shelly and the gang, before you lose them. You know you'll only end up with a bad case of — what is it you called it the other day?"

"FOMO. Fear of missing out. Point taken. Cool."

Before jumping in a cab, Tommy bought a bottle of mineral water from a convenience store. When he arrived at the ferry terminal, he walked to the taxi queue but found no sign of Mitchell. For a moment he wondered if he had already headed home, until he spotted the familiar figure bundled up and sitting alone on the stone steps leading down to the ferry terminal. When Tommy neared, he noticed Mitchell rocking gently backwards and forward.

"There you are," said Tommy, trying not to sound worried.

"Here I am," said Mitchell, his voice slow but not as slurred as earlier. "I'm a little drunk."

"I thought you might be. The incoherent text messages were a giveaway," said Tommy, pulling the water from his bag and unscrewing the top. "Here. Drink this."

Mitchell reached a hand up unsteadily and took the bottle. Tommy noticed a damp patch on the front of

Mitchell's plaid shirt but said nothing. Mitchell took a few tentative mouthfuls before offering the bottle back.

"Keep it," said Tommy. "Come on, let's get you home."

"Zane—?"

"Is fine. I said you weren't feeling well. He's out making new friends. Let's worry about you."

Tommy went to help Mitchell, who waved him off and managed to stand upright unassisted.

"I threw up a bit." On his feet now, Mitchell peered down at his shirt. "A lot, actually. I'm sorry."

"Probably for the best. You want to tell·me what happened?"

"No."

When Mitchell stumbled to his left, Tommy strode over to support him. With an arm around Mitchell's waist, Tommy led them to a red taxi. When the back door opened automatically, Tommy explained to the driver in Cantonese that his friend had a touch of heatstroke but was otherwise fine. The explanation appeared to placate the driver, and after Mitchell gave his address in very passable and, thankfully, coherent Cantonese, they set off.

"You stink of whisky vomit," Tommy murmured, fitting Mitchell's seatbelt.

"Twenty-five-year-old Baxter malt whisky vomit, to be precise."

"Didn't take you for a whisky drinker."

"I'm not. One glass of wine is usually my limit. And I've never had whisky in my life. But there it was. Even had my name on the bottle. So I decided what the hell."

"And I'm predicting that by the morning you will vow never to touch another drop again."

They sat in companionable silence as the driver negotiated the small roads rising to Mitchell's block. Some streets zigzagged left and right, and Tommy peered anxiously at Mitchell several times. His face retained an unhealthy pallor, but he appeared to be composed.

"I'm sorry, Tommy," said Mitchell.

"You said that already."

"I owe you. Once again."

Tommy turned to Mitchell.

"That list is mounting up in my favour. How about you swear off whisky on the wedding day?"

"That much I will gladly promise you."

When the taxi stopped outside the small courtyard housing Mitchell's apartment block, Tommy had a moment of recognition. But from many years before. Maybe he'd once gone home with a hook-up who lived there. The sex must have been good if he recognised the place by daylight. Most of his past shags began and ended during nightfall.

Seeing Mitchell struggle to pull money from his jeans pocket, Tommy paid the driver and helped Mitchell out of the taxi. When Mitchell finally punched in the door entry code and indicated the top-floor apartment, Tommy inwardly groaned but helped support Mitchell slowly up the narrow stone staircase. With both of them catching their breath outside, Tommy took the key from Mitchell and opened the door. After kicking their shoes off, Tommy used a hand to guide Mitchell inside. The space felt airy and cool, and for a moment Tommy wondered if Mitchell had left his air-conditioning running all day, but then he noticed the windows to the apartment stood in the shade of another block.

Mitchell had moved to the middle of his living room, looking dazed. Tommy drew level with him and placed a hand on his shoulder.

"Where's your shower?"

Mitchell pointed to a door leading off the living room.

"And what about your washing machine?"

He indicated the same door.

"Excellent. First, pick out something clean to wear, then go to your shower room, dump those clothes into the machine, then have a long, cold shower."

On his way to a different door, Mitchell emptied his pockets of wallet, lanyard, phone, a red postcard and a handful of coins onto the sofa before disappearing inside. Tommy took the opportunity to appraise the apartment. Somebody — the owner perhaps — had modernised the place beautifully. Even the air-conditioning in the living room was a modern split-level unit and barely made a sound. Decoratively, nothing stood out — neutral furnishings in either navy or grey. Even the rug beneath the gunmetal grey coffee table was a dusty oatmeal. Tommy realised the apartment was decorated the same way Mitchell dressed, purposefully understated.

Moments later Mitchell appeared from the bedroom, carrying a pair of track bottoms, a grey T-shirt and a white towel. Very slowly and gingerly, he paced towards what Tommy assumed to be the bathroom. After a few seconds Tommy heard the shower begin to run, water splashing into a basin, followed by gargling, perhaps Mitchell using mouthwash. Less than a minute later, still dressed, Michell returned to the main room. Tommy could see him struggling as he tried to unbutton his shirt, but his fingers refused to obey.

"Come over here, you big dork," said Tommy, stepping into Mitchell's space to assist. With his gaze lowered, concentrating on plucking at the buttons, he raised his eyes at one point into Mitchell's beautiful brown eyes, the emotion behind them unfathomable.

"If you say sorry one more time—" began Tommy, which had Mitchell grinning.

"I was going to say thank you."

Tommy finished unfastening the final button and nudged the shirt off Mitchell's shoulders. Beneath he wore a white undershirt and, although swaying slightly, he managed to pluck that awkwardly off over his head, leaving him bare-chested and his hair in an untidy heap. Only the belt to his jeans appeared to be giving his fingers trouble, and after watching Mitchell try three times, Tommy huffed out a sigh and stepped back into his space, unfastening the belt for him.

"I could almost believe you've done this kind of thing before," whispered Mitchell, his warm breath of mint tinged with whisky caressing Tommy's ear. The remark caught Tommy off guard. The soft words were sensual and arousing, not something he would have expected from Mitchell.

Emboldened by the challenge, Tommy held Mitchell's gaze while yanking the leather belt out from the jeans' loops, which jolted the bigger man slightly to one side. Still maintaining eye contact, Tommy dropped the belt onto the floor and reached to unclasp the top metal stud of Mitchell's jeans before unfastening the zipper. Colour had returned to Mitchell's cheeks. His dark eyes were fully dilated with an attractive mix of desire and fear before he peered down at the space between them.

As Tommy went to grab the waistband of Mitchell's jeans, Mitchell looked up, inadvertently brushing their lips. Instinct took over, and Tommy brought their mouths together, feeling Mitchell freeze for a split second before reciprocating hesitantly. Tommy could hear a distant voice in his head advising caution, a warning he chose to ignore. Instead, Tommy brushed his tongue against Mitchell's teeth, tasting a sour minty flavour, but that single contact seemed to ignite something inside Mitchell, who took a shuddering breath before roughly pulling their bodies together, opening his mouth and deepening the kiss. In an instant, control passed from Tommy to Mitchell, a transition Tommy found surprising but a total turn-on. Apart from the strong arms holding him in place and the tongue exploring his mouth, he could feel a hardness poking into his upper thigh.

A little roughly, Tommy yanked Mitchell's jeans down his thighs, then leant away and drank in Mitchell's body. Mitchell's build was what Devon labelled solid-framed, not overweight in any way, but big boned. His friend preferred his men not gym-toned but mature and naturally muscular. On this occasion, Tommy could see his point. Did Mitchell purposely dress down to hide his attractiveness? Because, beyond any doubt, Mitchell had a nicely proportioned body. Broad shoulders and thick forearms covered in the same dark pelt that covered his defined chest and coated his pectorals, the trail tapering down towards the noticeable bulge.

But in that moment, cold common sense kicked in. What the hell was he thinking? If they took things any further, wouldn't they risk ruining everything? And an ambient sound he had barely acknowledged finally demanded his attention—the shower water was still running. He looked up into Mitchell's eyes, seeing arousal clouded by a mix of fear and hesitation.

"Boxers," said Tommy, glancing down and trying to make light of the situation. "Tartan fucking boxers?"

Mitchell smiled, clearly relieved, and followed Tommy's gaze.

"What's wrong with them?"

"Who dresses you? Your mother?"

"They're comfortable."

"They'd have to be. Why else would you wear them?"

"Now who's being rude? They're good in this humidity. And some people like boxers."

"The Kennel Club?"

Mitchell looked puzzled for a second before catching on to Tommy's canine reference and laughing. The joke succeeded in breaking the tension between them.

"I'm sorry," said Tommy. "I shouldn't have done that."

"It's—it's okay. I didn't exactly put up any resistance."

"But I think it's best if we don't—"

"Of course. No, of course. We should keep this thing between us professional."

"Go and shower," said Tommy. "Before I relent and do something we both regret."

Mitchell didn't move for a moment, staring at Tommy, and for a second he thought Mitchell might be bold enough to take the initiative. And Tommy's resolve, which had never been steadfast, would have evaporated. After all, how often of late did he have a half naked, aroused and bluntly attractive man standing in front of him. Tommy could worry about the consequences later. But Mitchell, the gentleman, could not. Instead he smiled sadly, shook his head and headed into the bathroom, locking the door behind him.

"You are going to have one dreadful hangover in the morning," called Tommy, above the sound of the shower water and having no idea whether Mitchell could hear him. "Take it from one who knows."

For a moment, he considered quietly making his escape. Mitchell would understand. The more time he spent in Mitchell's presence, the closer he came to overstepping the boundaries of their friendship. But even in the short time they'd known each other, Tommy knew something had rattled Mitchell badly today. Maybe he just needed company and someone to listen.

Heading to Mitchell's kitchen, Tommy stopped at the sofa to reach down and pick up the red card with the Chinese characters that Mitchell had discarded. Tommy had seen similar slogans in his time, sometimes created on scrolls with auspicious sayings gifted to friends and family on special occasions. Some were hard to translate into English, but this one he knew well. Four words. *Adversity. Come. Follow. Receive.* When adversity comes along, receive it favourably. Or maybe a better translation would be to accept hardship with grace. But why would someone have sent Mitchell that particular idiom? Did they know he was going through a rough patch?

The kitchen had been modernised with black floor tiles, plush grey kitchen units, a large multifunctional microwave and a large, expensive-looking fridge in stainless steel. After filling and switching on the white jug kettle, he noticed other red cards stuck to the fridge door.

Opening cupboard after cupboard to orderly piles of chinaware and glasses, Tommy eventually found large mugs in shades of grey and smiled when he discovered a collection of teas, including a dusty glass jar of loose-leaf chrysanthemum. His grandmother swore the flower had medicinal qualities for those who had overindulged in spirits, Chinese wine or other potent alcoholic drinks. He remembered her telling him that finishing four full cups before bed would help lessen or even avoid a nasty headache and upset stomach in the morning. A cafetière sat drying on the draining board, so Tommy used that to brew the tea before bringing everything on a tray into the living room.

Mitchell eventually appeared, towel drying his wild mop of dark hair. At first glance he looked better, typically untrendy but comfortable in his baggy casuals. Only when he glanced over at the tea and mugs did Tommy notice his bloodshot eyes.

"How are you feeling?"

"Marginally better. Do you want to get back to your friends?"

"No, but I'll head off soon," said Tommy. "By the way, Zane wanted me to ask you if it's okay for him to attend rehearsals and hang out with members the theatre group."

"For heaven's sake. Of course it's fine. It was our idea."

"I know, but I couldn't tell him that. I think he needs to hear the words from you at some point."

"Lord knows what he's telling his mother—my sister. She's bound to call him today."

"Don't sweat it. I told him you probably had an upset stomach. Here. Drink this tea," said Tommy, holding up one of the mugs of freshly poured tea. "My grandmother swears by it to minimise hangovers."

Mitchell took the mug and sniffed the steam appreciatively before taking a sip.

"Do you know what this means?" asked Tommy, holding up the red card he had found on the settee.

"That one? No idea. My landlady keeps sending them to me."

"It's an older generation thing, little idioms, something my grandmother likes to send. Bumper sticker philosophy. This one translates as accepting hardship with grace."

Mitchell snorted sadly. "Yes, that sound about right."

Tommy put his mug down.

"Okay, Mitchell Baxter. Are you going to tell me what happened today?"

Mitchell heaved out a sigh and sat down heavily in a chair opposite.

"What do you need to know? I polished off an almost-full bottle of whisky —"

"And vomited. Yes, I know all that. My question was more around *why*."

Mitchell stared out of the window.

"It's a work thing."

"And you can't talk about it?"

"I'm afraid not."

"But it's bad enough to warrant you polishing off a bottle of spirits and clearly involves tough decisions somebody's making that you're just going to have to swallow."

Mitchell swung his gaze back to Tommy, clearly surprised at the words.

"How would you know that?"

Tommy held up the red card. "Because you just said so."

"Look, Tommy, I'm legally forbidden from talking to anybody about what's going on. But let's just say that I have a feeling that my days of living in Hong Kong are numbered."

An unexpected twinge pinched at Tommy's chest, the thought of losing a friend perhaps, or of something being unresolved.

"I understand."

"The irony is that in HR, we're constantly preaching to our workforce about embracing change, adapting and keeping up with the constantly shifting demands and needs of the business. But deep down, it's me who's uncomfortable with change. Don't worry. I still promise to be your plus-one for the wedding."

Tommy's phone interrupted them, pinging in his pocket. He read the message and held the phone up to let Mitchell see the words.

Zane: *Can you remind Mitchell about the theatre junk trip next Saturday. The dress code is anything nautical. I'll need to buy fancy dress.*

"Looks like we're on a junk trip next Saturday."

"We?"

"If I'm going—and I have no choice as one of the organisers—then so are you, Mitchell. Visibility, remember? And you need to be there to support your nephew."

"Oh, heavens. It never ends, does it?"

"You have no idea. But you said your nephew should socialise more."

"Nautical?" said Mitchell. "What the hell am I supposed to wear?"

"Don't worry," said Tommy, smiling. "I'm sure Zane will come up with something fitting."

Chapter Thirteen

On Monday morning, feeling better than he deserved, Mitchell left Zane sleeping and made his way to the office. He had no idea what time his nephew had returned because he had been fast asleep. Instead of potentially waking Zane with a text message, he left a scribbled note on the coffee table telling him to call if he needed anything.

During weekdays, Mitchell liked to arrive around seven-thirty, before anyone else, mainly to read messages, complete any overnight tasks and prioritise his day. That morning he picked up an extra-large coffee on his way in and was thanked his stars for the quiet emptiness of the office. His good fortune did not last long.

"Didn't think you'd make it in today," came Kate's voice across the otherwise empty open office.

"Whyever not?"

"I'd heard you were unwell yesterday."

Hong Kong's parochialism could be annoyingly intrusive. News travelled at the speed of light. On the flip side, that could sometimes be a blessing.

"Who told you?"

Kate appeared slightly embarrassed at the question.

"Girl gossip. I bumped into Shelly last night. She was out with her theatre people. Never mind about that, I have news. Remember I told you I was interviewing for a CFO position? The recruiter phoned late Friday night and told me the interview's this Tuesday. But I need your help."

"Go on."

"They asked me if there's anything in my current contract that might prevent me from starting as soon as my notice period has expired. Or if the bank might consider paying me out of the notice period."

"You're not going to find out what your redundancy package might be?"

"Honestly, Mitchell, it's not worth it. I've been through something like this before. This place will become toxic. And I doubt I'll get more than the standard minimum amount. I'd rather be working, especially with Angel to support. But I'd still like to swat up on my terms of employment, in case they ask at the interview."

"Don't you have a copy of your contract?"

"Somewhere. Home's a bit of a bomb site at the moment. I hoped you might be able to slip into my personnel file and check."

Mitchell sighed. "You do know you have a personal copy in your private portal account, don't you?"

"Yes, darling. But rather than me ploughing through screen after screen, unsure about what I'm looking for, you could use that huge brain of yours to dig the contract out for me."

"Okay, Kate. Let me check. And remember, you can't breathe a word or even entertain questions about what's going on here. Not to the people you're interviewing for or the recruiters."

"I know that. I'm legally bound. But just to give you a head's up, the recruiter did ask me a few interesting questions about rumours that have been circulating. I denied all knowledge, of course. But I don't think the secret is as secure as our people would like us to believe. And don't hate me, but she asked if you might ever think about moving on."

"What did you tell her?"

"Don't worry. I lied, of course. I said I don't know you that well and that she's going to have to approach you herself."

"And so it all begins."

"Yes. Fasten your seatbelt," said Kate. "Shelly pointed out your nephew last night. Nice looking lad. He seemed to be having fun."

Mitchell was thankful for the distraction.

"Apparently I got him totally wrong. He only arrived this weekend and he's already making friends. Tommy — that teacher friend of yours — has been a big help, actually."

"Has he now?" said Kate, with a grin. "That's good to know. When we met him and Shelly in the café, I sensed some indifference between the two of you."

"Indifference? Is that your polite way of saying that I thought he was a complete asshole? Turns out I was wrong there, too. He's not so bad."

"No, he isn't," said Kate, just as someone else appeared at the door to the office. She looked as though she wanted to say something more but stopped herself. "Excellent. I'll leave you to it then. Send me that stuff we talked about. Preferably this morning, if you can."

"Will do."

The new arrival turned out to be a manager from the bank's retail banking division. She'd wanted to speak to Pauline about the upcoming pay reviews. Pauline had delegated the task to Helen in her absence, but Helen had phoned in sick. He took the manager into a private meeting room to conduct the interview and sat listening attentively. All the while he felt like a fraud, knowing this woman and the staff member she had come to talk about would soon be gone, casualties of the coming cull. But he had an obligation to remain professional.

Thankfully the rest of the day went by largely without incident. But Kate had been right, and he had begun to hear whispers around the office during the afternoon.

With no Helen or Pauline around and a quieter day than usual, he left the office at about six. On his way out, he decided he needed to sound off to someone. He called a familiar number after finding an empty bench a few blocks from the office.

"Are you around for coffee and a chat, Harold?"

"Sorry, old man." Harold's voice sounded strained. "I've had a particularly bad day. Lot of pain. William's gone to get my prescription topped up. Can this wait until tomorrow?"

Mitchell felt instantly remorseful. Friends were dealing with far more significant problems than his own.

"Of course. Is there anything I can do for you?"

"Not really. Don't worry, it's not all doom and gloom. I believe William told you that they're bringing my op forward. The specialist had a slot become vacant. I didn't ask why. Does having a chat over the phone work for you? Would be nice to hear a friendly voice to keep me company."

Mitchell made up his mind because he needed to share his news with somebody he knew to be both pragmatic and discreet. He looked around to make sure nobody was in earshot before beginning.

"I shouldn't really be telling anyone about this. Everything's still confidential. Please tell me you won't say a word to anybody, including William. Promise me, Harold."

"Darling, you know me. I'll have forgotten all about it by the time I put down the phone. Especially once the pain meds kick in. What on earth has got your aussieBums in such a twist?"

Mitchell took a deep breath and blurted out his news.

"In short, the bank I've been working my ass off for is closing down the whole Hong Kong operation. Well, leaving behind a skeleton staff. And I'm being sent back to London."

"Okay," said Harold, sounding nonplussed.

Mitchell's indignation stalled. Harold's reaction had not been the one he had been anticipating.

"Countless people will lose their jobs," added Mitchell.

"I imagine that's goes with the territory. And?"

"It's just—" began Mitchell, but he hesitated again.

"Look, if it's sympathy you're seeking, then I'm probably not the right person. To my knowledge—and I'm no expert here—three or four international companies have shut up shop in Hong Kong over the past four years. And I'm guessing people would have lost their jobs then, too."

"Yes, but—"

"Which means that either other businesses have entered the marketplace or existing companies have recruited new staff—possibly the experienced staff who have been let go—to cope with the new demands from the customers who have been left high and dry. Isn't that how business works in our delightful capitalist society? If I was a wealthy Hong Kong investor who'd been relying on a particular international bank to service my needs, and that bank closed down or moved away, then I'd find another. I know some of these internationals claim to have a global online presence, but in my experience they're rarely as effective as having local experts on the ground. Or am I missing something?"

"No, you're doing pretty well. Carry on."

"Many of the people who lose their jobs will find new ones. Or decide to start their own businesses. Or realise they don't need to work at all. And the world will move on. But if there's one thing I have learnt about us Hongkongers it's that we are both practical and resilient in a crisis. While the world to-and-fro'd and hummed and hawed about wearing protective masks on the street at the outbreak of the coronavirus, everybody here was already masked up. We'd learnt our lesson with SARS. Being made redundant from my position with the construction company was the best thing that ever happened to me. I retrained and started my own property agency with the redundancy payout and, although I had to work tirelessly for months, I finally got the rewards I deserved for all the hard work I put in. Your position here will be gone, then?"

"It will. Although that, too, is confidential at the moment."

"And what will you do?"

"I told you. I have to return to the UK. They've found a position for me there."

"And is that a done deal? Can you not request redundancy? And have you considered other options? You are what used to be known as a company man, Mitchell. Loyal to a fault. Valued in the past but something of an anachronism in this day and age. You define yourself by your association with an organisation that sees you as little more than a foot soldier. One thing I love about so many of this new generation is that they are their own brand. They do not shackle themselves to one company, but promote the value of who they are and their individual skill sets. You're still young and eminently professional, you have extensive knowledge, years of experience and wonderfully marketable skills. And aren't you a local tax-paying permanent resident now?"

Trust Harold to state the obvious. Working in Hong Kong, Mitchell knew better than anyone that having been granted permanent residence meant he could stay in the region without requiring a working visa. He could also legitimately search for other employment or even set up his own business.

"Thank you for the reminder," said Mitchell. "Apologies, I'm still emotionally processing the change."

"Well, don't dilly-dally, old man. Treat this as an opportunity, not a death sentence. You are being uncaged and can do whatever you like if you're prepared to take a chance," said Harold before changing the subject. "Now, tell me how that nephew of yours is doing? Cheered up any? I hear on the grapevine that he's been drafted into the local theatre troupe. That must be a load off."

Once again Mitchell stalled a moment at how quickly news travelled. Who needed social media when you had friends like Mitchell's?

"I apologise for his behaviour at lunch, Harold. But, yes, he seems to be settling in well and making new friends. Tommy Chow, of all people, has been instrumental in helping out."

"As I have always said, sometimes a nudge in the right direction is all that's required," said Harold, as William's voice sounded. "Ah, that's my special delivery. Got to go. Please don't worry too much or overthink this predicament of yours. You'll do the right thing, darling. You always do."

The moment Harold ended the call, Mitchell already felt better. Kate had grabbed the bull by the horns and explored new career possibilities. He needed to do the same. He picked up his bag and had begun to stand when his phone sounded.

"Alec Janussen is in town," said Tommy excitedly, without even an introduction. "He says he has meetings with a supplier. Oh, I'm sorry. Can you talk right now?"

Mitchell snorted and sat back down again.

"I'm all ears."

"He's asked to meet me for coffee, says he has something a little delicate he wants to run by me."

"Maybe you won't need me after all," said Mitchell.

"No, I don't think it's that. There's something I haven't told anyone."

Tommy explained to Mitchell about an unknown but pretty woman holding Daley's hand in a society magazine photograph at the launch of a new sports product, one also attended by Alec. Mitchell smiled at being the one now handing out advice.

"I think you should leave well enough alone," said Mitchell.

"She's my sister. How can I?"

"Have you called Daley?"

"Repeatedly, but he hasn't been answering and I didn't want to leave a voicemail."

"There's your answer, then. Agree to meet Alec and ask him yourself. You say he's in the photo too. I bet he knows exactly who she is. Tell him about stumbling across the article and say you're just curious."

"What if he tells Daley?"

"What if he does? You *are* just curious, aren't you?"

The line went quiet, a sure sign Tommy was thinking.

"What's wrong, Tommy?"

"Will you come with me? To the coffee shop? I can introduce you before the wedding. Please, Mitchell. And I will count that as one less favour you owe me."

"When has he asked to meet you?"

"In half an hour. Told me to pick a venue. Somewhere we can talk."

Not that Tommy could see, but Mitchell rolled his eyes.

"I'm on my way out now. Tell him six-thirty at Coffee Maestro. I'll wait for you outside."

"What would I do without you?"

"I'm thinking more about what I would do without you."

* * * *

Alec Janussen was just as attractive as Tommy had described. Tall, blond and charismatic, he stood out in a crowd even when seated. The broad grin of perfect teeth that lit up his face when he singled out Tommy was infectious and natural. Mitchell understood Tommy's infatuation instantly, even though the realisation sent a ripple of defeat through him. They would make a good-looking pair—a power couple. Once Tommy had given Alec a brief hug, Mitchell held out his hand and had a firm handshake returned. To give Tommy a chance to speak privately, Mitchell offered to head to the counter to order coffee. When he returned, Alec appeared to be enthusing over plans for Daley's bachelor party.

"Tommy told me about your business venture," said Mitchell, placing Tommy's drink down. "Sounds exciting, doesn't it, Tommy?"

Mitchell noticed Tommy's knee bouncing up and down beneath the table.

"Can be," said Alec, nodding and smiling, then he talked about the range of sports his company offered. All the while, Tommy said nothing.

"What's the most dangerous sport you've attempted?" asked Mitchell.

Alec lounged back in his chair and looked at the ceiling, his thick, tan neck and large Adam's apple in full view.

"Toss-up between base jumping and ice climbing. Neither for the faint of heart. Have you heard of the Lyngen Alps in Norway? Yeah, probably not. I climbed a frozen waterfall there. They said what we were doing was for beginners then went on to scare the shit out of us, warning about the risks of getting buried alive in avalanches or plummeting to our death from a great height due to a misplaced footfall. Dude, that was one high-intensity experience."

"I might stick to waterskiing," said Mitchell.

"Well, we offer barefooting, which is a bit like waterskiing, but without skis."

"Sounds painful."

Alec laughed aloud, and Tommy's laughter followed like an afterthought.

"Funnily enough, stings less if the water's choppy. But the only injuries I've seen are when people take a tumble. Especially if they're bold enough to try slaloms or jumps. Hold up a moment. I've got a shot of me somewhere."

As Alec lowered his head to search through his phone, Mitchell tapped Tommy's foot beneath the table and twitched his head in Alec's direction. Tommy appeared to have zoned out. After admiring a couple of photos of a bare-chested Alec in nothing but surfer shorts, holding onto a ski rope with one hand, his muscled arms and legs covered in blond hair, Mitchell decided to take charge.

"Alec. In an edition of *StarAsia* magazine a couple of months ago—"

"Mitchell," warned Tommy.

"There was a picture with you and Daley in Bali. At a launch party for a brand of sports watch."

"JPY. Active Timepieces range. Yeah, that was us."

"And there was a girl in between you and Daley."

"Ellery Yeoh. That's right, mate." Mitchell didn't know Alec but felt sure a flicker of concern showed in his eyes. "She's the sister of the sports company owner. Daley went to high school with her."

"Why was Daley holding her hand?"

Alec's expression changed, going from neutral to sad.

"That's what I wanted to talk about, Tommy. But as I mentioned, it's a little delicate, so I asked to see you privately."

"Do you want me to leave?" asked Mitchell.

"No," blurted Tommy, looking startled at Mitchell before shaking his head.

"Okay, look," said Alec. "Daley wasn't holding her hand, she was holding his. I know that doesn't make much sense at the moment, but hear me out. Ellery works for an ophthalmologist practice, eye specialists, that Daley's family have been using for years. As you know Daley wears glasses, and he's had to visit the specialist a couple of times over the years. That day test results came back to confirm that he's suffering from a rare type of glaucoma, something that usually affects the elderly. It's early days, and most people don't even notice, but his vision is partially impaired, a bit like having tunnel vision. Most of the time you wouldn't even know and he manages unaided — flat surfaces that are well-lit and relatively even — but being on that uneven lawn at dusk was a challenge and Daley didn't want to spoil the event by face-planting in the turf. Hence the moment of hand-holding between him and Ellery, which happened to be caught on camera."

Tommy heaved out a sigh.

"See? I knew there would be a simple explanation. Sammi already knows about his eyesight."

"Yeah, but the tests indicate his condition's getting worse. That's why I wanted to talk to you first. He knows he needs to tell her — pretty bloody soon — but he's terrified she might want to reconsider marrying him. And I think that would just about kill him."

"My sister would never pull out of the marriage just because—"

"Wait a minute," said Mitchell, touching Tommy's forearm. "There's something you haven't told us, isn't there, Alec?"

"I'm afraid so. There's a good chance Daley will lose his vision completely within the next eighteen to twenty months."

Chapter Fourteen

.

Tommy singled Mitchell out as he stepped down from the minibus dressed as a pirate captain. From what Zane had told him, the sight should have been amusing, bordering on hilarious. With time on his hands during the week and apparently settling nicely into Hong Kong life, Zane had picked up their costumes and sent Tommy photos of each component part. Wearing long, black boots, grey-and-black-striped trousers belted in gold, a white silk poet shirt open and loosely laced at the neck, a three-cornered hat and a long black coat with gold trimmings, Mitchell should have looked ridiculous.

What he should not have looked was ridiculously hot.

Even his thunderous expression added an air of brooding sexual magnetism. Visions of unlacing the shirt while unclasping the belt and pulling down those breeches had Tommy forgetting to breathe for a moment. He quickly shook the thought away.

"You say one word, Tommy Chow," warned Mitchell as he drew near. "Just one word, and I get back on that bus."

"Aye, aye, Cap'n."

Finally, Mitchell cracked a smile just as Zane stepped off the bus, dressed equally impressively as a version of Sinbad the Sailor, complete with silver hoop earrings and a red and black bandana tied tightly around his head. His darker skin added a swarthiness and an air of authenticity to the costume.

Tommy had opted for a crisp French sailor costume of sleeveless blue-and-white-striped top — to show off his arms — with matching blue neck scarf, white sailor's cap and tight white shorts.

"Nice outfit," said Mitchell, raising an eyebrow. "Economical. Popeye?"

"Hilarious. Wait until you see Alec."

"Alec's here?"

"I invited him. He was supposed to head back to Singapore Friday, but he agreed to stay on because we're having a family dinner. And Daley couldn't be here."

"Does Sammi know about Daley?"

"I have no idea. And it's killing me."

"Let them work things out, Tommy. By the way, someone's waving at you."

Tommy turned to where Mitchell pointed.

"Shelly."

Tommy had been on more junk trips than he cared to remember. Varnished teak structures were a regular sight — usually at weekends — bobbing about in the harbour, taking partygoers to various destinations, including the outlying islands. Somebody, probably one of the show's producers, had secured a more modern boat. Shelly smiled a little too mischievously as they stepped aboard. Before he had a chance to ask, she began showing them around, starting in the galley below deck, a small room with a fridge and eskies — cooler boxes — full of cold drinks, an adjoining washroom and cooking facilities where the crew would be knocking up a range of food.

Most importantly, she told them, both the main and the upper levels had plenty of cover from the sun, the main deck with fixed bench seating and tables, the upper with foam-filled mats. After the tour, Zane was called away by three of his theatre friends seated in the main deck. Shelly finally led them to the upper deck, where they found Alec standing at the prow, taking a phone call, facing out to sea like a superhero figurehead.

Tommy gaped at his broad, muscular back, down the deep ridge of his spine and to his slim waist. He'd let his blond hair flow out that day, sun-bleached and reaching his shoulders.

"Isn't he a sight for sore eyes," said Shelly. "Blond Aquaman. Swims in the hotel pool every morning so he already had those orange budgie-smugglers with him. And I found some accessories buried in the costume and props box at school, dark green gauntlets from a Robin Hood production and that thick black belt. His legs are covered in green body paint and he asked me to brush in lines to represent fish scales. What do you think?"

"Hope you didn't use a permanent marker," said Mitchell.

Tommy snorted but then looked quizzically at Mitchell, who had been staring at Alec, unsmiling. Had that been a joke, or was he annoyed? Just then Alec turned and produced an award-winning smile before pointing at his phone to let him know he was busy and giving them a thumbs-up.

"I should have," sighed Shelly. "Once we reach Sai Kung, he'll be straight in the sea and all my beautiful handiwork will be washed away. Loving your outfit, by the way. Now, while Alec finishes his call, I have a surprise for Mitchell. This way."

Shelly led them back down to the main deck, to the back of the boat, the stern, which appeared empty apart from a couple of older people seated on the farthest bench, one in a wheelchair. Tommy wondered what Shelly wanted to show them until, next to him, Mitchell's voice called out in surprise.

"Harold? William?"

William turned around first and waved them over. Tommy did not appreciate being summoned. Mitchell didn't hesitate and headed straight across, leaving Tommy with Shelly.

"Why are they here?" he asked, unable to keep the annoyance from this tone. "I thought this was for the theatre group and friends, for them to get to know one another."

"Harold stumped up for the boat, the food and the drink. They've even provided a small motorboat and one of those inflatable banana thingies. How could I not invite the two of them? If I'm going to be honest, I didn't think they'd come."

"In which case," said Tommy, after an exaggerated sigh, "I suppose I have no choice but to say thank you. Get the pleasantries out of the way."

Tommy had never warmed to Harold. He'd meant what he'd said about finding Harold and his people judgemental and elitist. And he had never met anyone quite as pessimistic as William. At least his own group of gay friends—however superficial a person might think them—knew how to have fun out there in the world, running around and joining in, rather than sitting and judging or criticising from the sidelines like Harold and his cronies.

"Tommy Chow," said Harold. As he approached, Tommy realised Harold was seated in his electric wheelchair. He used a lever to turn the chair and assess Tommy. "How are you? I must say, of all the nautical costumes I've seen so far, yours gets my vote. Crisp, clean and muscular with a tantalising hint of *Querelle*."

Tommy smiled, even though he had no idea what Harold meant. "Thank you, Harold. And I'm doing fine. More to the point, how are you?"

Harold sighed with distaste. "Let's not talk about me. Mitchell tells me you helped get his nephew involved in this new play with people his own age. That was very kind of you."

"You've got to be kidding. He's helping us out. We need as many hands as possible backstage. And he's already a hit with the rest of the gang."

"I noticed that, too," said Mitchell. "He went straight off with them as soon as we arrived. I've no idea why his mother thinks he's such a loner."

"Maybe he just found his people," said Tommy. "I noticed him hanging around the same group at rehearsals this week."

"Do you think he might be having a little holiday romance?" asked Harold. "How delicious."

"Oh, heavens," said Mitchell. "Thanks for putting that thought in my head. As if I don't already have enough to worry about."

"Bad week, dear?" asked Harold.

"Let's just enjoy the day," said Mitchell cryptically.

And the day could not have turned out better. A gentle breeze rolled in from the South China Sea, tempering the heat and humidity. They set sail into the choppy waters of Victoria Harbour and made their way out to sea, following the headland towards Sai Kung Country Park. Only a few of the youngsters attempted to stagger from deck to deck as they left the harbour, the junk tossed around like a toy boat in the wake of larger vessels. At their destination, three similar sized sailboats moored a few hundred feet from the sandy beach. Tommy had visited the location once after a typhoon when the water had been a murky grey peppered with washed-up flotsam. Today, with barely a wave disturbing the surface, the sea sparkled blue, clean and inviting.

Harold had spared no expense with the experience. Once the crew anchored the junk, the kitchen staff served various drinks and barbecued foods, including meats, seafood and vegetarian options. Large trays of garlic bread and assorted salads accompanied the main food. They had even conjured huge aluminium trays of lasagne and stir-fried rice.

After eating and chatting with Shelly, Tommy wandered the decks to find Alec holding court with a group of youngsters that included Zane. Tommy stopped to listen momentarily as Alec captivated his audience with stories about his travel business and his various touch-and-go experiences. When Alec spotted Tommy, he seemed relieved. After a few words, he stood and excused himself from the group. Many seated took this as an opportunity to get up, and the group began to disperse. Alone with Alec, Tommy's brain went mush before shutting down completely.

Alec brought the remainder of his plate of food with him and led them to an empty built-in bench backing onto a window of the galley kitchen. Nobody else was around.

"Don't get me wrong," said Alec, sitting first and leaving just enough space for Tommy to sit close to him. Alec oozed health and confidence and coconut suntan oil. "Those kids are great, but they ask a shit ton of questions. Usually all at the same time. Thanks for saving me. By the way, I've been asked to remind you about the family dinner tonight."

"Sammi sent me the details," said Tommy, fighting to get his nervousness under control, the soft Australian accent and mere proximity of Alec making his knee bounce.

"Who's going to be at this intimate dinner?" asked Alec.

"Around forty-five friends and relatives. They wanted to host a kind of rehearsal dinner."

"Not so intimate, then?"

Tommy sighed. All week he had wanted to phone his sister and tell her what Alec had told him. But eventually he'd agreed that Daley ought to be the one to explain himself. That decision was his alone.

"How long have you known Mitchell?" asked Alec.

"Not long," said Tommy, grateful for the change of topic.

"You picked a right good bloke there."

"No. I mean, yes," said Tommy, chuckling nervously. "He is a good guy. But, you know, we're just friends. Nothing more."

"Friends? You two aren't intimate? Daley seems to think he's your boyfriend."

"I might have slightly misled people. He's a gay friend who's a boy. Mitchell's not really my type. I mean, you saw him at the café. Look at that hair and the way he dresses. One of our friends jokes that he stands out like bad shoes."

Tommy had been babbling, trying to make light of the observation, but Alec didn't smile. Tommy began to regret having said anything and backtracked.

"Don't get me wrong," he said, lowering his voice at a sudden clatter from the galley. "Mitchell's a really great guy, and a good friend. He's just not—you know—"

"Your type. I get it. Funny, I got the impression…"

Alec's handsome profile peered out to sea as his words trailed off. Eventually, he brought his gaze back to Tommy, his expression serious, his eyes alight. For one heart-stopping moment, Tommy wondered if he was about to snag his man.

"Look—and you can say no if you want—but a colleague of mine who's moving to Hong Kong in August is going to be at the wedding. Gerry's a decent bloke, nice-looking enough, but hasn't had much luck finding a fella. Well, not one that isn't an asshole. And I reckon Mitchell would be right up his street. Could you maybe give me a hand hooking them up?"

Tommy gawked at the decking between his flip-flops, trying to catch up. What had just happened? Alec wanted to pair Mitchell off with someone? But that was good, wasn't it? They needed to be apart if Tommy was going to have any chance with Alec. Except he had begun to wonder if Alec was even interested. And, for some strange reason, he wasn't sure how he felt about Mitchell being fixed up with a stranger.

"I'm not sure Mitchell's ready," he said before melting into Alec's beautiful blue gaze. How could anyone ever refuse him? "Let me think about it."

"Good man," said Alec before patting Tommy on the shoulder and handing him his empty plate. "Mind dumping this for me? I need to dive in and take a leak in that beautiful ocean."

Tommy tried not to overthink the dismissal. After disposing of their paper plates, he strolled to the rear of the main deck, where he was surprised to find Zane and a small cluster of his new friends with Harold and William.

Mitchell handed out drinks and glanced up for a moment, but then quickly looked away, barely acknowledging Tommy's friendly smile. His usually warm demeanour appeared rigid and cold, as if something had angered him. Harold sat at the centre of the group, his voice commanding everyone's attention. Perhaps one of his preachings had struck a nerve with Mitchell, causing this change of attitude.

"… and in 1997, the British returned the territory to China," said Harold. "I'm sure you must have seen television coverage of Chris Patten and Prince Charles in the pouring rain, waving from the deck of the HMY Britannia. From then on, Hong Kong became a special administrative region, a governance referred to as one country, two systems."

"What does that mean?" asked Zane.

"Harold. *Please*. Enough with the history lesson, I beg you," said Mitchell.

Harold chuckled.

"I'll make it brief. China, as in one country which includes Hong Kong. Two systems, as in China with its huge one-party socialist system ruled by the Chinese

Communist Party, allowing Hong Kong to continue operating with reasonable autonomy under its established capitalist system. Until 2047, at least. Simple."

"Simple? If only that were true," said William, with more than a hint of sarcasm.

"And everybody knew this was going to happen?" asked Zane.

"Of course."

"I don't understand, then. Why the protests? That's what your friends were arguing about in the restaurant, wasn't it? I mean, sure, protest if soldiers are threatening to march through the city, but not if it's something they've known about for years. I remember seeing pictures in the media of people running through streets fogged with tear gas. Mum wanted Mitchell to get on the first flight out."

"I like your nephew, Mitchell. We think alike," said William, his hand on Harold's shoulder. "The problem, Zane, is that like any other major city in the world, ours too has its faction of idealistic troublemakers."

"That's not the whole story," said Harold, gently clasping William's wrist. "The answer to your question is one of political ideology, I believe, and down to a divide between those who desire a self-governing Hong Kong with a democratically elected government, and those who are content to have Hong Kong fully integrated into China as another mainland city."

"Which is what the Chinese and British governments agreed to and what the people of Hong Kong knew was going to happen," said William.

"Back in the eighties. Without consulting the people. And China's agreement to allow Hong Kong reasonable autonomy didn't last long, did it?

Introducing a national security law that essentially restricts freedom of speech. In history, it's all too often that sense of futility that gives rise to protest," said Harold before releasing a heavy sigh. "But I do think there's something more fundamental. I believe Hongkongers consider themselves different from their mainland compatriots, see themselves as more independent and cosmopolitan. And I don't mean that to be insulting to their hard-working brothers and sisters. But they've experienced over a hundred years of trading freely and successfully on the international stage, building Hong Kong into a financial powerhouse and a world-class city. And I fear the generations who will inherit this metropolis believe that's likely to change for the worse. That means all of you sitting here. Let's hear what you think?"

Nobody volunteered to speak. Tommy wasn't surprised. He had seen the same thing repeatedly. Youngsters who were worried about voicing their opinions, fearing they might be ridiculed or, worse still, reported to the authorities.

"How about you, Zane?" asked Harold. "It's often difficult to get your head around something happening across the other side of the planet."

"I understand people falling out over politics. I couldn't vote, but I wasn't asleep when the Brexit referendum happened."

"But at least people got to vote," said Harold.

"Yes, and look at the mess that created," said William.

"My parents and their friends fell out big-time," said Zane. "Some still don't talk. But I guess what you're saying about Hong Kong is something only someone who lives here can truly understand."

Tommy watched as Harold, somewhat affectedly, clasped his hands in his lap on the red-and-black-tartan blanket and studied the horizon.

"You, of all people, might enjoy this, Tommy," he said, staring into the distance. "A retired teacher friend of mine back in England, who openly admits to oversimplifying things to get her point across, gave her class an analogy to try to help them understand why many Hong Kong people might be feeling the way they do. Imagine that, while imperial China was signing away the lease to Hong Kong back in 1842, a legal inclusion in the agreement—let's call it a legal cock-up or a loophole overlooked by the British—offered a reciprocal leasing to China of the Isle of Wight off the south coast of England."

Zane joined in the laughter. "Have you been there? The Chinese are welcome to it. Talk about snoresville. Except for the music festival, of course."

"You clearly haven't been there recently," said an Asian lad in Zane's group. "I visited with my parents last year. The place is way cool. Even without the attractions of Carisbrooke Castle and Blackgang Chine, there are some amazing restaurants and beaches."

"And before being colonised," continued Harold, "Hong Kong was little more than a fishing village. As I said, you need to be imaginative and consider what kind of a trading post the Isle of Wight might have become for the Chinese, and how the world might have changed, had they taken up the leasing agreement and put their stamp on the island."

This time, everyone fell silent.

"Let's pretend that what happened in Hong Kong in terms of administration, growth and expansion also happened on the Isle of Wight, an island overseen by a

China-appointed administrator. Children taught both English and Chinese in schools. Streets filled with Chinese merchant houses, hawker stalls with regional Chinese shops and restaurants. The island also known as San Kong, or New Harbour in Cantonese, named after the town of Newport. Shang Lin adopted as a loanword for Shanklin, and the same principle for other island towns. Shrewd and affluent businessmen from Canton and Shanghai seeing the opportunity for profit and pumping money into the island, building impressive structures and seaports to facilitate trading routes between Asian and European nations. Road signs erected in Traditional Chinese as well as English. Colourful Buddhist and Taoist temples springing up in towns and along sandy beachfronts. Streets hung at various times of the year with vibrant scarlet-and-glittering-golden lanterns. Let's also assume there would have been significant land reclamation on the sea-facing south side of the island and even a new international airport constructed. All the things we've seen developed in Hong Kong over the years happening on your doorstep back home. Culturally, I wonder if the people of the Isle of Wight might have ended up becoming something quite new and – to borrow a modern word – a hybrid Briton proud of both their Western and their Eastern heritages. Now fast-forward to current times, when new generations who have known no different, who have accepted life on the Isle of Wight as their norm, are hearing rumours about the UK government's plans to integrate them back into the English mainland and erase elements of their history. How do you think they might be feeling?"

"Pissed off," said Zane.

"Wait a moment," interjected William. "Apart from being total fantasy, Harold does tend to sugarcoat. Let's look at the other side of the coin. First of all, in all of history, China has never shown any appetite for colonising overseas territories, so the likelihood they would have acted upon this overlooked option would have been less than remote. Secondly, imagine the embarrassment to multiple British governments across the years, having this independent colony on their doorstep, ruled over by a nation often perceived as hostile. Which, admittedly might have done the British some good. Maybe they would have finally begun to understand how Spain and Argentina feel about Gibraltar and the Falklands. And how might the British government react if, as the lease draws to a close, these islanders begin protesting and demanding self-rule as an independent one-party communist state? Do you want me to go on?"

"As you can see," said Harold, "William loves to play devil's advocate."

"Somebody has to, dear."

"Maybe the answer lies in the uncertainty of change," said Mitchell. "Not knowing what the future holds."

Something in Mitchell's sullen tone struck a sad chord. Once again, Tommy peered quizzically across at him but Mitchell would not meet his gaze.

"Hear, hear," said Harold, clapping his hands together. "Now that we've put the world to rights, let's lighten the mood. Can somebody get me a top-up of that wonderful bright pink cocktail that I believe they call Seabreeze?"

With Harold no longer the focal point, individual conversations started up. Tommy noticed Zane's small group moving off past him. But not before Mitchell caught up.

"Okay, Zane," said Mitchell, holding him back. "Who's that local girl who has not left your side since you got on the boat?"

Zane's expression softened, blood rushing to his cheeks. Tommy said nothing, even though he had seen them seeking each other out at rehearsals.

"Her name's Emily. Mitchell, she is totally peng."

"Peng?" asked Mitchell, visibly surprised.

"Beautiful."

As soon as Harold and William snorted, Tommy understood why.

"Do me a favour," said Mitchell, grinning. "Don't use that expression in front of her. In Cantonese, the word peng means cheap."

"It does not!" said Zane, his expression one of mortification.

"Actually, your uncle's right," said Harold. "Although in context, you wouldn't normally use the word in connection with a person."

Tommy stuck around with Mitchell, Harold and William. Interestingly, he found Harold's company and conversation enjoyable even though he chose not to join. They had picked a nice spot shaded from the fierce sun, and Tommy nodded off for a few moments until he was woken by shrieks of laughter and cold droplets of water on his forearm. When he turned, Alec appeared before them like a bronze statue. Just as Shelly had said, the body paint had washed off his skin, and he stood in just his Speedo, a towel draped around his shoulders.

"What's all the excitement coming from the front of the boat?" asked Mitchell.

"They're playing silly-buggers," said Alec. "The way kids do. Singling out one of the group, pouncing on them and throwing them into the sea."

Mitchell looked up, and Tommy understood instantly.

"Is Zane with them?"

"I think he was the next victim."

Before Mitchell could say anything, Tommy was on his feet and running to the front of the junk. Only distantly did he hear Mitchell's panicked words to Alec.

"Zane can't swim!"

Tommy rushed forward and grabbed an armful of brightly coloured swimming noodles lying on a bench. Pushing through the group of youngsters standing at the prow, he jumped into the sea. Children's safety had been drilled into him at school for physical activities, and apart from being a first aider, he had been trained over the years to think quickly in emergencies.

From the amount of thrashing about, Zane had hit the water only seconds ago and remained on the surface. Emily swam nearby but appeared frightened, clearly not a strong enough swimmer to help. Those on deck had only begun to realise what had happened, and a few loud splashes followed Tommy into the water. Fortunately, other recreational flotation devices lay scattered around in the water. Tommy thrust a giant rubber ring at Zane and shouted for him to grab hold, grasping firmly as Zane clamped his arms onto the device. Although shock and fear filled his eyes, he stopped struggling and his panic began to subside.

"Are you okay?" called Tommy. He noticed Emily had swum over and trod water next to Zane while placing a hand on his shoulder. The poor kid looked more embarrassed than anything.

"I'm—I'm cool."

"It's okay, everyone," Tommy shouted to the watchers as he swam the ring and Zane towards the junk steps. In Hong Kong they had a saying about saving face, and Tommy decided to tell a white lie to explain away what had happened. "Zane's fine. He suffers from leg cramps. Best he stays out of the water for the rest of the trip."

"Thanks, man," muttered Zane.

When Tommy looked up, he saw Mitchell craning over the railings. His face had gone deathly pale, and, in truth, he looked more terrified than Zane.

Chapter Fifteen

On any other Saturday morning, Mitchell would have been up and about, making breakfast, doing housework or planning his day. Today he languished in bed, blinking at the ceiling fan, mulling over the string of dismal recent events. His days had deteriorated progressively from bad to worse. On rare occasions, a laboured week at work without much happening could feel like a month. Even though the last few weeks had flashed past in minutes, each retrenchment meeting had felt like a personal failure.

At unscheduled times during the days before the official announcement, members of staff from various departments had come to ask him if rumours about layoffs were true, and each time he'd had to lie and reassure them. As for recruiters, he'd finally refused to take their calls, sick of having to deflect questions. When all bank staff finally had the news confirmed in a town hall meeting, many faces had turned his way with contempt.

The following day, with ruthless efficiency, redundancies had begun.

Only last week an excited Kate had hauled him out for a coffee and shown him an email she'd received with the generous offer of a comparative role in a rival bank. Her interview had been successful. Charteris had even agreed to let her go earlier than her notice period. On the surface, he'd tried his best to look happy for her, but deep down he felt only a sense of sadness and loss.

With Pauline back in the office, he'd sat with his head bowed in the meeting where his colleague, Helen, had been told she would be the first casualty. For somebody usually quick to temper, she had taken the news with stoicism. While Pauline stepped out to attend another meeting, he had gone in to see Helen as she'd packed up the few personal items from her office drawers.

"*I'm so sorry, Helen,*" he had said from the doorway.

"*Don't be.*" She'd looked in remarkably good spirits. He'd wondered if she'd already known. "*I'm honestly relieved. I kind of thought I'd be one of the casualties, just not the first.*"

"*What will you do?*"

"*Head back home for a while. Take some time out. Rethink my life. Maybe look for a job there. Don't suppose you fancy working in Sydney, do you? We make a good team.*"

Mitchell had chuckled sadly. He would miss working alongside her.

"*We do. And the offer sounds tempting. Let's stay in touch. To be honest, I'm not sure how I'm going to survive the next six months without you around.*"

"*Poor Mitchell. Having to give people bad news day after day. I don't envy you. And I doubt Cruella will want to get her hands dirty.*"

By the time the day of the junk party came around, he'd felt emotionally shredded. If Zane had not been visiting, he would have made an excuse to bail. But putting on that absurd pirate costume and seeing Zane proudly wearing his own had conspired to improve his mood. Then, meeting Tommy in his sailor's outfit, looking as ridiculously sexy as ever — and remembering their moment from the week before — followed by genial chats with Harold and William, the array of colourful food and glorious sunshine, and the stress of the week had all but melted away.

Until his nephew had almost drowned.

Even before that, when he had gone to the galley to get drinks for Zane and others, he'd overheard Alec and Tommy as they'd sat and chatted, their backs to him, unaware of his presence. Objectively, he'd known Tommy wanted to connect with Alec, but hammering home Mitchell's dowdiness and unsuitability had bordered on insulting. Moreover, Tommy's agreeing to help fix Alec's colleague up with him at the wedding had felt like a betrayal. Mitchell's good mood had already begun to dissolve long before the near drowning incident.

He had made the naive mistake of letting himself to get too close. The kiss, however tentative, had stoked something in him, given him false hope, and he needed to take a step back and reevaluate their connection. He enjoyed their conversations, but how could he ever get past Tommy's superficial nature, his emotional transience and lack of any kind of depth or substance? Tommy had made plain that he saw nothing more than friendship between them. And even that would probably wither and die once their agreement to help each other was fulfilled and Zane had gone. No, he needed to put distance between them to maintain his sanity and retain a modicum of self-respect.

They had disembarked the junk at around four, with everyone still in high spirits. After helping William with Harold, they'd said their farewells. Zane, who had already forgotten about the incident, had made plans to head into town for drinks with his group, still dressed as seafarers. Undoubtedly photographs of their antics would appear later on social media. Mitchell had declined the offer to join. After waving to Tommy and Alec, who'd had dinner arrangements with Sammi and their relatives, Mitchell had headed towards the taxi queue, relieved to be going home alone. But not before Tommy had caught up with him,

"*Everything okay?*" Tommy had asked. Maybe he had sensed Mitchell's mood change.

"*Apart from my nephew almost drowning, you mean?*"

"*He should have said something. He could see what they were up to. He is a grown-up.*"

"*He's still a teenager. And he's in my care. While in Hong Kong, he's my responsibility.*"

"*You can't blame yourself —*"

"*Then who else can I blame?*"

Tommy had fallen silent. The couple in front of Mitchell had climbed into a taxi, making Mitchell the next in line.

"*I'm meeting Devon and Oscar on Wednesday evening,*" Tommy had said. "*Do you want to join us?*"

"*I'll pass. Going be busy for the next couple of weeks.*"

Tommy's obvious disappointment had made Mitchell's chest ache, and he'd almost caved. But he had made up his mind, which meant sticking to his resolve.

"*Alec's waiting for you,*" Mitchell had said, nodding to a point over Tommy's shoulder. "*You should go.*"

"You are coming to see the show, aren't you? It's my birthday on closing night."

"We'll see," Mitchell had said, opening the back door to the taxi. *"Zane flies home the following day."*

"What's going on, Mitchell?"

"I told you, I've got a lot on my plate. Look, don't worry. I'm still your date to the wedding – unless you get a better offer," Mitchell had said, waving to Alec. *"In the meantime, I'll see you when I see you."*

And with that, despite feeling conflicted, Mitchell had climbed into the back of the waiting taxi. He'd known Tommy stood watching him drive away, but he'd refused to look back.

Not everything had been doom and gloom. Zane had blossomed. His involvement with the theatre group had unlocked something in him, bringing him out of his shell and making him more vocal and animated. Mitchell had almost been envious, listening to his enthusiasm about his work backstage and his exploits around town with his new buddies.

One night during the past week, after an evening rehearsal, Mitchell had been checking the day's countless unread work emails and listening without comment, nodding occasionally, while Zane had sat cross-legged on the sofa and gushed about Tommy's fantastic stage set and how inspiring he was to work with. Mitchell had only looked up from his laptop when Zane had stopped talking.

"Why have you ghosted him?" Zane had asked.

"Ghosted?"

"Tommy says you're not answering his calls or messages."

"Work is crazy, Zane. You know that. Each day has been packed with redundancy meetings or exit interviews. I don't have time for much else. Certainly not socialising."

"You're coming to the final performance."

"I really hope —"

"No, Mitchell. That is not a question. Everybody needs a day off, even you. And I have a ticket for you. You're coming to see what all the fuss has been about and you're coming with me to Tommy's after-show birthday party."

Mitchell had laughed then.

"You know you sound just like your mother sometimes?"

"Say it, Mitchell. Say you're coming."

"Yes, Zane. I'm coming."

"Good." Zane had jumped up and headed towards the kitchen. "Talking of which, don't forget we've agreed to FaceTime Mum and Dad on Saturday evening. I'm grabbing a beer from the fridge. Join me?"

"There's a bottle of white wine open in there. Pour me a glass."

While Zane had disappeared into the kitchen, Mitchell had realised how much he would miss having his nephew around. But he also knew they had forged a new and enduring relationship. They'd sat up that night until one, with Zane telling him about the things he had seen and done with his Hong Kong friends, opening up about his determination to put the work in at university, to make his parents proud, and his gratitude to Mitchell at having invited him to Hong Kong.

Mitchell yawned then looked at the clock. Almost ten. He'd planned to have a day to himself. Enjoying his newfound independence, Zane would most likely be meeting up with his new friends. Maybe Mitchell would take his motorbike out for a spin. As he lay there, considering finally getting up, he heard movement coming for the main room, followed by a soft tap on his bedroom door.

"Are you awake?" came Zane's voice.

"Awake and decent. Come on in."

Zane entered, carrying a mug of tea for Mitchell. He was already showered, dressed and ready for the day, togged out in pressed khaki shorts and a long-sleeve shirt in red cotton.

"Mitchell, I need a favour. I've been invited to lunch with Emily and her folks. I haven't had a chance to tell you yet, but she's studying law in the UK. She's been offered a place at Bradford Uni. That's thirty minutes' drive from the campus in Leeds."

"I see. Does your mother know?"

Mitchell fought back a smile, knowing Tommy would have picked up on the ABBA song reference. But then Mitchell remembered his new resolve.

"My mother doesn't need to know everything."

"And this favour is what? Me not telling her?"

"No, of course not," said Zane, grinning. "Straight after lunch, we have the chance to get into the theatre where the play's being performed. We had a group message this morning. They've given us two hours for the lighting and backstage crew to go and see how everything works and get a feel for the space. The thing is, Emily really needs the lighting and set change plan, which is hanging on a clipboard back at school. I'd normally have asked Tommy, but he's not around today, doing something for his sister's wedding. I know it's a bit of an ask, but would you mind going to the school at midday — Shelly's there rehearsing with the rest of the cast — and bringing us a copy?"

"What, I'm your personal messenger now?"

"Please, Mitchell. We could go, but we'd miss the chance to have lunch with Emily's family."

"And the school will be open?"

"Head through the main entrance and straight down to the end. Except for us, the place is empty on Sundays.

Follow the sound of voices. There are two small studios next to each other that are normally used for dance classes. There are glass panels in the doors, so you'll see which one they're using."

"Okay. I wanted to take my bike for spin anyway. Where do I bring this paperwork?"

"Do you know the Hong Kong Academy of Performing Arts in Wanchai?"

"I do." The location was perfect. He could drop off the documents before riding his bike through the cross-harbour tunnel and eventually into the New Territories.

"We're in one of the smaller theatres. Text me once you reach the main lobby. I'll send Shelly a message and let her know you're coming to the school."

"Okay. Out of interest, where are the parents taking you for lunch?"

Zane smirked and folded his arms.

"I wondered if you'd ask. They're taking us to a local dim sum restaurant."

"And you're okay with that?"

"I owe Harold an apology. I wasn't in a good headspace when I arrived. But my friends have taken me for chow I would never normally have touched and I guess dim sum grows on you. I've even joined them for a seafood dinner, a place called Chilli Crab Under The Bridge to feast on something they call hairy crab. Sounds gross, doesn't it, but they're delicious served with chunks of deep-fried garlic. Emily even made me a breakfast of rice congee, which looks like rice pudding but is savoury rather than sweet—"

"I know what congee is, Zane. I'm just surprised you do."

"Are you kidding? Emily likens it to chicken noodle soup, something simple to eat if you're feeling under the weather. She made mine with shredded chicken, spring onions, ginger, soy sauce and added this local chilli sauce. We even had these fat noodle-covered doughnut sticks to dunk in. She's promised to make me some when we're back in England."

"Are you sure you want to go home?"

Mitchell had meant the comment as a joke, but Zane's face became serious.

"I'm definitely coming back, Mitchell. I can see why you like living here."

"There are pros and cons to living anywhere in the world. Believe it or not there are things I miss about the UK. And life can be significantly different in Hong Kong when you have to work for a living. But I'm glad you've come to appreciate why your uncle stays. Maybe your mother will back off a bit now I have you on my side."

* * * *

Mrs Lau's doorway stood open as Mitchell descended the stairs in his biking leathers, which meant she would be hovering inside. He called out a greeting and she appeared, smiling as ever. They chatted briefly about Mitchell's life and his nephew before she handed him a single letter.

"Nothing much today. Just another receipt from Mrs Zhang."

Mitchell carefully unpeeled the envelope in front of her and stared at the inclusion of a red card with gold lettering. Two rows of four characters. Without a word, she took the card from him and shook her head.

"How to explain this? I will translate each word for you. 'Timber already become boat; raw rice boiled into cooked rice.' I think it means that when some things are done, they can't go back to what they were originally. Does that have any meaning for you?"

"Maybe. I suppose we would say something like what's done is done. There's no going back. Not sure how that relates to me, but I'll keep you posted."

He pulled up outside the Sino-Anglo International School, where the tall aluminium gates appeared to be locked. Until he noticed a side gate left open. As he locked up his bike on the road, his phone rang in his jacket pocket. He assumed the call was from Zane even though the display read Unknown Caller. Maybe he was using somebody else's phone.

"Mitchell Baxter," he answered.

"Mitchell, don't hang up," came a female voice he recognised vaguely. "It's Gemma Chu from JM Recruitment Consultants."

A wave of anger rose in Mitchell. He'd endured weeks of dealing with work problems. Could he not just have one uninterrupted weekend to himself?

"How did you get this number?" he asked sharply.

"Look, don't be mad. I know it's the weekend and I'm sure the last thing you want is to discuss work. Your organisation is the talk of the town right now. But I wanted to speak to you personally. And privately. Can you give me five minutes? And actually, you gave me this number. When you were looking for a cryptocurrency specialist while you were visiting your Singapore office back in January."

Gemma Chu. They'd had four or five coffee morning meetings over the years, talking about filling critical positions. Professionally, she had climbed the ladder of the recruitment specialist agency with frightening speed, until she had become one of the partners. He admired her efficiency and used her regularly because she asked insightful questions about each role and listened, sending only suitable candidates for interview and keeping in constant touch throughout the process.

"Sorry, Gemma. You're right, my life of late has been a disaster movie. But just so we're not wasting each other's time, we're not recruiting anyone right now."

"No," said Gemma, laughing. "But we are. That's why I'm calling. We have a brand new position for a full-time senior recruitment manager coming up, someone who has in-depth knowledge of the banking sector. Would be a bonus if this person also had human resources experience and could turn their hand to training on general office topics. Can you manage a breakfast meeting before work on Monday? With me and our head partner. Say seven-thirty?"

"Wait," said Mitchell, confused. "You want me to interview—"

"Not interview, Mitchell. Our consultancy knows everything there is to know about you. This is for a fireside chat and to see if what we're offering could entice you to join us."

"I—yes, I can meet with you both."

"Do you know Coffee Maestro on Montague Street?"

Mitchell laughed. "I know it well. See you there. Seven-thirty Monday morning."

After Gemma signed off, Mitchell stared at his display. Harold's words came back to him about the world moving on and how Mitchell had marketable skills. Until that point, an inertia had overtaken him as though he was standing unmoving in the darkness. But now the sun peeked over the horizon. He might not like what they offered, but the chat would be a first step to get him moving forward.

After expelling a deep sigh, he stepped through the side gate and up the steps to the school entrance. Just as Zane had said, the door pushed open. Inside, the municipal corridor of grey and lemon yellow stood empty. Noticeboards with colourful posters and flyers, and intermittent classroom doors, lined the walls.

As he made his way down the wide passage, oddly familiar smells of paints or crayons and other indescribables reminded him of his childhood. At odds with what Zane had said, a student was practising scales on a stringed instrument somewhere in the depths of the building. Only as he moved farther into the school did the child begin to play the opening strains of a tune. Walking to the open doorway on his right from where the sound flowed, Mitchell decided to poke his head in and perhaps wave a quick hello to the young musician.

Except he found not a child sitting there but Tommy Chow.

Tommy perched on a plastic chair at the far end of the vast empty gymnasium, dressed in white shorts and a hot pink T-shirt, an elegant cello cradled between his thighs. Mitchell marvelled at how comfortable and natural he appeared. His body swayed with the all-too-familiar melody issuing from the instrument as the bow moved back and forth across the strings. Originally written for the violin, the haunting theme from *Schindler's List* took on a whole new meaning for Mitchell, played on the mournful cello.

He began to retreat but stopped. Something drew him in. Each precise and sorrowful note filled the empty hall with such eloquent sadness, bringing back memories. Instead of leaving, he leant against the sharp frame of the open door and closed his eyes.

The night of his death, Joel had dragged Mitchell and three of their friends to see a late showing of *Schindler's List* while they were undergraduates at

Warwick. Joel had sat mesmerised through the whole film, holding painfully tightly onto Mitchell's hand and unashamedly letting tears flow. Afterwards, Mitchell had refused drinks, claiming tiredness from pulling all-nighters and wanting to go home to bed. Joel had been buzzed and insisted on staying out to party, promising to get a cab home.

Mitchell still remembered being awakened the following morning by a call from Joel's parents. They had been contacted by the police in the early hours to tell them about their son. A lorry driver who had fallen asleep at the wheel and ran a red light had crashed into the back of the taxi carrying Joel back to their digs. Despite valiant efforts of the emergency services team, Joel had died on the way to the hospital.

Memories came back to Mitchell of the boyfriend who had seen the good in everyone and everything despite experiencing his fair share of hate and discrimination, who had loved nothing more than making dinner, dancing and singing along to music like some cheesy character from a Disney movie, someone who had loved life—and Mitchell—with all his heart, and had carefully mapped out their future in his head.

And the loss got worse over time. Tins of food no longer carefully lined up in cupboards with their labels facing forward like a well-stocked supermarket. The bookshelf lined with Joel's collection of wolf memorabilia comprising figurines, framed photos or picture mugs, all left to gather dust. No more insistence on kisses and cuddles before lights out, no catching Joel in the kitchen after cleaning the floor, ballroom dancing around the room with the mop while using a tea towel tied to each foot to dry the floor tiles.

At Joel's funeral they'd played the theme tune to *Schindler's List* as the curtain had slowly closed around the coffin. Mitchell had sat pale and impassive through the whole ceremony. Joel's mother and sister had both been sobbing messes, holding onto each other, permitting him to ignore himself and concentrate on doing his best to console them.

On his way to and from the car park he had walked beneath a black golf umbrella through torrential rain. Not a single droplet had touched him. His shoes had only become wet because of random puddles. At the time, the rain had been like his numbness, shocking, elemental and never-ending, but something he could protect himself from. Maybe he should have collapsed the umbrella and let the rain soak him to the skin.

Hindsight had become his tormentor, and guilt and blame were ingrained in him. Why had he had to be selfish about being tired when he could have stayed out a little longer to enjoy drinks with their friends? What hardship would that have been? Or why hadn't he insisted they go home together instead of surrendering so easily to Joel's stubbornness? At the inquest, he couldn't even feel anger towards the lorry driver who had also died, a single-parent father of four kids working insane hours to put food on the table.

Dark weeks had followed. Bad food habits and insobriety had become his sanctuary, a way to lose himself, the inevitable hangovers a deserved punishment.

Intervention had appeared in the form of his sister. No shouting, no lectures, no rationalising his emotional state—everything he would have expected from his firm and pragmatic sibling. Instead she had broken down in front of him, told him she forbade her brother from giving in to despair like their mother had. She needed him strong, needed to know that he would be there for her and her family in case she had to face dark hours of her own. She would not leave until he had promised.

Before she'd left, he had tried to soothe her by shaving, showering and changing into clean clothes, as well as swearing off drinking. Although the anguish had remained, he had buried himself in his studies, attained a respectable degree, good enough to get him onto a graduate programme with a leading bank, and worked at surviving. When he'd first seen the position advertised internally, a role based in Hong Kong, he had barely paid the posting any notice. Until one night, as he had lain awake, images of Joel had danced across his vision. The following day, without consulting anyone, he had applied.

In his head, he had rationalised that he could escape his pain by fleeing to Hong Kong. A new life, a new start, a safe Mitchell. If he could immerse himself in work and prioritise his profession, his company would protect him. He would honour Joel's memory by never getting close to anyone. And he would stay away from vain and heartless men like Tommy Chow, who had no emotional depth and who, if he let them, could hurt him deeply.

He could almost hear Joel's exasperated voice telling him he had everything wrong. Joel would have wanted to be remembered as a force of nature, his life filled with laughter and love, not a cold stone statue to be worshipped.

Mitchell had been wrong about so many things.

For the first time in as long as he could remember, as the music echoed through the hall, he allowed himself to cry, quietly and privately, not wanting to alert anyone and especially not wanting to give Tommy cause to stop playing.

As he took a deep breath and dabbed at his eyes before stepping away and moving on down the corridor, he heard words in his head, words wrapped in Joel's voice.

Enough.

You can let go now.

Chapter Sixteen

As the house lights went up for the cast's final bow of the last night, Tommy stood out of sight in the wings, scanning the stage and ensuring everything went to plan. Maybe the performances were over, but the backstage crew would keep working until the last person had left the auditorium. He raised a thumb to the lighting booth before stepping over to a blind spot and looking out to the audience.

Familiar faces climbed to their feet, giving the actors an ovation. His gaze flashed past Kate, Beth and Mark in the fifth row, who were applauding wildly. William stood in the aisle at the end of the same row, clapping politely. Although Tommy could not see him, he knew Harold would be there, sitting in his wheelchair, hidden behind those on their feet in the row in front. Zane had told him Mitchell would be there, but Tommy had not expected the surge of pleasure at singling him out, smiling and happy.

The week after the junk trip, Tommy had become furious with him. How dare Mitchell ghost him? Who the hell did he think he was? How much time and effort did typing a simple response take, even if he was busy? Tommy had raked over the day of the boat trip time and again, wondering if he'd pissed Mitchell off in some way by doing or saying something offensive. Each time, he came up with nothing. When the weeks of being incommunicado had rolled by, he'd begun to mourn their exchanges, missed Mitchell's face, seeing him break into a smile or laugh at something Tommy had said, usually unwittingly.

As the cast cleared the stage, the band played the last notes to the closing number, 'Cabaret, and a single spot shone on a lone black chair draped with a swastika flag in the centre of the stage. With a final crescendo, the music stopped and the spotlight extinguished, leaving the stage in darkness and signalling the show's end.

Tommy was thankful for no significant mishaps that night playing to a packed house. During the whole run, Zane had controlled the props like an obsessive. Everything in its place, used and returned to its rightful position before he went home for the evening. Set changes had been slick and seamless. Cast members had fluffed lines on the opening night, which was nothing new, but the prompt had worked well to get things back on track. The computerised lighting had been spectacular, even if cast members occasionally forgot their stage positions and delivered lines in partial shadow. The only major cock-up had come on Friday night, when the sound effect that should have been distant machine gun fire was instead the sound of a gaggle of geese honking, raising titters from the audience. Fortunately, that had only happened once. He'd been in shows where phones had not rung on cue, clocks had not chimed, or worse still, when gunshots had not sounded at crucial moments.

A scattering of applause came from those audience members who had stayed until the band's last note. Typical of community theatre, they'd had a run of only five performances—four evenings and one matinee. After tirelessly rehearsing over the past three months, after all their hard work, everything was over in the space of days.

Spirits would be high in the dressing rooms, but Tommy needed to remind people that the theatre closed promptly at ten-thirty, and everything had to be packed and removed from the building. Official group photographs had been taken with actors in costume at the dress rehearsal or between the matinee and evening performances. People had no real reasons to stick around except to natter. Shelly had devised the idea of giving each cast member a free first drink ticket for the after-show bar, valid until ten-fifteen. No better way to get people moving than the promise of a free drink.

"Shelly sent me to come and tell you to bugger off," said Shelly's principal assistant. "Her words, not mine. The costumes and props are packed away, the set's being dismantled and we've roped in people to help with the heavy lifting. There are a few hangers-on but we can chase them out. Go enjoy your birthday."

Relatives of cast members crowded around the stage door, welcoming their offspring with hugs and praise. Tommy made his way to a familiar group, realising how much he had missed the smile Mitchell produced when he approached. And something had changed. He appeared genuinely elated to see Tommy.

"Come on, birthday boy," said Zane with Emily in tow, throwing his arm around Tommy's shoulder.

"Let's get our talented stage manager a well-deserved drink."

"Excellent job," said Mitchell, as they finally strolled together across a footbridge towards the nightlife.

"So. You're speaking to me now, are you?" said Tommy.

Mitchell peered around at those in front and behind before leaning in close.

"I'm sorry. In my defence, this has been the worst three weeks of my working life in Hong Kong. But that's no excuse. My silence was a misjudgement. Let's talk later."

Somebody — probably Shelly — had reserved a section of Pink Propaganda for the private after-show and birthday party. Tommy spotted Sammi while the doorman was ticking off his name. She pushed through the crowd to throw herself at him, kissing him on the cheek before taking his arm and dragging him away to meet their friends. A few teacher colleagues wished him a happy birthday on the way. Due to the late hour, he'd agreed that the family celebration for his birthday would be lunch the next day.

"That was flawless tonight," said Sammi, almost shouting to be heard above the crowd. "Brilliant performances. Everyone said so. And the set was amazing. The best you've come up with by far. Kate says she's in talks with the organisers of the Edinburgh Fringe Festival. They might want to put the show on over there."

"Hang on. You were in the audience?" Tommy asked, surprised. She'd already been to both the Thursday and Friday night performances.

"Even with his crazy schedule, I made Daley fly in," she shouted, pointing to her fiancé chatting with Oscar.

"I loved the show so much, I demanded he come and see for himself. And we wanted to catch up with you."

The bar was too bustling for him to get a read on his sister. Had Daley or Alec mentioned anything to her about the magazine article? Either Sammi was putting on a brave face, or she was still oblivious. And had Alec told Daley that they had spoken? Right now might not be the best time to ask, but one thing was for sure. The not knowing was killing him.

"And you never told me Mitchell Baxter was such a hunk," she said as Tommy hugged Alec. Even through that close body contact, he knew his attraction to Alec had changed, as though the opportunity had passed.

"Mitchell?" said Tommy, releasing Daley and frowning at Sammi. Even though he had begun to feel a growing attraction to Mitchell, he was not about to give himself away. "Are we talking about the same person?"

"You see what I mean, Sammi?" said Devon, his arm tightly around Oscar's waist. "Your brother doesn't know a good thing when he sees one. Just because the man doesn't wear designer labels doesn't make him unappealing. Never begrudge a book because of its cover."

Sammi looked puzzled for a second before slowly nodding her agreement. Oscar smiled and shook his head at Sammi before leaning in and kissing Devon on the temple.

Tommy took his time greeting everyone, telling the actors how brilliantly they had performed, accepting birthday cards and presents from friends and having a few drinks along the way. All the while, he avoided Mitchell until he had seen everyone and could have him to himself. But that didn't seem to be happening, so eventually, he decided to pull Mitchell away from his group, telling them he needed his friend to help with something urgent and private.

Almost tripping over a beer crate, Tommy dragged a curious Mitchell into a darkened corridor leading to the bar kitchen, pushed him up against the wall and kissed him hard. Mitchell did not hesitate this time and returned the embrace, which began to get messy.

"You know it's my birthday?" asked Tommy, pulling away and wiping a thumb across his own lips.

Mitchell hiked in a breath, his face mimicking shock, before slapping his forehead. "So that's why they have a big banner with Happy Thirtieth Birthday Tommy Chow taped to the wall at—"

"Shut up and listen. For my birthday present I want you in my bed."

"I've already—" began Mitchell, laughing at first before he registered Tommy's earnestness. "Are you drunk?"

"Not even halfway."

"Are you sure about this, Tommy?" said Mitchell, his pupils wide but his expression apprehensive. "Is that going to complicate things between us?"

"I don't care. If you're going to be my wedding date, then I believe it's only right and proper that we consummate this arrangement. And I need to warn you that if you refuse to come home with me, I'm going to pull down your pants and blow you right here, right now."

"Let me get my jacket."

"Meet me out the front of the hotel, along the road," said Tommy. "I'm going out the back. Otherwise my friends will never let me leave."

"See you in five."

* * * *

On spotting Mitchell hurrying down the street towards him, Tommy stepped into the road and hailed a taxi. Without waiting for Mitchell to reach him, he climbed into the back. Mitchell clambered in after him, buckled up and turned to Tommy.

"Sammi was asking where —"

"Shut up and kiss me," said Tommy, reaching over and grabbing Mitchell, ignoring the taxi driver's attention.

* * * *

Tommy's apartment sat in a modern block on the eastern part of Mid-Levels, with a glossy marble entrance hall and shiny aluminium elevators. His grandmother owned the property, which differed from Mitchell's modest home. Mitchell began to reach for him the moment the door closed, but Tommy held him at bay with a hand to his chest, prodding the button for the sixteenth floor before raising his eyes to the tiny camera in the corner of the ceiling.

"They have CCTV in all the lifts and that old bastard on the front desk doesn't miss a thing. Maybe we can use this time to talk." Getting fresh in the back of a taxi when he would never see the driver again was very different to giving a free performance to the regular — and allegedly gossipy — night porter. "What did I do? For you to ghost me?"

Mitchell smiled sadly and looked at the panel of floor numbers.

"Nothing. I had a really crap few —"

"Bullshit. What did I do, Mitchell? I need to know, so I don't lose my friend again."

"A mountain of things happened, Tommy. Work pressures, friends quitting work, Zane being thrown into the sea. But then I overheard you talking to Alec about me. My fault. I got it into my head that we were becoming more than friends and when I heard what you said, I decided I needed to put some distance between us. Especially hearing both of you planning to fix me up with one of Alec's friends. "

"Shit. You overheard that?"

"Not intentionally. I was getting drinks for Zane's friend when you two were sitting outside the galley chatting."

"I never agreed. And I never will. You're mine tonight."

The lift doors parted on Tommy's floor and he stepped out first to open his front door. Once inside with the door closed, both kicking off their shoes, Mitchell pushed Tommy up against the wall, kissed him and pushed the length of his body against him. He felt Mitchell's body tremble. With an effort of will, Tommy pushed away and led them into his bedroom, flicking on the bedside lamp. Tommy thanked the stars he had tidied that morning, knowing he might be home late. Mitchell stood momentarily, taking in the wall posters and the decor before his hungry gaze turned to Tommy. Something had definitely changed in Mitchell. His usual reserve was gone, replaced by a new and frankly delicious wildness in his eyes. Tommy moved across the room and stood in front of him.

"I'm going to undress you," he said.

"Hurry up, then. But no snark about my underwear."

Tommy snorted. "Wouldn't dream of it."

Mitchell didn't move as he let Tommy unbutton his shirt, unzip his jeans and pull down his boxers. On his knees, he looked up into Mitchell's dark gaze, at the man he had once dismissed as boring. How wrong could he have been? Mitchell's arousal already stood to attention, thick, straining and eager. Tommy grabbed the base of his cock and, while staring up at Mitchell, opened his mouth wide.

"No," said Mitchell, cradling Tommy's chin and smiling down at him. "Not this time. Tonight *you* get blown, birthday boy."

"I thought maybe you might want to fuck me."

Tommy began to unzip his jeans but Mitchell stayed his hand and, very gently and painstakingly, began to unbutton his shirt and undress him, leaving him naked.

"Oh, I will. But only after you've let me blow you. Do you have condoms?"

"The drawer to your right. An assortment of lubes and condoms. But I'm on PrEP."

Mitchell stopped unbuttoning for a moment, a puzzled expression on his face, before continuing.

"I don't know what that is. But I'm used to condoms, if that's okay?"

"Whatever. Just stop talking."

Mitchell snorted and picked up the pace. Not once did he touch Tommy's skin, just a soft, warm breath on his chest, in his ear or against his upper thigh as he removed clothing. What at first Tommy thought he might find infuriating became the opposite, awakening every nerve ending in his body, raising goosebumps on his skin. His cock grew so hard he feared that a single touch of flesh on burning flesh might make him explode.

Mitchell sensed the tension because he reached a hand behind Tommy, roughly squeezed, then slapped his rear cheek before kneeling on the floor. Tommy definitely had had mild-mannered Mitchell all wrong. There was no way he could last long, feeling the heat and rough surface of Mitchell's tongue slide up the underside of his cock. He even clamped his hands onto Tommy's backside, caressing his glutes and repeatedly pulling him in. Tommy's orgasm, however incredible, happened far too quickly. He wanted the sensation to go on all night. Mitchell pulled away and stood while wiping his mouth with his fingertips.

Before Tommy could voice his disappointment, Mitchell lifted him bodily from the floor and threw him onto the bed. Mitchell removed the last of his own clothes before crawling along Tommy's body.

"That wasn't even foreplay. I am going to touch and taste every inch of you, Tommy Chow," said Mitchell, lifting one of Tommy's legs and kissing the underside of his foot. "Until you're begging me to fill you. And in case I never get the chance again."

"Bring it on, Baxt — ahhh."

Mitchell had lowered his head and sucked on Tommy's big toe. Rarely in his life had Tommy been lost for words. But at that moment he lay back and allowed his body and mind to switch off, to succumb to the sensations. Strong but careful fingertips brushed his gooseflesh, soft lips kissed the sensitive skin behind his knees and his inner thigh and sensual raindrops fell from the skies. After humming his approval, Tommy gasped when Mitchell began to use his talented tongue to lick the crevasse between his ass cheeks and moisten his entrance. Soon, a finger joined the tongue and slipped inside, heading directly for his sweet spot.

Tommy wasn't used to being prepared with such care and wanted to shout at Mitchell to hurry up and cut to the chase, but Mitchell knew what he was doing, stroke by careful stroke. Every time the build-up of sensations stopped abruptly and Tommy raised his head with irritation, he saw Michell's gaze burning into him.

"Bastard," muttered Tommy.

Mitchell grinned before moving up Tommy's body until they came face to face. After a tender gaze, he brought their mouths together. Tommy lifted his head and deepened the kiss while bringing his legs up to clamp around Mitchell's naked midriff to hold him in place.

Tommy had been with enough men to recognise a generous lover. Mitchell wanted to focus on pleasing him, listening and feeling for signs of pleasure, raking fingertips down his body, squeezing the flesh and nuzzling nooks. Each time Tommy reacted appeared to fuel Mitchell's own fire, and finally Tommy felt a firm pressure against his entrance. Once again, Mitchell looked intently into Tommy's eyes as he moved his hips slowly forward. This time, Tommy surprised a groan out of Mitchell by tightening the grip of his legs. Once Mitchell had slid fully inside and stopped, they both gasped with surprise. Tommy had been with more endowed men, but Mitchell filled him, the feeling natural even with the condom.

Mitchell began a slow rhythm without breathing a word, never dropping his gaze from Tommy's. He moved his hips fluidly, the sensual dance occasionally pushing in different directions until his cock ignited a spot inside Tommy that made his eyes flutter wide and a slight gasp escape him. Mitchell smiled at the reaction and lifted Tommy's ankles onto his shoulders. Tommy squeezed his eyes closed, threading his arms around

Mitchell's neck and pulling his head onto his shoulder. His erection, which had returned to life, repeatedly rubbed up against Mitchell's firm navel. They fit together perfectly, their chests touching, Mitchell's upper body swamping his own.

Just as Tommy felt the delicious tightness of what promised to be an intense climax begin to erupt, Mitchell stopped moving. Tommy's eyes flew open with irritation to find Mitchell's face hovering over his again, smiling slyly.

"I *will* kill you," said Tommy.

Mitchell laughed aloud before his gaze darkened and he resumed the dance. This time, they almost finished together. Tommy came undone, groaning loudly, shooting a sticky mess between them. Mitchell climaxed moments later, soundlessly, his whole body shuddering on top of Tommy, warmth filling the condom. They stayed glued together until Mitchell withdrew very slowly and carefully and lay next to Tommy. Neither spoke for so long that Tommy began to drift off into a post-coital slumber.

"I should go," said Mitchell, sitting on the side of the bed and reaching for his underpants.

"Or you could stay." Mitchell looked almost as surprised as Tommy felt at the words he had spoken, but he meant every one. "I mean, if you want."

"I do, I really do. But Zane flies home tomorrow —" said Mitchell, pulling on his underpants before squinting at his watch face. "I mean, today. And I need to be there for him. Help get him organised."

Tommy nodded his understanding and pulled himself to sitting, watching Mitchell putting on each item of clothing, unexpectedly savouring the view, especially when Mitchell turned to grin shyly at him.

Once fully clothed, he came around the side of the bed and perched at the end by Tommy's feet before bringing a wrapped box from his jacket pocket.

"What's this?" asked Tommy, leaning forward to accept the artfully wrapped gift.

"A small present. To celebrate your birthday."

Tommy opened the packaging to find a Tom Ford Eau de Parfum bottle. Like a kid at Christmas, Tommy ripped away the cellophane wrapping. After pulling the bottle from the box and spraying a slight mist onto the inside of his wrist, he inhaled the distinctive scent.

"This is too much, Mitchell," he said, grinning. "You didn't need to do this."

"I know, but I wanted to. I was short with you after the boat trip and this is my way of apologising as well as celebrating your significant birthday. I also wanted to prove to you that I do listen. Tom Ford is your favourite, after all. It's not the most expensive — heavens, the price of some are more than I earn in a month — but I'm reliably informed this is a classic."

Tommy took another sniff, and when Mitchell stood up, readying to leave, Tommy's heart sank. He wanted to say something more, but the words wouldn't come.

"Look, Tommy," said Mitchell. "I don't want you to think this has created any expectations or messed with my head. If this was just a one-time thing, then I'm fine with that. I'm really glad we had this night together, but I know where your heart lies. I'm just grateful to have my friend back."

"Me too," was all that Tommy said, even though he wanted to say so much more. Instead, he looked up into Mitchell's smiling eyes.

"And I'll even agree to you giving me a makeover for your sister's wedding."

"You will?" said Tommy, his eyes lighting up.

"I will."

Mitchell stopped in the doorway and turned back, a pained look on his face.

"Just, please, Tommy. Promise me you won't dye my hair blond."

"I promise."

Chapter Seventeen

As quietly as possible, Mitchell opened the door to his darkened apartment. In the taxi on the way home, he'd been tempted to text Tommy to tell him how much he had enjoyed their one and only night together, but he'd decided not to complicate things. Besides, being almost three in the morning, Tommy would most likely be asleep. Smiling to himself, Mitchell couldn't remember the last time he'd done the walk of shame but he felt entirely unrepentant, as though his physical union with Tommy had somehow broken down an internal emotional barrier.

No lights shone in the apartment or from beneath Zane's door. Even so, Mitchell crept across to his bedroom in darkness and only switched on the bed lamp once he had closed his bedroom door. As he undressed for the second time that night, he gave himself a self-satisfied smile in the wall mirror before climbing into bed.

As soon as his head sank into the pillow, he slept soundly and deeply. At seven-thirty, the alarm on his phone beside the bed emitted a soft peal. Even at weekends, Mitchell set his phone alarm to go off at the same hour. The temptation to kill the alarm and sleep through came and went. Even sleep-fogged, priorities nagged him. His nephew had to fly home that day. After switching to silent mode, he stuffed the device into his dressing gown pocket. The flight wasn't until after lunch, but he'd need to get Zane breakfast, help him pack, organise a taxi and get him to the airport in good time for his journey home.

He showered, dressed and completed his usual morning rituals as quietly as possible. Feeling more alive and awake, he filled and switched on the kettle, waiting until eight-thirty before tapping lightly on Zane's bedroom door.

"Wakey, wakey, sleepyhead. You've got a long journey ahead of you."

Nothing. This time, Mitchell knocked a little louder.

"Zane. Come on. You need to get moving."

After still getting no response, he opened the door. Not only was Zane not there, but his bed had not been slept in, although his case appeared already packed and ready, sitting in the corner of the room. For a second Mitchell froze, until he calmed himself and allowed logic to take over. He yanked out his phone and checked for messages. Nothing. First of all, he fired off a quick note to Zane. His nephew had taught him about the ticks on the bottom corner of messages to indicate whether the note had been received and read.

Nothing changed. When he called Zane's number, the phone rang repeatedly, eventually going to voicemail. Why wasn't Zane picking up? Mitchell shook away the fearful thoughts beginning to fill his brain. He would not allow himself to panic again like the morning he'd heard about Joel. Instead, he calmed himself. There had to be a simple explanation. If something had happened, somebody would have contacted him. Think, Mitchell, he told himself. He needed to contact one of the crew members Zane had befriended. Or somebody who might know how to get hold of them.

Tommy.

After six rings, just as Mitchell was about to abort and rethink his options, the call was picked up.

"'Lo," came a gravelly voice.

"Morning, Tommy. It's Mitchell. Mitchell Baxter. Yes, you probably gathered that. Sorry, I know you love your Sunday morning snoozes, especially after a night of—um, well, let's not go there. Look, I wouldn't call if this wasn't urgent. I need a very quick favour. Zane didn't come home last night. I have no idea where he is and he's not answering his phone. As you know he flies home today and I'm a little concerned. Could you ping me over the phone numbers of any of the stage crew you might have, Shelly and maybe Emily? I'm really sorry to bother—"

"Let me ring round. Then I'll come over."

"No, you don't need—"

"I'm awake now, Mitch. Make yourself useful while I get dressed. Head down to that little coffee shop at the end of your road and order me the biggest latte they serve. And one of their awesome Danish pastries. I'll get a taxi and meet you there. Shall we say forty-five minutes? Taxis are a little harder to come by from here on Sunday."

"Thank you," said Mitchell before a thought came to him. "Look, about last—"

But before Mitchell had a chance to speak, Tommy rang off. Mitchell stared at the display for a second before jumping into action.

* * * *

The barista in the café had just called out Mitchell's order when he noticed a taxi pull up outside the café. Somebody was leaning across the back to pay the driver. Not knowing Tommy's pastry of choice, he had ordered an assortment of baked goods, including cinnamon, apple and peach custard Danish tarts to accompany their coffees.

"Are those all for me?" Tommy's humoured voice came as he approached the table.

"I wasn't sure what you liked. So, I got a selection."

"Well, you guessed perfectly. I love cinnamon Danish, but any of these would have done. May I?"

"Be my guest."

"First of all, relax," said Tommy, sitting opposite and taking the pastry. Mitchell felt almost grateful for the diversion, eclipsing any awkwardness from the night before. "Zane would not be the first nineteen-year-old to stay out all night. At his age, overnighting at the weekend was the norm for me. Although I would usually let my mother or sister know."

"Exactly," said Mitchell. "And I doubt you'd have done so the night before you're due to catch an important flight. What did you manage to find—?"

"Hang on," said Tommy, placing his phone on the tabletop. "Can you let me have a sip of coffee first? I'm gasping."

Mitchell waited patiently while Tommy blew on the surface of his coffee, took a couple of sips and released a groan that sounded a lot like the ones Mitchell had wrung from him in bed earlier that morning. As Mitchell crossed his legs, his knee knocked painfully on the bottom of the table. Tommy didn't appear to notice.

"Nobody seems to know what happened to him. Shelly says he spent the latter part of the evening stuck to Emily. She tried Emily's mobile but she's not answering. Apparently, she lives in Tai Po. One of Emily's friends who worked on the theatre set lives nearby and her father has offered to drive her to Emily's apartment." Tommy stopped speaking when an unfamiliar pop melody issued from his phone. "Hold that thought. I think this might be her now."

Tommy grabbed the device, stood and walked away from the table to take the call. Mitchell could see by Tommy's expression and brief sigh that the news wasn't helpful.

"Yes, that was the friend calling back. Emily lost her phone last night. But she got home in the early hours — alone — and slept in her own bed. They'd all gone to Causeway Bay for karaoke after finishing at the bar. That's where she thinks she lost her phone. Anyway, she told the friend that her and Zane had said their goodbyes on the street outside the karaoke bar at around one. Zane took a separate taxi and she assumed he was heading back to you."

"Then where the hell is he?" said Mitchell, feeling panic begin to rise. "And why is he not answering his phone?"

"Mitch. Calm down. Panicking is going to help nobody. Emily's going to check with the crew members they were out with last night. Did he mention the names of any other friends he'd made, ones he might have partied on with? Or any places he liked to hang out?"

"If there were, you'd probably know better than me," said Mitchell.

"Emily was his closest. Before rehearsals, they used to meet at a bubble tea shop in Soho. How about we start off looking down there while I wait for her to get back to me? Do you want to book an Uber?"

"No need. I came prepared."

Mitchell reached beneath the table for his open rucksack and placed a white crash helmet before Tommy. Unfortunately, he didn't have his phone camera to capture Tommy's expression.

"As you said yourself," said Mitchell, "taxis are scarce this time of the morning. And as we have an emergency, getting around will be much faster on my bike."

Mitchell felt bad about rushing Tommy, but the hour was already nudging ten. Later that day, the plane carrying Zane would take off from Hong Kong airport with or without him. Zane's father had already messaged to confirm he was picking his son up from Heathrow. How would Mitchell explain to him and his sister that Zane had gone missing?

While Tommy packed the remaining pastries into a bag, Mitchell started the engine on his bike and waited for Tommy to climb aboard. Mitchell had never carried a passenger before, but after having had Tommy in his arms last night, feeling his rigid body crushed up against his back now and his arms snaked tightly around his midriff felt utterly right. Less than a minute into the ride, Mitchell felt Tommy's body soften against him and his grip loosen.

They arrived at the tea shop in Soho in good time. Even though the place appeared packed and buzzing, they saw no sign of Zane. Tommy handed his helmet to Mitchell and told him to stay outside. He reasoned that he could converse better in Cantonese, but Mitchell guessed that he didn't want him interrupting, especially in his present state of mind, and potentially freaking out the store employees. Mitchell watched him march up the counter, pull out his phone and show the screen to the staff, most likely a photo of Zane. One of the female servers nodded once but then grimaced and shook her head.

Mitchell's heart sank. But Tommy wasn't deterred and tried the same tactic in other cafes and coffee shops along the road. Each time, he reappeared, shaking his head.

"Look," said Tommy eventually. "You need something to keep you busy. Why don't you head home, make sure he's packed everything and wait for him there. He's bound to show up sooner or later. He may even be home already. If worse comes to worst, you'll need to speak to your family and see if they can rebook his flight. I'm going to meet up with Emily in Causeway Bay. She has a few suggestions of places I can check."

"I hadn't thought that far ahead," asked Mitchell, feeling powerless. "Do you want me to drop you off at Emily's place?"

"Not for this. The MTR will be quicker. Mitchell, you need to remember that your nephew's not an idiot. If anything had happened, he would have gotten word to you somehow. Let me do this on my own. You go home and get everything ready. I'll call if I find anything and you can phone me know if he turns up. Agreed?"

"Okay."

"Now head home and wait to hear from me."

Mitchell rode his bike slowly down the slope to the bustling Queen's Road, checking pedestrians as he passed. He could hear his sister's voice in his head, berating him for breaking his promise to take care of her son. If anything had happened to Zane he would never forgive himself. As he drove through traffic past a row of shops, he noticed a familiar figure farther down the pavement.

William, dressed conspicuously in one of his casual but stylish and distinctive Shanghai Tang outfits, stood outside a convenience store, a small plastic bag dangling from his hand. He looked lost on his own, as though he was unsure of his surroundings and location. Mitchell realised he had rarely seen William without Harold. Catching a break in the traffic, Mitchell pulled up along the pavement and lifted his visor.

"Morning, William. Is Harold not with you?"

"Mitchell. Good morning. No, I left him at the hospital." William looked paler than usual, the hand holding the goods shaking slightly. "He was admitted at four this morning."

"Heavens, I had no idea his operation was today."

"Neither did we. The specialist surgeon had a late cancellation, so they called us up. Woke us in the early hours. All a bit of a rush to get there."

"Are you on your way home?"

"Actually, I'm not quite sure what I'm doing at the moment." William peered down at the bag he held, and Mitchell felt a tug of sympathy. Tommy had been right. William and Harold were two halves of a whole. No wonder he felt so lost.

"How did it go? The operation? When can we go and see him?"

"I have no idea." When William met his gaze, Mitchell wondered if his pallidness was not due to tiredness but to fear. "They told us three hours, but it's been almost five and Harold's still in the operating theatre. The duty nurse sent me home, told me to get some rest. I half suspect they got fed up with me stopping them and asking questions."

William's attention was drawn to something over Mitchell's shoulder, and he turned to see what William was looking at but saw only random pedestrians.

"Where's Zane?" asked William. "Isn't he with you?"

"Tommy and I are trying to find him. He's disappeared off the face of the earth."

"He isn't at home?" William frowned and checked his watch, which seemed a strange reaction to Mitchell, but something he put down to William being distracted..

"He stayed out all night. And his flight's later today. But don't worry, William. You should get yourself home and get some rest. Or something to eat. I'm sure they'll call you the moment there are any developments —"

"When we left for the hospital, he was still fast asleep in our spare room."

"Who?"

"Zane."

"Wait. What? Zane spent the night at Harold's place?"

"Yes. And, technically, the property belongs to me."

"Why was he at yours?" he asked.

"Another of Harold's grand ideas," said William, smiling sadly. "Mainly because of you and Tommy. When your nephew came to bid us goodnight at the bar, he asked if we'd seen you. Earlier that evening, as Harold was backing his wheelchair out of the disability toilet, he saw you and Tommy in the passage behind the bar getting intimate — although I think Harold used a more vulgar expression. Tommy slipped out the back way and I remembered seeing you head quickly out the front, avoiding people. Harold, of course, put two and two together. Zane was overjoyed when we told him. Honestly, ever since that dreadful Repulse Bay cocktail party, Harold has been obsessed about hooking the two of you up. Cajoling Kate and Devon into finding a way to bring you both to the beach clean-up and using Zane to get you onto the junk trip. He and Devon were trying to figure out how to force you to the MacLehose hike together, but by some miracle or another you managed to arrange that yourselves. Anyway, being who he is, Harold offered Zane a bed for the night once he'd finished with his friends, to give you two time to finish what you needed to do, so to speak. We left him fast asleep in our spare room when Harold and I packed a bag and took a cab to the hospital this morning."

"He's not answering any of my calls," said Mitchell, dumbfounded.

"Ah, that might be my fault. I do apologise. I should have messaged you, but I have been somewhat distracted this morning. When your nephew turned up last night, he said his phone had run out of juice and asked for a charger. I was half asleep and plugged the device into our study charger down the hall. Said I would wake him at seven the next morning. Would you like to come back and check if he's still there?"

"Do you mind?"

"Oh, please," said William, stepping into the road to hail a red taxi. "I need something to keep me from going insane. If I were a braver sort, I might even agree to ride pillion on that monstrosity. Let's go find that errant nephew of yours. I'll meet you there."

Mitchell fired a quick message off to Tommy before trailing the taxi back to William and Harold's apartment. He had been there a few times over the years for dinner parties. An older property, like the one Mitchell rented, their building had the addition of an ancient elevator with a criss-cross metal barrier. The tenth-floor apartment had three bedrooms and a panoramic view of the harbour from the living room. They, too, had renovated and decorated exquisitely. Mitchell had always assumed, incorrectly as it turned out, that Harold had bought the property with the proceeds of the sale of his business.

"I never correct guests when they assume the flat belongs to Harold." As the elevator rose, a ride Mitchell had assumed they would take in silence, William began speaking. "To be honest, I think of the flat as belonging to us both. But the truth is Harold helped me sell the place my father left me when he passed. That's how we met. Then he arranged all the renovations. He has a keen eye for detail. Although the bricks and mortar are legally mine, the property has Harold's elegance and style stamped all over it."

William's voice trailed off. Mitchell didn't know what to say, so he placed a comforting hand on his shoulder and gave a squeeze. The gesture felt strange and awkward. Mitchell could not remember having touched the man before, even to shake his hand. William turned towards him and smiled sadly.

"Everything is meaningless without him."

"I'm sure he'll be fine, William. He's in the best place now, in professional hands."

"I keep telling myself that. I just hope we're both right."

Inside the apartment, William pointed down the hallway to the end bedroom. Mitchell opened the door to the darkened room and flicked on the light.

"Wassup?" came the shocked voice of a bleary-eyed Zane, sitting up and shading his eyes with a hand.

"Nothing much, chum."

Mitchell strode over to the window and pulled open the curtains, letting sunlight join the assault on Zane's vision.

"Except the plane you're flying back to London in," said Mitchell, before peering down at his watch, "is leaving Hong Kong in around two and a half hours' time."

Chapter Eighteen

Tommy's teaching colleagues from overseas invariably remarked about the number of public holidays Hong Kong citizens enjoyed, the region commemorating Chinese and English celebrations. On the first day of July, a public holiday called the Hong Kong Establishment Day to celebrate the return of Hong Kong to China, Tommy and his friends had created a tradition of meeting for a Handover Day lunch. Some laughingly referred to the event as Hangover Day on the rare occasion the holiday fell on a Monday and leisurely celebrations took place the day before, often dragging on late into the evening.

That particular Monday's Establishment Day, just over a week since Zane had been the last passenger herded onto the plane for his flight home, Tommy met Mitchell for his image transformation beneath the Times Square clock in Causeway Bay. As Hong Kong malls went, this popular one would do nicely to shop for Mitchell's wedding clothes. Once they had those sorted, hopefully before one o'clock, they would meet

Oscar, Devon and a couple of their friends for lunch on the tenth floor. For the afternoon, Tommy had already planned out the places to take his makeover subject.

In preparation, Tommy had sent Magenta, his hairdresser, phone photos of Mitchell and emphasised his friend's somewhat conservative nature. Magenta, in turn, had sent back shots of a series of model and celebrity hairstyles, ranging from outrageous and clearly unacceptable to short, clipped and even shaven. Tommy had vouched for something in between that would push Mitchell's boundaries but not freak him out. And, of course, no colouring — as instructed. He hadn't told Mitchell yet that the day would conclude with a full grooming, including a wet shave, eyebrow waxing, a mani-pedicure, and culminate in a ninety-minute shoulder, back and foot massage.

Mitchell seemed tired and subdued when they met — like a lamb to the slaughter, perhaps? Tommy hoped not. He suspected Mitchell's working week had not been kind. The last time they had been together, Tommy had spent much of his Sunday helping find Mitchell's nephew. Tommy wondered if their time together had made Mitchell feel obligated, because he had made no bones about Tommy's plan to reinvent him.

Zane crashing at Harold's place still made little sense, but Tommy hadn't pushed for an explanation. With William's help, Mitchell had managed to get Zane to the airport just in time for his flight. Zane had texted Tommy the moment he'd landed at Heathrow, thanking him for his friendship, making clear his intention to return at the earliest possible opportunity and asking Tommy to look out for Mitchell — as if he needed looking after.

"Once we've picked out the right suit," said Tommy on the long escalator leading up into the mall. "I am convinced everything else will fall into place. If we had enough time, I'd take you to see my tailor in Tsim Sha Tsui. But he'd need at least a week for fittings and adjustments. And, more importantly, we'd need to have a style in mind and I have no idea what suits you best. At this boutique we can pick out a selection in your size and get you to try them on."

Before he'd moved back to Canada, a friend of Tommy's had worked at one of the men's designer fashion stores. They specialised in off-the-peg branded clothing and Tommy still had a discount card. Tommy tried to read Mitchell's expression as he pulled one suit after another from racks, but Mitchell seemed distracted that morning.

"Okay, catwalk time. We have a decent selection to be getting on with. Try each of the six I've hung in the dressing room. Let's check out the styles, and see what feels and fits you best."

After a full five minutes and a fair amount of huffing and grunting from the small changing room, the door opened and Mitchell stepped out. Tommy almost dropped his iced caramel macchiato. The first suit comprised a tuxedo jacket and matching trousers covered in scarlet sequins with black velvet trimming — an outfit that might have looked good on a Cantonese pop singer, but not on Mitchell.

"How's the fit?" said Tommy.

"I appreciate that I should be grateful you didn't pick anything out in hot pink, but there is no way on God's green earth — to borrow your turn of phrase — that I would be seen wearing anything like this in public."

"Red is an auspicious colour in Chinese culture. My family—"

"Tommy."

"Okay, okay. Try the next one."

Fair play to Mitchell, he donned Tommy's choices obediently and patiently, without once refusing or complaining. Mitchell looked more relaxed when he stepped out wearing a traditional black tie ensemble, but while Mitchell cited James Bond, Tommy considered the look too dull, too much like Mitchell's usual business attire. Moreover, his old uncles would be wearing similar outfits. Neither the sage nor the tan suit appealed to either of them. Tommy smiled and nodded at the burgundy two-piece, but Mitchell shook his head and, after a huff, Tommy waved him back inside. As the hour ticked on, and Tommy loudly drained the last dregs of his drink, Mitchell finally stepped out wearing a distinctive blue three-piece number that even drew the male salesclerk's attention.

"It's a brighter tone than I would normally choose," said Mitchell, the single-breasted jacket open as he smoothed a hand down the front of the waistcoat while looking at himself in the full-length mirror. "What shade of blue is this?"

Tommy rolled his eyes. "Royal."

"I like the fit."

"Me, too. And the colour. Not an obvious choice for you. Everything works. This is the one. We're going to need to coordinate and accessorise—"

Mitchell's head whipped around.

"I am not carrying a male clutch bag or whatever you call—"

"Shirt, cufflinks, tie, shoes. Have a little faith."

"Fine," said Mitchell before turning to the clerk. "How much are we talking?"

"Don't be vulgar," said Tommy. "The right fashion choice does not come with a price tag."

"I think you'll find it does. More importantly, my savings account is not bottomless."

"Think of this as an investment."

"In what?"

"In you, the new Mitchell. Worth every Hong Kong cent."

Tommy noticed Mitchell's smile broaden as he admired himself in the mirror again before nodding to the clerk and heading back into the room to change.

"What about you?" came Mitchell's voice.

"What do you mean, what about me?"

"Are you going to buy anything?"

"My whole outfit was chosen, bought and paid for two days after my sister announced her big day."

"Of course it was."

Once Tommy had the suit colour, everything else felt instinctive. For him, at least. Convincing Mitchell to accessorise with a white wing-tip shirt, dark red bow tie with matching top-pocket hanky and cufflinks took some doing. Mitchell cited sustainability and lack of opportunity to reuse. Even the light shade of brown shoes and matching belt had him pulling a face. Eventually Tommy got his way and, after asking the clerk if they could store the bags in the boutique— Tommy did not want Devon questioning any of his fashion choices—they made their way to the top-floor restaurant.

"I hope you're fine with Japanese. This tiny ramen noodle bar called Oishi Ramen is tucked away in the corner. Devon calls the place his secret haven. One that everyone seems to know about—"

"I've been there. Many times. I know the place well."

"I know he's my friend, but Devon's hopeless at keeping secrets."

"Oh, I don't know," said Mitchell cryptically. Tommy peered around at Mitchell, but his gaze was elsewhere, scanning a poster outside the glass front of the building.

They arrived a little after one. The head waiter informed Tommy that the rest of their group of six had already been seated, causing him to wonder who else Devon had invited. Hopefully not Aaron, who would surely make a snide remark about Tommy being out in public with Mitchell. As he rounded the corner and caught sight of the other guests, his jaw dropped open in shock.

Sammi and Daley sat at the back of the semi-circular booth—as though holding court—with Oscar and Devon to their right, leaving room for Tommy and Mitchell. They had already ordered a pot of green tea and clay cups. Tommy felt a creeping dread seeing Sammi and Daley sitting there, solemn and maybe even nervous.

"Why are you two here?" he blurted before either had a chance to speak. "I thought you would be doing last-minute—"

"Sammi asked if they could join us," said Devon.

"Is everything okay?" asked Tommy, fearing the worst. He looked directly at Daley. "I've been trying to call you—"

"Sit down, Tommy," said Sammi. "We need to talk to you. Both of us."

A cold dread filled Tommy and for a moment he felt unable to move. Until Mitchell nudged him into the booth and scooted in next to him.

"Do you know what this is about?" Tommy whispered to Mitchell.

"I think so," said Mitchell, touching Tommy's knee. "And I think you do, too."

"Oh, shit," said Tommy, throwing himself back in his seat and putting his hands over his eyes. "Please don't tell me the wedding's off."

"What?" came Devon's voice.

Mitchell gently pulled Tommy's hands away from his face. "Don't be so melodramatic. Sammi, for goodness' sake, whatever you have to say, speak up and put your brother out of his misery."

"Tommy, I knew about Daley's condition. But neither of us had read the magazine article, not until one of my bridesmaids showed me. Later on Alec told us about your concerns, my silly but darling brother. Daley and I have spoken privately with Mum and Dad and we wanted to talk to you in person at the after-show party. But you disappeared before we had the chance. Apparently, you—and the rest of Asia—got to see a photo of my husband-to-be holding hands with some supposedly random woman. I had no idea, by the way, when I handed you that garbage magazine. But there is a story behind the photo. Daley, do you want to explain or shall I?"

"No, I'll take over," said Daley. "Let's start at the beginning. Everyone knows that I've had trouble with my eyesight. What most people didn't know— including me—was just how serious it had become."

Daley went on to tell them almost word for word what Alec had divulged, and about the friend called

Ellery, who had helped Daley negotiate the uneven lawn.

"What you need to understand, Tommy, is that I love your sister beyond measure. And I would never keep something this serious from her. I told her as soon as I knew. In case she wanted to rethink our wedding plans."

"And I told him he doesn't get off that easily. I had to remind him that we've been in love since college and that our vows would include the words in sickness and in health. But I am also insisting on two things. Firstly, that we get second opinions from other ophthalmologists. Daley's specialist tells us the Czech Republic has become a world leader in ophthalmology. He's already in contact with some global experts on Daley's condition. We aren't giving up hope of a cure, are we, love?"

"No, bride-to-be," said Daley, smiling. And at that moment, the truth he had always known hit Tommy hard. His sister and Daley were meant to be together.

"And the second thing we wanted to announce is that we're going to waste no time starting a family, to ensure Daley gets to see his firstborn."

Tommy felt as though the whole restaurant had fallen silent. He rarely showed emotion, but seeing Devon burying his head into his napkin and a tearful Oscar leaning across to give Daley a friendly hug, he felt the sting of tears, made worse when Mitchell placed a warm arm around his shoulders.

"How do you feel about being Uncle Tommy?" asked Mitchell, which at least raised a few chuckles. "Now there's a sobering thought."

"Can we please order?" announced Daley, finally breaking the mood. "I had lukewarm scrambled eggs for breakfast on the plane ride over and could frankly eat at least three bowls of ramen."

A huge weight lifted from Tommy's shoulders. Feeling back to his old self, he winked at the young waiter to catch his attention before waving him over to give their order. Everyone appeared to relax into lunch. Once the food had reached the table, they finally asked what he and Mitchell had been doing. Tommy explained and, as expected, Devon and Sammi demanded to know where the bags were, insisting on inspecting the purchases.

"No can do. You'll have to wait until the big day."

"Surely you already have suits, Mitchell," said Oscar.

"Boring work suits," answered Tommy before Mitchell could respond. "And before you ask, I had his permission to help smarten him up for the wedding."

"Tommy believes my sense of style is questionable," said Mitchell.

"Really? I think you look perfectly fine," said Oscar.

"Fine, but unremarkable. And, in my opinion, he could look so much better," said Tommy, refusing to become defensive.

"I think what Oscar is trying to say is that if it ain't been fixed, maybe it's because it ain't broke," said Devon.

"Don't you mean, if it ain't broke —" began Daley, but Oscar placed a hand on his shoulder.

"He knows exactly what he means."

"But the way things are going, Oscar," said Mitchell, "with Tommy's expensive tastes, I'm likely to be broke before the day's out."

"You'll thank me one day," said Tommy to Mitchell before returning his attention to the rest of the group.

"Anyway, we have more to do. Look forward to seeing you all Saturday."

Daley insisted on picking up the tab, and after Tommy gave everyone hugs, they made their way to Mitchell's apartment to drop off his purchases before heading out again. While there, Mitchell told Tommy to sit while pouring them a couple of cold drinks.

"What do you think?" asked Tommy, taking a glass of water from Mitchell. "About Sammi and Daley?"

"Like you said before. They're meant for each other."

"I know, right?"

"But it's not going to be easy. They're going to need your love and support, Tommy."

"That goes without saying."

Mitchell's smile seemed sad as he sat beside Tommy and spoke in a lowered voice.

"Look, I know what happened after the show doesn't change anything between us. I'm not delusional. Anytime we go anywhere, I see how people single you out. The salesclerk and the waiter in that restaurant. Whereas I might as well be invisible. I like you, Tommy, genuinely, but I need you to know that I have no expectations. And I don't want there to be any weirdness between us."

Tommy wasn't sure how he felt about Mitchell's explanation. Was he trying to let Tommy off the hook, to convince him he had no expectations? Their night together had meant something to Tommy, but he had yet to process exactly what and how much.

"There isn't. You do realise the flirting is all for show? Nothing more."

"I do. But if you get your shot with Alec, I would recommend you reel in that particular quirk. I've never had that problem, but some people might come to resent their partners getting that kind of attention."

"If I *were* to get a shot with Alec, I imagine he'll get just as much attention as me."

"Fair point."

"Come on, let's go. We've got a lot more to do."

Magenta's salon happened to be a short walk from Mitchell's place. Tommy noticed Mitchell's eyes widen when Magenta met them at the door. With black spiked hair containing pink and purple streaks, black-painted fingernails and deep purple lipstick, he looked more like a punk rocker than a hairdresser. But Tommy knew that Magenta had an impressive list of loyal clients who used him and talked him up regularly.

Tommy had barely settled Mitchell in the stylist's chair when a call came through. The musical group hired for the wedding had planned to rehearse the number with him on Sunday afternoon. But one musician had been asked to fill in at a last-minute church event that afternoon.

Tommy felt insecure about his abilities and had been the one to insist they practice together before the ceremony. The trio had made a special arrangement around the melody his sister had chosen, and he needed the reassurance that he would not cock anything up.

"Magenta, darling. Can I leave my friend in your capable hands?"

"Of course, darling."

"Where are you going?" asked Mitchell, turning to him in a panic.

"An emergency to do with my sister's wedding. If it wasn't urgent, I wouldn't go. I want more than anything to see this transformation. I'll call you during the week, but I probably won't see you until the day of the wedding. Hope that's okay?"

"No colouring!" said Mitchell sternly.

"No colouring. Tell him, Magenta," said Tommy.

"Don't worry, darling," said Magenta, pulling a white cloth around Mitchell's neck. "I have my instructions. Masculine style, with a full manicure. Now take off your shoes and socks, love."

"What? Why?"

"Because while I style your hair, my assistant, Ophelia, will wash your feet, then give you a pedicure followed by the best foot massage you've ever had."

Tommy turned as the door closed behind him, catching a glimpse of Mitchell's alarmed expression through the shop window. He couldn't help but laugh and blew an exaggerated air kiss to him before continuing on his way.

Chapter Nineteen

On the morning of Sammi and Daley's wedding, Mitchell stood in front of his full-length mirror, putting the finishing touches to his outfit, grateful that Tommy had insisted on an uncomplicated clip-on bow tie. Once it was straightened, he stepped back and winced. The new shoes pinched uncomfortably and would need time to wear in, time he didn't have. He had an agreement with Tommy to showcase every item they had picked out, even though a pair of his work shoes would have provided more comfort.

During the week, colleagues had stared at his new haircut, and some in his department had passed favourable comments. A minor miracle considering the morale. All he saw when he looked in the mirror was an overdressed man in his late thirties desperately trying to regain his youth. The hairdresser had even waxed and shaped his eyebrows, removing the barely noticeable hair between them to provide more definition. Thank goodness Ellie hadn't been invited to the wedding. His sister would most likely have choked with laughter. They would FaceTime tomorrow, and she would undoubtedly provide him with her candid opinion whether or not he asked.

Joel would have approved. Wholeheartedly. Not only at the Mitchell upgrade but also at the selfless act of Mitchell helping Tommy to connect with Alec, no matter how sombre the thought made him feel. Joel had been the one to badger a reluctant Mitchell into various fancy dress costumes for college parties. Another door that had closed with his passing, until Zane had coerced him into that ridiculous pirate costume. The thought made him smile. Hopefully, Zane would be on the call again tomorrow and would not only approve but applaud Tommy's makeover choices.

Funny thing, but the silence of the apartment following Zane's departure had hit Mitchell hard. Only a few times during his nephew's stay had Mitchell yearned to have his space back. Standing there alone now, he missed asking Zane's opinion, missed having him pad barefoot across the room to grab a bottle of water from the kitchen, headphones still in place, or join Mitchell on the sofa to watch a programme, sitting cross-legged while peeling an orange.

Mitchell gave himself another critical once-over just as his phone rang. Gemma from the recruitment agency. He stared at the display, unsure whether to take the call. The meeting with her local boss had been cordial. He'd been honest about the position they would create for Mitchell, which felt more like a sales role. The basic salary would be minimal, supplemented by the number of hiring placements he successfully completed each month. The arrangement made him uncomfortable, but Gemma's boss had come from a similar background to Mitchell. They had left him to think about the offer while they sought a final sign-off from their supervisor. Taking a deep breath, Mitchell answered the call.

"Hi, Mitchell. Are you free to talk?"

"Go ahead. I'm getting dressed for a wedding on the front lawn of the Repulse Bay. But the ceremony doesn't start for another couple of hours."

"Oh, I see. In which case, this is a huge ask, but our CEO is in town from Vancouver and flies out later today. We want to offer you the recruitment position, but he's asked if there's any chance he could meet you in person before he heads to the airport. I've been showing him around Stanley, so we're not far from the Repulse Bay. Could you jump in a taxi and pop over for fifteen minutes?"

Mitchell checked the time. Stanley was about half an hour's taxi ride from home, and the venue was only ten minutes from Stanley. The meet-up would be doable if he could catch a ride immediately.

"Give me thirty to forty minutes. And you'd better let him know I'm going to be overdressed. Where should I meet you?"

Gemma gave directions to a bespoke coffee shop in Stanley Plaza as Mitchell locked his front door and made his way down the stairs of his apartment block. Fortunately, the door to Mrs Lau's apartment stood firmly closed today, and he escaped undisturbed into daylight. Catching a taxi on Saturday morning proved to be a trial. Fortunately, Tommy had recommended a local taxi app, and he plugged in his details. Sure enough, a driver responded a few minutes later, and he waited for his pick-up. Tommy had also put him right on wedding gift protocols, a red envelope containing cash being the custom, and far easier to transport than the often bulky and overpriced presents from wedding lists that had become the norm at Western weddings.

* * * *

Mitchell found Gemma and the CEO at the back of the air-conditioned coffee shop. During the short walk from the taxi drop-off to the café, he had felt perspiration caused by humidity trickling down his spine. He had also garnered amused looks from people, overdressed as he was.

Gemma gave him a hug as though they were old friends, and the CEO gave his hand a firm shake. Mitchell almost laughed when she pushed a large mug of his favourite caffè americano toward him. In discussion, the man appeared more concerned about Mitchell and allaying his concerns. Mitchell took an instant liking to him as he talked about his own journey setting up the business before highlighting the success of their Asia Pacific operations. He also made no bones about the hard work and long hours involved. Time flew by, and eventually, Mitchell had to make an excuse to leave.

"Off you go, then. Enjoy your day. Just know that you come highly recommended, Mitchell," said the CEO. "And you'll have an offer in your inbox Monday morning. Isn't that right, Gemma?"

"Already drafted and ready to send. Just needed your digital sign-off, boss," said Gemma, grinning at Mitchell.

Grateful for a dose of the café's air-conditioning and caffeine, Mitchell had to wait only a few minutes for a taxi. When he arrived at the Repulse Bay, the ceremony appeared to be about to begin. As the taxi driver pulled away, Mitchell hurried to the entrance, where an attendant checked his invitation before ushering him towards the cordoned-off area. Just before the last row of seating, a good-looking older lady in a beautiful sleeveless cheongsam of red silk and embroidered florals stepped forward to greet him.

"Good afternoon," she said, taking in his attire with her approval plain. "I'm the grandmother of the bride. And who might you be, young man?"

"Lovely to meet you," he said, holding a hand in greeting. "I'm your grandson's date."

"Tommy?" said the woman, her surprise plain.

"Sorry, yes. Tommy."

"Heavens. He said he would bring somebody to make me proud today, but he really has outdone himself. Do you have a name?"

Mitchell laughed and introduced himself properly. The woman appeared to process his introduction before meeting his gaze and asking if he lived in a very particular block of apartments on the island.

"How would you know that?'" he asked, more curious than offended.

"Well," she said, grinning mysteriously. "This is a strange coincidence. I'm your landlady, Mr Baxter. I know we've never met, but I believe you know my friend, Mrs Lau —"

"You're Mrs Zhang? Who sends me Chinese proverbs on cards?"

Mrs Zhang put a hand to her lips and giggled like a young girl.

"I do that for all my tenants. Do you like them?"

"Mrs Lau translates them for me. My fridge door is plastered with untold amounts of wisdom you've sent to me from across the years."

"And which is your favourite?"

"Too many to pick. But there was one you sent that didn't mean much at the time. Right now, though, with my current situation, the words make perfect sense. It reads something like timber already being a boat and rice already being cooked. In English, I suppose, we would use the expression, what's done is done. There's no going back."

Mrs Zhang nodded and spoke a few words in Cantonese. "And what about your current situation makes that one so meaningful, Mitchell? Can I call you Mitchell?"

"Of course," he said before staring into the crowd. "Decisions have been made in my professional career that I have no control over. My job is on the line, which will affect my income, which in turn may affect my ability to stay in Hong Kong. I fear I might have to give notice on the apartment soon—"

"No," said Mrs Zhang, placing the fingers of her right hand over Mitchell's heart.

"I'm sorry?"

"That will not happen. You've been an exemplary tenant over the years, so if you have short-term financial concerns, you let me know. Besides, your story is not yet told. I can see this in you, even though we have only just met. You have a good heart and more to give. Just be patient and positive."

"We'll see," he said, amused and touched by the sentiment. "But thank you for those kind words."

"Now go and take a seat. The ceremony is about to begin."

A member of the serving staff offered flutes of champagne and soft drinks. Bearing in mind the heat and humidity of what was likely to be a very long day, Mitchell thanked the young girl and plucked a chilled sparking water from the tray before moving to an empty seat on the back row.

A sea of bare heads and a hodgepodge of colourful hats faced an archway of white flowers on a low podium with the South China Sea as a backdrop.

Matching floral displays on pedestals bordered each of the rows across the lush front lawn. Some guests read from the wedding programmes while most used them to fan themselves. Agreeing to forge ahead with plans had been a serious gamble considering the threat of a super-typhoon reported in the region and heading their way, but one that had paid off because Mitchell saw barely a cloud in the sky. Daley and his groomsmen — minus Alec, the best man — already stood on one side of the stage looking out to the audience while a trio of identical-looking women opposite played Vivaldi, slowing to a stop at the nod from the celebrant.

As Michell scanned the crowd, a red-haired man sitting on an aisle seat a few rows in front caught his eye and waved. Mitchell didn't recognise him, assuming the gesture was probably in response to Mitchell's tardiness, but he returned a smile. After a furtive glance down the aisle, the man stood and came over to Mitchell, who moved a seat along to give the stranger space to sit.

"Cutting it a bit fine, Mitchell?" The man had an Australian accent. He dressed like most of the men, in a black dress suit. Only his flaming red hair stood out from the crowd.

"I am a bit," said Mitchell. "Sorry, do I know you?"

"I'm Gerry, or Gez," said the man, shaking Mitchell's hand. "Mate of Alec, the best man. He told me to look out for you. Said you'd be here on your own. Nice togs, by the way."

The name rang a bell. Was this the guy Alec and Tommy had wanted to set him up with? Did that mean Alec and Tommy had already gotten together? He should have phoned Tommy to check yesterday instead of working into the night.

"Thank you," Mitchell replied. "You too. So you probably already know I'm a friend of the bride's brother."

"Nice."

Mitchell scanned the crowd but couldn't spot Tommy. Not that he expected to. Even though they would sit together for the wedding meal, Tommy had other duties to perform such as attending the pre-wedding games and participating in the ceremony. On their shopping day together, Tommy had tried to explain Chinese wedding etiquette to Mitchell and how weddings involved something referred to as door games, a set of often silly pre-ceremony challenges for the groom, devised by the bridesmaids, to demonstrate his devotion and commitment to his soon-to-be bride.

Even after the ceremony, Tommy had been enlisted to help with guests. Not-so-discreet Devon had let on to Mitchell and Oscar that Tommy would be playing the cello to punctuate the bride's entrance, although Devon had no idea what song he had chosen.

"Ladies and gentlemen," called the celebrant, finally silencing the crowd, "welcome to the wedding of Daley Tan and Sammi Chow. Please make yourselves comfortable and enjoy this glorious day. Before the ceremony begins, we have a small surprise for you. The bride's brother has agreed to join the musicians in accompanying the bride's procession with a song chosen especially by and for the couple. Please put your hands together for Tommy Chow, accompanied by the Melody Triplets."

Mitchell hadn't noticed Tommy until he stepped onto the small stage. Alec moved before him and placed a wooden chair in front of the three standing musicians. Tommy, holding his cello and bow in one hand, lowered himself into the chair. In a gesture that would have been innocent involving anyone else, Alec squeezed Tommy's shoulder and whispered something to him, and was rewarded by a smile and Tommy's free hand patting the top of Alec's. Mitchell squeezed his eyes shut for a moment and took a deep steadying breath.

He opened them again when music began playing. Alec had moved across the stage to stand by Daley's side. Tommy had the large cello between his legs and sat with his head lowered and hands frozen in place on the fretboard, waiting as the three female violinists played an ethereal introduction, unknown and yet at the same time vaguely familiar. Tommy wore a light purple suit with a double-breasted embroidered waistcoat and matching bow tie in deep purple. A white rose buttonhole added a further touch of elegance. He looked incredible, and—for today, at least—Mitchell felt proud to call Tommy his date. Visually, the ensemble blended beautifully together, the three female violinists wearing matching milky-peach flowing gowns.

"That him? Your friend?" asked the man, Gerry, next to him.

"Yes. That's Tommy," said Mitchell, unable to stop smiling.

"Alec was right. He's a stunner."

Gerry's comment soured his mood only momentarily, because when Tommy began playing, swaying as he infused the main melody, raising an appreciative murmur through the crowd, Mitchell's chest filled with pride. "*A Thousand Years*" by Christina Perri filled the air with the mournful cello picking out the vocal line. Maybe the song had been employed at countless weddings around the globe, but the outdoor setting with a gentle breeze blowing across the lawn and the sea glistening in the distance provided the perfect union. The arrangement sounded faultless, with violins plucked or playing countermelodies dancing around the central theme.

Preceded by the bridesmaids, Sammi's father accompanied her down the centre aisle before helping her onto the stage then retreating to his seat in the front row.

The ceremony played out during the next forty-five minutes, with vows spoken, rings exchanged and finally, the kiss that had everyone applauding. In the end, the newlyweds descended the steps and strolled unhurriedly down the aisle, frequently chatting with congregation members and showered by rose petals on their way to the waiting white Rolls-Royce. Before they had reached the final row, Gerry nudged Mitchell.

"Wanna grab a cold one at the Hyatt?" he asked, standing and stretching. "Alec tells me they're serving drinks in the lobby bar. And those taxis will soon be snagged if we don't shake a leg."

Mitchell stared above the sea of heads coming their way but couldn't see Tommy. Or anyone else, for that matter. Maybe they had already left. Mitchell sighed in resignation. Getting Mitchell together with Gerry had been the plan, after all.

"Why not? A quick drink can't do any harm. Lead the way."

Chapter Twenty

The moment the ceremony ended, as the bride and groom made their way down the aisle, Tommy thanked the violinists before jumping down from the stage. Overheated from wearing his suit in the midday sun and eager to grab a cold drink and find Mitchell, Tommy locked his cello and bow into their case. Once he had stashed the instrument securely, he headed for the small white tent where his friends sheltered. Huddled around a tall table, he found Devon, Oscar and William—but no Mitchell. With Harold still recovering in hospital because of complications with his surgery, Mitchell had asked if William could be invited.

"You're a dark horse, Tommy Chow," said Oscar, patting his shoulder and shoving a glass of bubbly into his hand. "You play beautifully. Heaven only knows how my boyfriend managed to keep that amazing talent of yours a secret."

"No need to cover for me, darling," said Devon, pecking Oscar on the cheek. "Tommy knows how hopeless I am at keeping secrets. I told him you'd be playing, Tommy, but made him swear to tell nobody. Honestly, I didn't even know if you would go through with the whole playing-to-an-audience thing."

"Sammi would have killed me if I'd backed out. Where's Mitchell?"

Not that Tommy didn't appreciate his friend's praise, but he wanted Mitchell's opinion.

"Nobody's seen him," said Devon, trying to hide his concern. "But don't worry. I'm sure he's around here somewhere."

"She looks beautiful, by the way," said Oscar, maybe to distract Tommy. "Your sister."

"Like a modern day Princess Grace of Morocco," said Devon, adding a sigh. "And their vows almost had me in tears again. Come on, Oz. Let's go over and say hello before they're chauffeured off to the reception."

Oscar and Devon sauntered across the lawn, arms around each other. Once again, Tommy scanned the grounds to see if he could spot Mitchell.

"What the hell did you do to him?" asked Aaron, appearing through the crowd. Sammi had told him that Aaron had managed to snag an invitation courtesy of his cousin, one of the bridesmaids.

"Devon?" asked Tommy, following Aaron's line of sight to an row of seats at the back of the lawn.

"Baxter. He certainly washes up well," said Aaron, nodding his approval. "You managed to turn an ugly fuckling into a swan."

"I did nothing. Mitchell Baxter," said Tommy, irked at Aaron's tone, "has a unique brand of attraction."

"If you say so. He's certainly looking delicious today."

"Where is he?" asked Tommy.

"Alec's friend seemed to think so," said William. "Practically drooling on him."

"The haircut, the designer clothes, the makeover," said Aaron, rubbing his chin. "I don't think I've ever seen him looking more..."

"Uncomfortable?" finished William, staring off into the crowd. Tommy glared at him but saw only pity in his eyes. "Thank goodness Harold wasn't here. He'd have been mortified."

Had Mitchell looked uncomfortable? If only Tommy hadn't been in such a rush that morning, he could at least have checked in with him. But Mitchell had willingly volunteered to dress in the clothes they'd picked out together. He'd sacrificed his usual plain style to improve his appearance. Or had he only agreed because he'd wanted to make Tommy happy?

"Where the hell is he?" asked Tommy.

"Poor thing. About to lose his job, too," said William, either oblivious to or ignoring the remark.

"William. Where's Mitchell?"

"I think him and Gerry went to the Hyatt," came Alec's voice behind him. "One of the bridesmaids saw them getting into the back of a taxi together."

Tommy's heart sank. When he turned, Alec studied him with sympathy. Tommy had texted Mitchell a couple of times during the week, but they had not spoken because of Mitchell's stupid work issues and Tommy being roped in after school to carry out last-minute wedding chores and entertain relatives.

"Sorry, Tommy, mate. My fault. I told Gerry to keep an eye out for him. But they can't be more than fifteen minutes ahead, if you want to go now."

"There are things I need to say. But I told Sammi I'd stay behind and help any stragglers find their way—"

"Don't be a dick," said Alec. "I can do that. And I'm sure I can rope in others give me a hand. My job was to help Daley and Sammi welcome guests at the other end. I'll text Daley and tell them we swapped roles. Trust me, he'll understand."

"If it helps, I have an Uber waiting," said William, his expression as blank as ever. "I can give you a lift."

"Go," said Alec.

Tommy downed his champagne and thumped the glass onto the tabletop. "If you'll excuse me, gentlemen. I have a wedding date to rescue."

Tommy didn't quite hear the Aaron's comment, but he was sure he heard a murmur of encouragement from Alec. Either way, he didn't care. At least for today, Mitchell had promised to be his date.

Once they climbed into the back of the Tesla, Tommy realised he had never been alone with William. Even though William appeared happy to let the journey go by in silence, Tommy felt obliged to make conversation.

"It's kind of you to share your ride."

"Yes," said William, staring out of the passenger window. Tommy thought William might ask more, but another few minutes went by.

"How's Harold doing?" he asked.

"I'm going to see him at four. We're hoping he'll be discharged early next week. But this is only the first round of operations."

"Must be difficult? For you?"

"I'll survive. I'm more concerned about Hal."

"Please give him my best when you see him."

William said nothing for a few seconds.

"Do you remember that dreadful cocktail party in Repulse Bay? Back in April?"

Tommy snorted. "How could I forget?"

"That night, after you'd both left, Harold told me that you and Mitchell would make the perfect couple. I told him he was talking out of his arse."

"I would have told him the same. But things change."

"That much is obvious."

Even though Tommy kept his gaze focused on the road ahead, he felt William turn to scrutinise him. William eventually spoke as the car turned into the lane leading up to the hotel entrance.

"Go and find Mitchell while I tip for the driver. But promise me you'll be kind. Of all of us, he alone has loved and lost. Mitchell may have a huge heart, but it's also delicate."

"His sister told me the same thing."

"You know his sister?" asked William.

"Not personally, but Zane must have said something because she called me last week. Said almost exactly what you just said, word for word."

"And what did you say?"

"I promised her, too."

Signs for the wedding punctuated the hotel lobby. Tommy followed them and the accompanying gold and red balloons to the Grand Ballroom, where Sammi and Daley stood to greet guests. While chatting to one of their uncles, Sammi noticed Tommy and smiled before pointing back the way Tommy had come. From the words she mimed, he realised she wanted him to head back to the hotel's champagne bar.

Other guests had congregated there, and Tommy found Mitchell in a quiet corner chatting together with a ginger-headed man wearing a traditional black tux. Even from the back, Mitchell looked stunning, the haircut and the clothes suiting him perfectly. As Tommy approached, he clenched his teeth clenched and curled one of his fists. The flame-haired ape with the lecherous smile had just brushed a speck of something from one of Mitchell's shoulders. Who the hell did he think he was?

"Mind if I talk to my wedding date?" asked Tommy, not bothering to introduce himself nor hiding the hard edge to his tone. Mitchell twisted around in surprise, a glass flute clutched to his chest.

"Date?" asked the carrot-top idiot, his gaze fixed on Mitchell. "Thought you said he was just a friend?"

"He is," said Mitchell, eyeing Tommy curiously. "But we had an agreement to be each other's dates to the wedding, rather than attend alone."

"And we need to talk," said Tommy.

"Go ahead then, mate," said the idiot with a smirk, not budging. "Don't mind me."

"*Privately*," said Tommy.

"Whoa," said the man, holding his hands up and backing up a step. "No worries. Need to find the dunny, anyway. Let's catch up later, Mitch."

The idiot had the audacity to wink at Mitchell as though sharing a private joke before sauntering across the room. Tommy glowered after him.

"*Sei puk gai*," he muttered, turning to see Mitchell grinning at him. "What are you smirking at?"

"Nothing," said Mitchell, gently shaking his head before sipping from his bubbly. "Nothing at all. You did amazingly well today, Tommy. I was running late and arrived just as the ceremony began. But I heard you play. You were sensational up there."

Tommy's foul mood melted instantly. Mitchell owned his new outfit, but what Tommy enjoyed most was hearing Mitchell's voice and especially his praise. Without asking, he took the glass from Mitchell's hand and drained the remains of the champagne.

"This is me doing you a favour," he said, handing the empty glass to a passing waiter. "Today's going to be a long one and I need you sober. I came to find you for a few reasons. Firstly, I wanted to apologise. I realise I strong-armed you into doing this makeover —"

"Hold on a second. I love the suit, especially with the matching bow tie and pocket hanky. And, believe it or not, the new haircut. None of which I would have chosen, but sometimes we all need to try something new. The shoes are as unforgiving as a trip to the dentist, but the pain is finally beginning to subside, even though I'll probably have blisters in the morning. The only thing I'm truly uncomfortable with is the amount of attention I seem to be drawing."

"You deserve to be seen, Mitchell," said Tommy softly, and he meant every word. "But there's something missing. The final finishing touch, if you will allow me. Sorry I didn't get the chance to do this earlier."

Tommy reached into his pocket and pulled out a small box.

"Like me, close male family members are wearing white rose buttonholes. But when I saw this, for some reason, the cute little accessory felt entirely right for you."

Tommy lifted a lapel pin from inside and showed Mitchell. The golden head of a wolf had caught his eye during their shopping trip, and he'd immediately thought of Mitchell, the measured stare he gave people, quietly sizing them up, the way he had almost passed unnoticed through Tommy's life. Mitchell's reaction was not what Tommy had expected. At first, he appeared startled, his brows creasing together and eyes beginning to glisten with tears.

"Or not," said Tommy, pulling the pin away. "Not if you don't like—"

"No," said Mitchell, grabbing Tommy's hand. "It's perfect. Just—unexpected. I love it, Tommy. I really do. Can you do me the honours?"

While Tommy fumbled to pin the broach in place, he could feel Mitchell's steady gaze on him. Once Tommy had finished and their eyes met, Mitchell surprised him with a peck on the lips.

"What was that for?"

"Partly for keeping up appearances. But, in all honesty, for proving me wrong about you. For how much I value our friendship and your company and, most of all, for you just being you, Tommy Chow."

Tommy stared at Mitchell as something inside him melted. Mitchell might have been wrong about him, but Tommy had also misjudged Mitchell. Maybe Aaron and others might finally have noticed him today, but Tommy had been lucky enough to spend time with him and get to know the real Mitchell.

"Then at least let's do this properly," said Tommy, putting his arms around Mitchell's neck and pulling him in for a kiss. Mitchell's lips felt warmly familiar, tasting of sweet champagne while his body smelled of the ever-present scent he loved to wear. Mitchell broke the kiss first.

"What about Alec?" asked Mitchell.

"What *about* Alec?"

"I thought we were hatching a plan to get you into his pants."

"Priorities change. I'm not sure Alec and I are compatible. He's never seen a single *Toy Story* movie. Says he always thought they were for kids. Besides, someone else has caught my attention of late. Even if they do prefer Adele over Beyoncé. Something we can work on. I remember telling you that sometimes people are meant to be together, however strange their partnership might appear to others. Take Oscar and Devon, and Harold and William, for example. What I'm trying to say is that I want you by my side for the rest of the day, and even longer, if you'll have me. But today I want you with me talking to guests as they arrive, sitting together through the dinner and speeches, and with me on the dance floor. And in my bed, later tonight. They've booked me a room here, by the way."

"I didn't bring a change of clothes," said Mitchell, looking adorably bewildered.

"Really? That's all you picked out from my heartfelt soliloquy?"

"No." Mitchell chuckled. "I mean, yes, of course I want to be by your side and in your bed. Why would I want to be anywhere else? And I would be honoured to meet the rest of your family. And if you're not tired tonight, maybe we could watch a movie—"

"The hell we will. And, by the way, if *Dexter's Laboratory* comes within ten feet of you again—"

"Who?"

"The ginger prick I just caught laying his hands on you. If he comes by again, I swear by my ancestors, I will set my grandmother on him."

Mitchell's humoured expression turned serious.

"Don't laugh, but I met her today. Your grandmother. You never told me she's also my landlady."

"She's what?"

"My landlady. The person who owns the flat I rent."

"Yes, I know what a landlady is," said Tommy, and he sighed as the penny dropped. "That explains it. I knew I'd been to your apartment block before. Thought maybe for a random hook-up. But she has six apartments she rents out. As a teenager, to earn extra pocket money, I used to help her clean and redecorate them whenever a tenant moved out."

"Small world."

"Welcome to Hong Kong," said Tommy, before linking his arm with Michell's. "Come on, we have a job to do. Let's go greet the guests."

Chapter Twenty-One

Although he would openly admit to being no saint, Tommy had confided in Mitchell that he had never knowingly trespassed. But right now, four weeks after the wedding, Mitchell had them skulking beneath lamplights on the Victoria Peak trail like a couple of secret agents, waiting until nobody was in sight. Mitchell had begun to enjoy occasionally shocking Tommy.

"We don't have to do this. You could just tell me," said Tommy.

"No, this is a rite of passage. You're the only person I've ever brought here," said Mitchell before hopping over the barrier. "Quick. Now. Follow me."

Mitchell heard the rustle of leaves behind him as Tommy followed his lead. When the street lighting from the main path began to fade, Mitchell used the light of his phone to find his way.

Lights twinkled below, stars and moonlight reflecting off the harbour waters. After repeatedly searching the carvings on the old rock's surface, he wondered if his had been erased. Until he stumbled across the faded lettering. Reaching out a hand, he showed Tommy the inscription, explaining the Sunday in his past when he had been at his lowest.

"Before I go on, I have something for you. For us," said Mitchell, pulling Tommy down so they both sat with their backs to the rock. Once they had settled, he reached into his backpack and pulled out two cans with a distinctive blue and silver design.

"One for you," said Mitchell, handing over a chilled can.

"Moscow Mule? Where the hell did you find it?"

"Let's just say your sister is very resourceful."

In unison, they snapped back the ring pulls and clicked their cans together before sipping. Mitchell, never a fan of fruity cocktails, found the taste too sweet for his liking but said nothing, instead enjoying the camaraderie.

"Back to your story," came Tommy's voice. "You obviously stayed."

"I did. Once I'd finished mutilating the rock face, I remember watching the sun finally rise. I'd been sitting the way we are now with my back against the rock when a native bird landed in a bush nearby and started twittering loudly. A nice sound actually, the birdsong resembled laughter. Then another joined the first, adding to the dawn chorus. The two performed some kind of ritual, touching either side of the other's beak like crossing swords. When they finally flew off, I turned to face the sun of a new day glistening off the skyscrapers and harbour."

Mitchell pointed down to the dark waters of Victoria Harbour.

"And that's when it happened. I'm a rational person by nature. I knew I was alone, but I sensed someone else sitting near me. Imagine the way you and I are sitting together right now, but neither of us touching, talking or looking at one another. I can't hear your breathing above the sound of the wind, or feel the heat coming off your body, but I know you're there. That's exactly how I felt. You've been around me enough by now to know that I am not given to flights of fancy. But in that lowest of times, I knew beyond any doubt that Joel sat beside me. I swear I could even smell faint traces of the distinctive lotion he used for his dry skin. And I began to cry, not with sadness, but happiness. Because without needing to turn my head I knew that Joel had always been with me, keeping me company and guiding me. It's hard to explain but I'd felt the same comforting presence with Joel so often when he was alive, when he and I used to watch a film together or simply sit either end of a sofa with our legs up on the coffee table, reading our books. And in that moment I knew what he was trying to tell me."

Mitchell turned to see Tommy's eyes glistening in the moonlight.

"That I was going to be okay. I didn't need to finish up my contract and go home, because I was already home."

Mitchell reached a hand out and took Tommy's fingers in his own.

"That Monday, everything changed," said Mitchell. "Kate started working for us. Colleagues began inviting me to lunch and social events and introducing me to other native English speakers and friendly locals. Eventually, everything would fall into place. I realised I just needed to be patient."

"Well, you're going to have to be patient with me, Mitch," said Tommy. "I'm not used to being with anyone for more than—"

"Two months. Yes, you told me. Nothing's guaranteed, Tommy. Daley might lose his sight in the next couple of years. Harold may lose his chance to walk again or even his life. But they'll both fight because they have partners they care about. I believe that if someone's worth the effort, exercising patience is the easiest thing in the world. We can tell people we're friends if that's easier, as long as I have you in my life."

"Oh no you don't. We're boyfriends. My grandmother already knows and approves."

Mitchell laughed and squeezed Tommy's fingers before letting go and reaching into his pocket with his free hand to bring out a scarlet card.

"Talking of which, Mrs Lau gave me this postcard your grandmother sent. When I visited Harold in hospital, he taught me how to say this in Cantonese. I've tried to learn parrot fashion, but my accent is probably terrible."

Mitchell rattled off the eight syllables the way he had been taught.

"Hold hands with you, grow old with you," said Tommy, squeezing Mitchell's hand. "Not bad. Hong Kong's your home, then?"

"As long as she will have me and as long as I have you."

"Then we need to make a few changes," said Tommy, getting up from the ground and dusting off his backside before pulling something from his pocket. Mitchell wondered what Tommy was doing, scratching something on the rock surface until Tommy leant back to admire his handiwork.

"What did you do?"

"I've crossed out JASMIN and scratched in TAMSIN."

"Tamsin? Who or what is Tamsin?"

"Your engraving now reads — Tommy And Mitchell Staying in Hong Kong. I Promise."

Tommy settled back down next to Mitchell and bumped his shoulder playfully. After moments of staring out into the starlit sky, Tommy linked their arms together and rested his head on Mitchell's shoulder, intimacy he had never shown before.

"Can you believe Devon and Oscar have been living together for two months?" asked Tommy. They had been to lunch with the pair only a week ago.

"I know," said Mitchell. "Oscar's really happy. He says Devon brings out the best in him. And Devon told me after only a week he felt totally at home in Oscar's place, like — "

"A fish to the slaughter?" added Tommy.

Mitchell's laughter became a sigh, staunched only when Tommy spoke.

"Maybe we should consider doing the same."

Mitchell had no words and had temporarily lost the ability to breathe.

"Move in together, I mean," said Tommy, his silhouette turning to Mitchell. "What do you think?"

"I mean, I would love that," said Mitchell quietly, his heart filling. "But only if you're ready. I'd hate you to feel trapped — "

"Look, even before I turned thirty, I had this nagging feeling I'd been missing out. But I couldn't figure out what I didn't already have. Enter Mitchell Baxter.

Didn't take long for me to realise that my fiercely guarded independence is also a source of loneliness. But ever since we started hanging out, something's changed. I find myself looking forward to seeing and talking to you, And when I'm alone, I laugh about times we've spent together or things we've discussed. It's been strange but nice actually getting to know someone before jumping their bones."

"And about the bone-jumping? Am I enough? And how do you feel about waking up next to the same face every morning?"

"Like I said, my motivations have changed. I find these things hard to articulate, but you're my missing piece, Mitch. I'm more worried that I won't be enough for you—"

"You are already more than I could ever have hoped for. And to answer your earlier question, I've heard that two can live much better and cheaper than one person living alone."

Mitchell smiled into the night sky. The past four weeks had been his happiest in Hong Kong, having Tommy in his life. They were still cautious around each other, and even though Mitchell had considered them living together, he would never have dared to bring up the idea. Having Tommy thinking along the same lines made his happiness complete.

"I love Hong Kong," said Tommy. "I know it's my place of birth but I love living here. Back when I was younger and foreigners asked what country I came from, I would always say Hong Kong, and none of my family ever corrected me. I just hope we're not relegated to a backwater, an ageing movie star or a has-been that has had her time in the limelight and is now rarely mentioned in the tabloids."

"Norma Desmond," said Mitchell.

"I don't know who that is."

"Precisely."

Mitchell felt Tommy shiver next to him and pulled him closer.

"If this is your way of cheering me up, Mitch, I need to tell you it's not working."

"Things can change in a heartbeat," said Mitchell. "Neither of us can predict the future, baby. Maybe we'll still be here twenty years from now, maybe we won't. But if that means moving to some other place on the planet, then so be it. Right now, the only place I want to be is by your side."

"Me too," said Tommy, who appeared to stifle a yawn beside him.

"Okay, I think we should go. Get you home and into bed—"

"Wait. Look. Shooting stars. Quick, make a wish," said Tommy, hiking in a breath and using his hand to direct Mitchell's gaze to the brief light show in the sky. "Do you think one day people might be living up there on the moon or among the stars? Nothing seems beyond the realms of possibility these days. How would you feel about us being extraterrestrial expats living together on another planet?"

"Tommy," said Mitchell, laughing.

"Yes, Mitch?"

Mitchell smiled as he shook his head, pulled Tommy's hand down into his own and squeezed before kissing each of the knuckles.

"Don't point at the moon."

Want to see more from this author?
Here's a taster for you to enjoy!

Companion Required
Brian Lancaster

Excerpt

Kennedy
London, England, August 2016

Two triple-shot espressos down and Kennedy Grey massaged his fingers into his temples. Dull throbbing had begun to resemble a migraine. Not because of the coffee—his lifeblood most days—but because the previous candidate had tried his patience to the limit. *'Is the food safe to eat? Isn't Singapore in China? Aren't gays banned in China? And will there be any fringe benefits?'* Questions about food safety he could accept, especially if a candidate had allergies. He could even appreciate them not being familiar with the geography of the travel destination. For that very reason, he had brought along a one-page map of Asia highlighting Singapore. But asking if there would be any fringe benefits had tipped him over the edge. The advert had been straightforward enough on the subject of remuneration.

Not for the first time that afternoon, Kennedy considered throwing in the towel and abandoning the whole precious idea. Maybe this was the year he made a change. After all, the signs of madness were everywhere, what with a game show host being chosen as the official Republican candidate to run for the US presidency and the people of Britain filing for divorce from Europe.

As a penniless young man straight out of university, he would have trampled heads for a heaven-sent dream of a job like this. On the laptop, he scrolled down to the UK Gay Society billboard and reread the contents of the advert.

Gay Holiday Companion Required

Based in or around London. Must have full ten-year passport with at least seven months remaining and be freely available to travel overseas for the whole month of September 2016. Candidate should ideally be between 21 and 25, non-smoking, social drinker, drug free, and must be able to pull off the role of dutiful boyfriend in front of male sponsor's close-knit circle of friends. Acting experience a distinct advantage. Any ethnicity considered.

Successful candidate will receive an all-expenses-paid holiday to Southeast Asia, starting with round-trip flights from London Heathrow to Singapore's Changi Airport, a three-night stay in Singapore, followed by a 14-night gay cruise to Hong Kong. After a two-night stay in Hong Kong, the holiday will culminate in a flight to Bali, Indonesia and eight nights staying at the sponsor's private luxury villa.

Candidate will receive a guaranteed five thousand pounds in cash for services rendered, and a discretionary bonus, should the candidate's performance exceed expectations.

If you are interested, please respond to gayvaccom@mooddle.com with a recent photo (headshots only, thank you) and CV, to arrange a mutually agreeable time for an interview.

So what if the advert bordered on politically incorrect? Marketing staff at UKGS had assured him that he had breached no advertising codes or legal regulations. Besides, the 'exceed expectations' line had only been tacked on this year, a suggestion from his best friend, Steph — a safe enough addendum, since for the past three years no one ever had.

Moreover, the advertised list of requirements told only half a story. He peered up and scanned the coffee shop. Even a couple of the young men sitting at various tables could have made the grade. In his head, Kennedy had an unspoken list of other requirements, undocumentable, such as the companion being a toned, blond twink, pretty as a royal wedding, but with a relatively low IQ. They should be no more than five feet six, and definitely shorter than his five-ten. Most importantly, they needed to be totally and utterly compliant to Kennedy's whims and wishes. And finally, once they had been paid off and returned to dear old mother England, he never wanted to see or hear from them again.

Since his split with Patrick, his partner of nine years, he'd made a point of continuing to join his friends' annual sojourn to different parts of the globe — his one break each year from the office and the boardroom — but now with a beautiful young acquaintance. Yes, perhaps bringing along a twink companion smacked of vanity, or desperation even, especially for someone in his early forties whose dark hair had begun to display grey streaks at the temples. But the simple truth was that while Kennedy found meeting and conversing with people for business purposes effortless, he found socialising awkward, especially on his own, and had always relied on Patrick to be the catalyst when meeting friends, old and new. Hence, for the past four years, he had paid for a companion to join him.

Palm Springs gay festivals, Hawaiian island hopping, gay tour of Barcelona and Sitges, cruising around the Greek islands with a week in Mykonos.

Pure culture? Maybe not. But a welcome respite from a punishing work life.

Ollie, his first post-Patrick choice, had turned out to be perfect. Previously an intern at Kennedy's corporate security company, the blond Adonis had flirted shamelessly with Kennedy and all other male staff, whether straight or gay. And even though Kennedy had been flattered and tempted, he had never succumbed. After the placement had ended, however, he'd made a point of keeping in touch. Once Patrick had decided to walk, Ollie had been his natural choice as lab rat companion. Perfect, as things had turned out, because Ollie had recently lost his job, so Kennedy had sweetened the deal by offering a sum of money to accompany him. Which was how the arrangement had first begun.

That first year the holiday had gone so well, Kennedy had not only stayed in touch but had invited Ollie along for a second helping. A huge mistake, as things transpired, because Ollie had incorrectly translated the gesture to mean that not only were they equals, but that they were going steady. And Kennedy no longer did 'steady' with anyone.

If his friends suspected anything, they said nothing. Only Steph knew the truth. And he made a point of telling any candidate the arrangement would be strictly nonsexual, unless they wanted more — which was how the idea of the playing card had come into being. But more than anything, he wanted a companion, not an escort. If the rationalisation might have meant anything to any of them, he would have cited Forster's novel *A Room With A View* and the chaperone arrangement between the two main female characters. But after he'd mentioned the reference to Ollie, and had then been lectured about that *'old James Bond movie they keep showing on Netflix'*, he'd stopped bothering to explain altogether.

For the first time since Patrick had walked out, he had been in two minds whether to ditch the charade, to simply bite the bullet and turn up alone. Only five friends had signed up for this year's sojourn—after last year's debacle—and one of those was Leonard Day. Kennedy not only had feelings for him but respected his business acumen. Maybe this year he would finally make his feelings known. If only Leonard didn't come with baggage of his own.

But Kennedy accompanying a plaything had become something of a tradition, a joke among his friends, and he wouldn't want to let them down.

"S'cuse me. You Kennedy Grey?"

Kennedy peered up from his thoughts to find an extremely blond, extremely buff young man standing over him. Steroid buff, Steph would have labelled him.

"I am, yes. And who might you be?"

"Who might I what?"

"Who… What is your name?"

"Francis."

Kennedy glanced down at his notes. Francis Slade, twenty-five years old, three o'clock appointment. Ten minutes ahead of schedule. One point in his favour. Kennedy swore by punctuality.

"Ah yes, Francis. Please sit down. So do you prefer Francis, Frank or Frankie?"

"Francis."

"Great. You've read the advert?"

"Yep."

"Good. So let me go into a bit more detail, give you a few minutes to relax. Then I'll ask you a few questions and finally let you ask any questions you may have. I've got other candidates to see, but I'll let you know whether you've been successful or not by Friday. How does that sound?"

"S'all okay."

Taking the response as his cue, Kennedy went into further detail about the holiday, explaining that in Singapore they would be staying in Kennedy's parents' house. However, the person would be introduced as a friend and would have their own bedroom. Whenever he delved into specifics — especially the rawer aspects — he always studied the candidate's face carefully to see if any of the information caused a reaction. Francis' flat face appeared incapable of showing any kind of emotion.

Whenever Kennedy got onto the subject of the cruise and his friends, he found himself becoming defensive. Yes, they could be a bitchy bunch, and a couple of companions had found them bordering on rude, but they were his long-time friends.

Bali, at the end of the holiday, was not only the cherry on the cake, but the icing, marzipan and ornate decoration. If the companion managed to survive until then, they would be able to enjoy the delights of that magical Indonesian island. By then Kennedy would usually be ready to get back to work, so would spend most of the last week either on his laptop, mobile phone, or writing up proposals.

"So far, so good?"

"Yep," said Francis, yawning and stretching his hands above his head. When his tee pulled tight,

Kennedy spotted the outline of nipple rings beneath the material. Tick. Another point in the boy's favour.

"How tall are you?"

"Five-seven."

"Nice," said Kennedy, reaching next to his laptop for the supplementary document. "So here's a list of other requirements. You'll need to take a medical examination before you travel."

"Why?"

"A precaution. To make sure you're in good shape, physically."

"I'm negative, if that's what you're asking."

"That's not…" Kennedy huffed out a sigh. "Look, the year before last, my travel companion came down with acute appendicitis three days into the trip. And due to severe rupturing—which was touch and go for a while—he had to spend six days in a private hospital in Florida after which, quite naturally, he wanted to fly straight home to be with his family. If he had taken a medical examination before the trip, it's likely the appendicitis would have been diagnosed early, avoiding his suffering and my equally ruptured bank account."

"Ain't got an appendix. Got it removed when I was eleven."

"That's not the point—" Kennedy ran a hand through his hair. "I need to make sure the person accompanying me is fit and healthy in all respects. And that condition is non-negotiable. So if it's a problem for you, then you need to let me know right away."

Francis stared down at the paper for so long that for a moment Kennedy thought he'd changed his mind.

"You'll pay?"

"Sorry?"

"For the medical?"

"Of course."

"'S'okay, then."

"Great. Any other questions for me?"

"How old are you?"

"Forty-two."

Francis grinned then. At least, that was what it appeared to be to Kennedy. Either that or the lad had wind.

"You like 'em young, then?"

Kennedy had to stop himself from answering that more than anything, he liked them compliant. And most younger guys tended to be less free-willed, more willing to please, mainly because they needed the money.

"Is that a problem?"

"Nope. I'm into Daddies."

Oh, heck, thought Kennedy, *Steph is going to have a field day if Francis becomes this year's chosen one.*

"So I've got your number. I'll be in touch Friday."

When Francis stood, whether purposely or not, he yawned again and stretched his arms above his head so that the bottom of his tee rode up slightly to reveal a ripped stomach and a dark-blond trail of curly hair running down and disappearing beneath the waistband.

Kennedy almost handed him the job right there and then.

About the Author

Brian Lancaster is an author of gay romantic fiction in multiple genres, including contemporary romance, paranormal, fantasy, crime, mystery, and anything else that tickles his muse's fancy. Born in the sleepy South of England where most of his stories are set, he moved to Southeast Asia in 1998, where he now shares a home with his husband and two of the laziest cats on the planet.

Brian loves to hear from readers. You can find his contact information, website details and author profile page at https://www.firstforromance.com/

Sign up for our newsletter and find out about all our romance book releases, eBook sales and promotions, sneak peeks and FREE romance books!